VINTAGE VAMPIRE

SOUTHERN RELICS COZY MYSTERIES

BELLA FALLS

EVERMORE PRESS

CONTENTS

*All audiobooks available are narrated by the wonderful and talented Johanna Parker

For a FREE exclusive copy of the prequel to the Southern

Charms series, Chess Pie & Choices, sign up for my newsletter!

Share recipes, talk about Southern Charms and all things cozy mysteries, and connect with me by joining my reader group Southern Charms Cozy Companions!

CHAPTER ONE

Sweat trickled down my neck, and strands of my hair stuck like glue to my skin as I assisted Bubba, our newest employee, in securing an old writing desk in the back of one of our business trucks. The humidity hung in the air so thick that I might as well have skipped the shower I took earlier. With all the things we planned to sell tonight, it took longer than usual to load up the truck.

I wiped my face off on the sleeve of my shirt. "I hope this is all. Whew! I'm sweatin' like a hog!"

"Should I take offense to that?" Deacon snuffled his flat nose at me as he waddled up next to the vehicle.

My cousin used to be one of the biggest players

with women I'd ever known until the night he messed with the wrong witch. Somehow, she'd cursed him into the form of a pig, saying he deserved to be what he truly was before she took off forever. Ever since then, none of us had been able to free him from his animal form and return him to normal no matter what we tried. Until tonight.

I moseyed over to the edge of the truck bed and sat down on the opened tailgate, swinging my cowboy boots as I talked to my cousin. "You know I wasn't talking about you, Deac. Even in that pig form of yours, you gotta feel that it's hotter than a pepper sprout. If we had a pool out here, it'd be boilin' by now."

"That's what mud's for. A good wallow will keep me cool most days. *Oink. Snort.*" My cousin squealed his enthusiasm. "Of course, Dad gave me a good hosing off so I could look good tonight."

After promising my aunt and uncle that we would put all our focus on finding a cure for Deacon, we'd experienced more frustration than hope. Even with Auggie as the coven's new librarian, the former professor hadn't been able to track down an effective spell or magical method to change my cousin back other than to track down the original

2

witch who cast the hex in the first place and convince her to reverse the curse.

"Your skin is practically glowing," I complimented. "I'll bet you get lots of attention at the market."

"It won't be anything like before," he grunted.

In his human form, Deacon used to make heads turn wherever he went. Even from his teenage years, men admired him for his strength and women swooned over his devilish good looks.

"Well, your mother and sister have all their fingers and toes crossed for you, and Granny Jo sends you all her love." The pendant around my neck warmed against my skin. I pulled on the chain to retrieve it with my fingers. "Oh, and Granddad insisted he wanted to come with us. You wanna wear the medallion for good luck?"

My thumb stroked the outline of an elephant on the brass coin that my ancestors had made into a necklace. Because of its magical nature, any of the numerous family ghosts had the ability to occupy the object and "ride" in it, especially if we were doing something related to the family business. Granddad still liked to help find the best bargains when he could.

"Nah, you keep him with you," Deacon insisted

with a grunt. "You'll feel his influence quicker than my tough hide. And we need all the help we can get."

A shrill whistle interrupted our conversation, and Uncle Jo waved his hat in the air as he approached.

Bubba came over, checking off a list in a small notepad. "Do you think we've got everything we need, Mr. Jewell?"

"Yes," my father and uncle replied at the same time.

With a snicker, I jumped down from the tailgate. Dad eased himself off the back of the truck with more grace than me. "All the pieces we're bringing with us are secure. But I don't think we'll have enough room for everyone to ride." He glanced at my cousin.

"That's okay, we can follow behind in Ol' Bessie," I offered, pulling my keys from my pocket. "Give me two ticks and I'll bring her around."

Buddy, our resident barn cat, chased after me as I hustled with quick feet to my little cottage situated on the back of our family's land. Even though the place was small, it possessed the best view of the Bogue Sound and was the perfect size for just me. Plus, it had the advantage of not being crowded with ghosts.

The cat meowed and scratched at my front door before I got into Bessie's front seat. I sighed and gave in to his begging, scratching him behind his ear. "Is it too hot for you, Bud? I swear, you're gonna turn into a terrible barn cat if you keep coming to my place to enjoy the air conditioning."

The second I unlocked the door and opened it just a crack, the cat zipped inside and disappeared. I'd taken to leaving out a bowl of water and some kibble in the kitchen just in case, so I left him to the cooler air and locked the door.

It took an extra try and a heap of patience to get Bessie's old engine to turn over, but once it did, the whole vehicle shimmied with every step on the gas to rev her to life. Easing her onto the dirt road, I drove the old pickup back to the barn and parked it behind the loaded truck.

Uncle Jo and Dad carried a large slab of wood they'd found somewhere in the recesses of the barn. After dropping the tailgate, they leaned the lumber against the truck and adjusted it to the perfect angle.

With the engine idling, I opened my door to see if I could help. Uncle Jo walked to the middle of their makeshift ramp and jumped up and down. "See? I told you it was sturdy enough."

"It's not an issue of whether or not it'll hold me,

Dad," Deacon complained. "When you said I was going with you tonight, you didn't tell me it would be in the back."

My heart ached for my cousin. I didn't blame him for his resentment even when we were trying to help him.

Walking to the back, I crouched down so I could look Deacon in the eyes. "I know that you've been in this state far too long. I think we always assumed the solution would present itself to us sooner or later. I'm sorry it's been so much later." I scratched the tufts of thick, wiry hair on the top of his head.

The pig leaned close enough to me he almost knocked me over. "I know you've all been trying, *oink*. I just want my life back."

I kissed his hammy forehead. "If you climb into the back of Ol' Bessie, then we can be on our way to the Midnight Market. It's a new moon plus a solstice. I'd say our luck is supercharged."

My uncle nodded at me in gratitude as his son lumbered up the ramp into the back of the truck. On the bed, Dad had stacked some moving blankets we used to transport furniture, giving Deacon a comfortable place to settle.

"Let's get on the road," Uncle Jo commanded, crawling into the passenger side with me. He shimmied the window at the back of the cab open so he could talk to his son if he needed to.

I placed my straw cowboy hat on my head and slipped the tape I'd selected from the glove box into the cassette player. Music from one of Deacon's favorite bands blared out of the speakers, and I risked my uncle's and my hearing by cranking the Florida Georgia Line's song about cruising loud enough for my cousin to hear. Rolling the windows down, we let the melody and wind blow past us on our way.

When we approached the designated area for the market, we slowed down to talk to a guy sitting in the middle of an empty field. He finished his sip of his drink and slid the can back into the holder in his camping chair. With a grin, he shoved himself out of the hammock-style seat and strolled over to talk to my father in the truck ahead of us. After a few minutes, he waved our first vehicle through but held out his hand in front of us.

"Howdy, y'all. Name's Pete." He grinned wide, revealing a few teeth missing from his smile. Taking a more authoritative stance, the man straightened and cleared his throat. *"Cicadas chirp their nightly tune. The stars, they twinkle in the sky."*

I looked to my uncle to provide the response to

the secret code. He shoved a meaty hand into his pocket, then checked the other one in a panic.

"Oh shoot, Buck's got the paper with the code words written down with him." Uncle Jo crowded closer to me and yelled out the window in his friendliest tone, "Don't suppose my brother's pass could extend to us as well. You should find our names on the list. That'd be Jewell with two L's."

Pete shook his head. "No, I'm sorry. Either you have the key to get in or you don't. Can't let you stay out here neither."

I retrieved my spell phone but cursed under my breath. "It won't work this close to the market." If Uncle Jo couldn't remember the rest of the code, then we wouldn't be going any further.

While I repeated the phrases to my uncle, the guard got a little bored and took a closer look at the contents in the back of our truck. "You fixing to sell a pig tonight? Must be something special about it."

"I'm not an it, I'm a he," Deacon corrected, causing the startled man to jump back a few steps.

"Well, I'll be. A talking pig. Don't that beat all," Pete mused, taking his trucker hat off his head to scratch it. "I'll bet he'll fetch a pretty penny to the right buyer."

My uncle glanced at his watch. "It's getting close

to opening time. Is there any way you could let us in this one time?"

Pete sighed. "Rules are rules, I'm sorry."

My stomach dropped, and I wondered how we'd get word to Dad that we were stuck outside the market. Worse yet, how would I be able to lessen the blow to Deacon.

"But," the guard continued. "Since you made my night with a talking pig, I'll give you a clue." Pete pointed at the field.

Uncle Jo huffed in exasperation. "I don't see anything other than a dark field.

"Shh," Pete scolded. "Just hush and watch. Whaddya see?"

I turned off the engine and stuck my head out of the window. A night breeze battled the humid heat that still lingered after a long, hot day. Crickets chirped and the buzz of cicadas filled the air. Tiny lights hovering close to the ground blinked on and off across the entire expanse.

"Ooh, I think I've got it," I said, slapping the side of the truck. "Say the first part again."

Pete chuckled and obeyed. "*Cicadas sing their nightly tune. The stars, they twinkle in the skies.*"

Squeezing my eyes shut, I repeated the words under my breath. With a snap of my fingers, my eyes flew open, and I recalled the rest. *"My way is lost without no moon unless I'm led by fireflies."*

"Well done," the amused guard complimented. "You know your country song history."

Turning the engine over with a roar, I let the truck idle. "I've got some family members who like the oldies." I thought of Granny Jo singing off-key in the kitchen while frying food in the skillet.

Pete pointed down the dirt road in front of us. "Follow it until you pass through the veil. Feel free to pull up closer to the entrance to unload before you park."

I thanked him with a tip of my hat, and he bowed a little in response. We pulled forward and bounced over potholes and other divots in the dirt until we reached the edge of the woods.

The pressure of magical energy tingled over my hands and down my arms as we drove through the glamour cast to hide the market. The bronze of the elephant coin warmed, and I braced myself for the full effect.

"Hold on, Deac," I shouted through the small window at the back.

It felt a little like what I imagined toothpaste would when being squeezed out of its tube. Once past the magical barrier that kept out mortals, we drove through the woods until we spotted some glittering lights up ahead.

Breaking through the dark thicket of trees, we entered the parking area in front of the Midnight Market. Several large tents of varying bright colors stood in the middle of the clearing. On the east edge, open-air stalls offered more room for the smaller goods to be sold. A few food trucks lined the west side, and the scent of food wafted through the open window. I hoped we'd find what we came for fast enough for us to at least try some samples.

A ginormous guy who looked like a mix between a troll and a Sasquatch wearing a bright orange vest stopped us with his enormous paw of a hand. He leaned down to see through my window.

"Buying or selling?" he asked in a deep, rumbling voice.

"Both," I replied. "My dad should have already checked in for his slot. Last name's Jewell."

The giant of a man ran a thick finger down the sheets of paper, tapping the clipboard. "Here you are. Yes, you've been checked into space 147, which is under the green tent over there." He gestured in the right direction.

Uncle Jo leaned across me. "Has the seller Mystic

Misty checked in yet? We're supposed to meet with her."

With another look, the guy nodded. "Yes, looks like she's in one of the outside stalls." He stepped to the side to take a gander into the back of the truck. "Is it for sale? Your animal?"

"No, *he's* not. We're here to purchase something specifically for him tonight," I said, hoping not to get interrogated with more complicated questions. "So, we'll be bringing him with us."

The guy scratched his chin. "That's a bit unusual, but I guess not out of the realm of tonight's market." He tore off a piece of paper with an orange tag stuck to it and handed it to us. "This will let you park in the lot around back with the other sellers. Please make sure your animal's secure and won't run loose or cause problems."

"I can control myself, thank you, *oink*," Deacon complained.

The protruding brow of the troll-like man lifted into his shaggy hairline and he guffawed with merriment. "Well, all right then. Take the path to the right of the tents to the parking lot in the back, please."

Uncle Jo pointed out a free spot at the very end of the first row of vehicles. He hopped out and directed me so I could back the truck into the space.

The tailgate was dropped by the time I secured the cab and got out. My uncle and I positioned ourselves on either side and assisted Deacon onto solid footing on the ground.

My cousin shook his entire body from snout to curly tail and smacked his chops a couple of times. "You know, this is the first time I've been out late at night in too long. I wonder if this Misty we're looking for is cute."

"Seriously?" I barked at him. "Need I remind you exactly how you got yourself into that form in the first place?"

Deacon cocked his bulbous head toward me. "Hey, give me a break. I can't help being who I am despite my outer appearance."

Uncle Jo shrugged his shoulders when I looked to him for support. "Let's stop wasting time and make our way down the outside stalls. I'd like to make the transaction before things pick up." He slung a bag full of Deacon's clothes over his shoulder just in case we found what we needed to return my cousin back to his former glory.

I followed behind my uncle, keeping careful watch over Deacon and whoever eyed him with a little too much interest. We'd already been asked twice if he was for sale, and I didn't want anyone else getting any ideas. Once the market opened at midnight, the place would be teeming with potential buyers, and more than a few would probably offer a hefty price for a talking pig.

Uncle Jo led us down the middle of the two rows of outside stalls facing each other to make sure his pig of a son didn't bump into one of the tables by accident. Several of the different sellers caught my eye with their enticing displays of jewelry and other handmade goods, but I forced myself to ignore them to stay focused on our mission.

An adolescent girl helping to drape bracelets over a display model squealed with delight. "Mom, look at the size of that pig!"

Deacon lifted his snout in the air with the same attitude I'd seen him put on when he walked into a bar on the prowl for a date.

The young girl raced around the corner of the table and rushed out to pet my cousin. "Nice piggy." She giggled when Deacon snorted just for her. "He's so well-behaved."

I snorted. "That's debatable."

"Emelia, what have I told you about running up to animals without asking permission?" her mother scolded, pulling her daughter's hands away. She glanced at me with a shy smile. "Is it okay if she touches your pet?"

I pointed at the pig. "Oh, he's not a pet. And you'd better ask him yourself."

Deacon oinked and snuffled with excitement at being the center of attention again. "I don't mind," he grunted.

Little Emelia backed away with wide eyes. "Mommy, did the piggy just talk?"

"I sure did," my cousin admitted. "And I like the ribbon woven into your hair. Blue is my favorite color, too."

I looked to the heavens for help. Whatever color a pretty girl wore always ended up Deacon's favorite hue of the night. All his time as an animal hadn't dampened his skills to charm.

The mom remained cautious, but her daughter grinned back at the pig, fingering the silk woven into her braids. "Mom did it. Why can you talk? Are you like a prince who's under some spell and needs a kiss from a princess to break it?"

The little girl's guess floored me. Uncle Jo and I exchanged knowing glances, neither of us able to come up with a better explanation.

"*Oink,* I sure am. How about we see if you have

what it takes." Deacon bowed his head closer to the girl.

She looked to her mother for permission, and when she received it, the girl threw her arms around my cousin's brawny neck and kissed his forehead a few times.

"Aww. It didn't work," she pouted, patting my cousin's head. "Guess I'm not the right princess, piggy."

"Come on, honey. Let's leave these people to their business," her mother insisted, heading back to their table. "Don't make me regret taking Meemaw's advice to bring you tonight." She mouthed a thank-you at Uncle Jo and me.

"Bye, Emelia," Deacon snuffled.

The little girl giggled one more time and blew a kiss at the pig. "My friends call me Emmie."

Uncle Jo, eager to move on, read the signs on the nearby stalls. "She's gotta be here somewhere."

"I'll bet she's closer to the end," I replied, patting my uncle's arm in encouragement.

We strolled down the end of the booths until we spotted a sign with various Celtic and made up symbols hung on a tie-dyed banner. The name *Mystic Misty* was painted in a white font with swirls and filigree. The tagline on the bottom sparkled in rainbow colors and read, *Specializes in crystal healing and enlightenment.*

Stones of all different shapes and sizes gleamed from their settings in different pieces of jewelry. I couldn't help but be distracted from our purpose by the shiny pretties, and I leaned closer to get a better look at a particular bracelet. The large, translucent orange and yellow oval contained flashes of brilliant colors that almost looked like burning flames from the inside.

A petite woman wearing a flowing black skirt and a corseted bodice with a leaf pattern laced over a white puffy shirt stopped fussing with the plastic containers full of her wares and approached.

"Ah, you've found one of my favorite pieces. It's a fire opal," she said with a smile. "They're said to encourage creativity and help in your business endeavors, but they can also protect you from danger, too. And if you've got a sweetheart, they can help warm up the romance. Although I see you already have a beautiful token on your finger." She nodded at the ring Luke gave me.

My fingers longed to touch the bracelet, but Uncle Jo cleared his throat. "My name's Josephus Jewell, and I contacted you on the recommendation of the leader of the Crystal Coast Coven."

"We start with amethyst, which makes for an all-around great grounding stone. Smoky quartz helps protect against negative energy, so I chose that to maybe help block the overall effects of the spell."

"Curse is more like it," Deacon grunted.

Misty continued with a sympathetic nod. "This green stone is chrysocolla, and it increases the confidence and manifests courage to overcome obstacles. Call it a natural boost to your ego."

"That's the last thing my son needs," Uncle Jo chortled.

"Now, this stone with the blue-green flash to it when you turn it in the light?" The woman turned the piece to show off the colors. "It's Labradorite. It really helps with transformation and can guide you to connect to your higher self."

"As long as I transform into my *real* self, I don't care about anything else," Deacon snorted.

Misty gazed down at the pig. "But real change takes true effort," she challenged. "Let me put it to you another way. If you want your outsides to change, then you might have to alter how you think about yourself and your place in the world."

My cousin snorted and snuffled in frustration. He bumped into me in his agitation, and I reached out to pat his hide for reassurance.

"Listen, I'm not here to rain on your parade." Misty leaned over the table in an awkward position just to scratch my cousin's head. "I truly do hope my work can be integral in helping you. All I'm saying is that it'll take some effort on your part to ignite the magic."

Deacon accepted her words and pushed his head into her touch. "Okay, I'm listening."

Misty scrambled back into place and finished her explanation. "These last stones at the center are a mix of garnet and jasper. Red is the color of the root chakra, and both types of stones should help ground you in your true self. I set them during the full moon, so I'm hoping that supercharged them."

"Your craft is really beautiful," I complimented.

"Thanks. I have to admit I'm a little nervous." She grimaced at Deacon. "I really want this to work."

"You and me both," my porcine cousin grunted.

Uncle Jo reached into his back pocket and drew out his fat wallet he always stocked when going to the market. "Four hundred I believe was the agreed-upon price." He counted out several bills and laid them on the table.

Misty stared at the money. "I feel like it's unfair for me to take anything. Not without knowing for sure." She bit her lip and asked Deacon, "Would you mind trying it out first?"

Her question surprised me. If it worked, it could be a huge endorsement for her and bring in more potential buyers tonight. But if it didn't work, I didn't want us to hurt her business. That was too many *ifs* to be betting on.

Deacon took a couple of steps away from the table. "But what if it doesn't...you know?"

"Then I can see for myself and assess what's working and what isn't." Misty gathered the long piece in her hands and scooted around her table to stand in front of my cousin. "We'll keep trying until we get it right."

"Sounds like you might end up spending a lot of time with me," Deacon flirted. "You sure you can handle it?"

"Pfft." Misty waved off his doubt. "I'm half witch and half elf. I've faced tougher challenges than you. Besides, I get the feeling that underneath it all, you're just a big ol' pussy cat." She scratched him under his chin, her eyes sparkling with coy teasing.

"Darlin', if you could see the real me, you'd know I'm definitely a big—"

"Maybe you should put the necklace on him and

see what happens," I interrupted, not wanting to hear my cousin finish his sentence.

Misty crouched down and stretched the long necklace across Deacon's jowls. Holding an end in each hand, she encircled her arms around his neck.

Before she stood up, she paused to gaze at him with her head tilted. "What?"

"Nothing. Been a while since I've had a cute girl's arms around me," my cousin admitted.

"Now, that's just sad. Here, hold this in place," she instructed, waiting for me to grab ahold of the two ends.

With her hands free, the jeweler wrapped her arms around my cousin's pig body and leaned into him with her eyes closed.

Uncle Jo watched over his son with surprise and approval. My cousin had taken for granted all the attention he'd garnered most of his life. When Deacon grunted in approval and nuzzled into the young woman's touch, I realized how starved he must be just for regular affection. The coin around my neck warmed against my skin in approval.

Squeezing him tight, Misty leaned her head against his hide. "Everybody should get hugs," she declared, before releasing him and taking the clasps examine this exquisite ring," she said, twisting my wrist so she could get a better look. "As old as it is, there must be an incredible story. I'd love to know what it is."

A prickly heat rose in my cheeks, and I distracted the bubbly girl with a quick embrace and a promise to tell her later. Although Luke had shown me a sliver of a piece of his former life, he'd clammed right up again after we'd gotten engaged and he'd slipped his sister's ring on my finger, avoiding talking about her at all cost.

I rubbed my chest to ease the ache in my heart. I couldn't help but agree with Misty as I followed my uncle and cousin deeper into the market to find my father. There was a bigger story behind the ring. And I intended to find out what it was.

CHAPTER TWO

Cate tapped the side of her empty glass with a spoon and slurred at our friend behind the bar, "Hey, Harrison. We need more medicine."

"Another round of Painkillers coming up," the new partner or Riki's Tiki Tavern agreed, hitting the switch on the blender.

Dani Jo groaned and held her head. "We should get some food if we're going to drink more."

"Ooh, maybe we can get Pops to send us over some burgers and fries," I agreed, chewing on the wedge of pineapple hanging off my drink. "Hey, Harrison. Can you get Pops to send us food?"

Our friend shook his head while he mixed our drinks. "What's wrong with our menu here?"

I blinked a couple of times, considering his question. "We already had an order of jalapeño poppers and some nachos. But I want an Ellie burger!" Everything shook on the table when I slammed my hand down for emphasis.

"Yeah, Ellie burgers for everybody," Crystal demanded. "And I don't want a Painkiller. Ooh, let's do shots."

Wesley, Harrison's best friend, brought over a pitcher of water and refilled all of our glasses. "I think you ladies should hydrate yourselves."

My cousin Dani grasped her water and drank it down in gulps, but Cate and Crystal gave him the stink eye and shooed him away.

I snickered and sipped on more water. "I think they want to butter me up to get me to decide on a wedding date."

"And to choose which one of us is gonna be her maid of honor." Crystal jutted her thumb at her chest, failing to wink in a spectacularly drunk fashion.

Cate shook a finger at her. "You're already married. You can't be a maid. Unless you're an old maid." She giggled at her own joke and kept repeating the derogatory term to herself.

"I am not old!" Crystal complained.

Dani Jo hiccupped. "But the technical term would be matron of honor."

"Aw, heck," Crystal whined. "Matron does sound kinda old. But I'm married to a good man."

"A *great* man," I emphasized. "Odie's completely awesome."

Crystal closed her eyes and grinned with pride. "Yeah, my boo bear is that and a whole lot more. Especially when he takes me into our bedroom and—"

"Shots!" I called out, cutting my friend off. "We definitely need some shots over here."

We definitely did *not* need more alcohol, but I didn't need to hear about my friend's escapades with her husband.

Harrison pinched the bridge of his nose, getting a little irritated at our increasingly drunken demands. We'd managed to chase out a few other tables with our antics. "What kind do you want?"

"Something with rum," Cate said.

Dani Jo pointed around us with wild gesticulations. "We're in a tiki bar. Everything comes with rum."

"How about a Kraken?" Harrison asked. "It's got coconut rum plus dark spiced rum, some lemon, and some orgeat syrup."

"Ye-e-ah," drew out Crystal. She turned to face our bartender friend and spoke in her best pirate imitation. "Release the Kraken, matey!"

She knocked over her water when she swiveled back around, dousing the table and all the innocent napkins, plates, and glasses. "Man overboard," she cried out each time she picked up an ice cube and tossed it back into the glass with a clink.

"Why don't you ladies move to the table by the window. It's a nicer view," Wesley suggested. "I'll clean this up."

I cupped his chin in my hand. "You're a good man, Wes. I don't know why you can't find a good woman to settle down with." My friends moved tables and squealed with joy when Harrison brought the drinks and shots over.

"Because the good ones are already taken, like you, darlin'," he flirted back, pulling free from my grip and retrieving a folded napkin from his pocket. "Besides, I got the number from the blonde chick who was sitting at the bar before she left."

I tilted my head and blinked at my friend's two blurry heads. "But don't you want something more meaningful?"

"Don't you want to set your wedding date?" Wesley deflected, nodding at my ring. "You're the one that's engaged, and yet you don't seem to be in the typical girly rush to walk down the aisle."

I frowned and stopped teasing my friend. "It's complicated." My fingers twisted the metal band around my finger.

"Yeah, well, I like a very *un*complicated life." Wesley wiped down the mess from our former table. "But I'll be happy to attend your wedding. Whenever you finally decide to have one."

I grumbled to myself as I checked my phone for any further messages. When I'd asked Luke to join us at the tiki bar, I'd gotten a very short response that he was busy. More avoidance. More mystery.

"Come on, girly." Crystal patted the seat next to her. "Pull up a chair and tell us your woes."

Cate closed one eye and pointed at me. "Because you've got a serious woe-face on. Is it something to do with your hunky vampire man? Like why he wouldn't come out with us tonight?"

Dani Jo flashed me a knowing glance. I'd talked to my cousin a little bit about my worries but had made her promise not to say anything.

"Maybe," I admitted. "He says he's busy." Holding up my phone, I showed them the quick message.

Cate attempted to read the text by squinting but gave up. "He's probably working on someone's car."

"True." I sipped on my fresh glass of water. "Although he normally tells me when it has something to do with work."

Crystal ripped the drink out of my hand and traded it with a shot. "Enough of your moping. We're your friends and we're here to cheer you up. So, first, let's do these shots to get you all loosened up."

I pushed my rising doubts deep down and raised the tiny glass in the air. "Release the Kraken!"

The other girls repeated the phrase, and we all tossed the liquid into our mouths. We slammed the shot glass on the table and sucked in air to cool the burn.

"Smooth," I rasped, licking my lips. "And coconutty." A warm buzz raced through my veins and relaxed me a little.

"Now that we've got your lips a little lubricated, spill." Crystal rubbed my arm. "What's going on? Why are you avoiding all wedding talk?"

I leaned my elbows on the table and placed my chin in my hands. "Because I think Luke might not really want to marry me." There. I'd finally said the fear that twisted my gut more and more.

Dani Jo stumbled off her stool and raced over to comfort me. "That's not true. He's totally devoted to you." She rubbed my back with vigorous insistence.

All my emotions I kept hidden welled up and burst out of me with accompanying tears. "It's supposed to be a happy time for us, and yet I feel like it's driven a wedge between us. I catch him sometimes staring at the ring on my finger, which I know belonged to his sister Isabella. But when I ask him to tell me about her, he shuts down. How am I supposed to promise to be with him as his wife when he refuses to share anything with me? I mean, forever is a pretty loaded word with Luke." My shoulders shook with my sobs.

"Hey, now, what's this?" Pops asked, approaching our table. He set down baskets of burgers, fries, and other goodies. "I thought tonight was a celebration and here I find you pretty ladies crying."

I grabbed one of the napkins on the table and wiped the tears from my face. "I'm okay, Pops. Just having a little man trouble."

The older man raised one of his bushy gray eyebrows. "You need me to have a little one-on-one with him, if you get my meanin'? Or do you need me to tell him about how Ellie and I ended up together? Two totally different approaches to try and get to the same outcome."

Giving me a ring that once belonged to her was… well, touching. Made me feel like he really trusted me."

"What do you know about his sister?" Cate asked.

I shrugged. "That her name was Isabella. Luke loved her so much. Still does, I think. And that her death was a deep blow to him."

"She was a vampire, right? How could she die?" Crystal set her drink down and dragged the basket of fries closer to her.

I'd asked Luke the same question. How had his sister died? It had to be something pretty serious to still upset him centuries later.

I blew out a long breath. "The truth is, I don't know. And that's why I haven't set a wedding date. Granny Jo's ready to hit Luke upside the head with one of her skillets, but Dad told her that sometimes a man needed patience."

High-pitched giggles burst out of Dani Jo, and I stared at my cousin. "What's so funny?"

"The thought of our ghostly great-grandmother laying into a vampire. I almost want it to happen," she tittered.

"Want what to happen?" Gloria asked, dragging a stool over to join us. Azalea followed her lead and squeezed in between Cate and my cousin.

I gave both the new girls sloppy high fives across the table. "What are you two doing here?"

Azalea waved at her husband. "Harrison called because he figured none of you should be driving. So, we'll act as your lifts home."

Gloria dipped a fried pickle into the ranch sauce. "Now, if nobody else is claiming this Ellie burger, I'm gonna eat it while you catch us up."

Even the addition of two sober minds didn't help us come up with a solution to my problem. Unwilling to let my worries drag down our girls' night, I steered the conversation to safer waters and let them suggest what types of wedding dresses they thought I should wear. In the midst of discussions about mermaid styles, A-lines, and long trains, my mind waded back into the murky depths of doubt to wallow.

Azalea filled us in on all the ins and outs of her wedding preparation as she drove Crystal and me back to our places. The two of us managed to guide our stumbling friend safely into the hands of her big bear shifter of a husband. Once Azalea aimed her car in the direction to take me home, I became tangled up in my thoughts again.

"Don't give up on hope. I think you and Luke are perfect together. All you guys need to do is to talk things out. Be clear with one another," she said as she slowed down to pull into the long driveway onto my family's land.

"You're right," I said, a new idea taking hold. Grabbing Azalea's knee, I startled her. "Would you mind driving a little farther down the road?"

"Sure." My friend turned on her blinker and pulled back into traffic. "Where am I taking you?"

"The garage." Emboldened by my decision and the alcohol still coursing through my body, I became more secure in my plan. "I'm gonna go in there and make him pay attention to me and not some car. I'll refuse to leave until he answers all my questions and tells me everything. Which might be a lot since he's lived so long. But still...no more mysteries. No more secrets."

The sign outside the garage Luke worked for loomed up ahead. Even in my inebriated state, I could tell that all the lights were off inside the customer service area. Azalea's car dipped as she turned into the parking lot.

"Maybe he's done for the night," she suggested, slowly driving past the darkened office area.

"When he gets working on cars after hours, he's usually there all night. And if he got done early, why didn't he come out to the Tiki?" I held my hand over my churning stomach. "Drive down there and we'll see if he's using one of the extra bays."

Luke's boss Walter let my boyfriend take on private contracts for work on his own time for a small cut of his fee. And sometimes, Luke liked to work on one of his personal vintage cars that he kept secret in a custom garage on his property.

We rolled past each bay with the garage doors all down and secured. "He's not here," I admitted in defeat.

Azalea stopped the car and turned to face me. "What do you want to do? Should I take you home?"

I bit my lip while thinking. Confronting Luke and talking things out remained a good idea, but maybe not while alcohol still fueled my decisions.

"Yeah, take me back to my place and I'll sleep it off. Sober Ruby Mae will be much better at having a rational conversation than me right now." I sighed and stared out the window as we headed back.

We approached the turnoff for Luke's house, and I wondered if maybe I should at least see if he was home. A strange sight caught my eye, and I grabbed onto Azalea's sleeve. "Turn here. Down this driveway."

My friend took the turn a little fast, and we bumped over a little of the curb as her tires squealed

"Luke?" I asked, recognizing the tenor of his voice. I pulled my hand behind my back and allowed the magic to fizzle out.

The heated discussion stopped abruptly. "Ruby Mae? What are you doing here?" Irritation laced his question. His usual Southern accent was replaced by something more foreign.

For a second, I wondered if I'd invaded someone else's house. Turning on the lights to be sure, I found Luke standing in front of the refrigerator with a strange man climbing out behind him. In all the time I'd been dating Luke, he had only revealed his underground lair to me very recently. Who was this man that my boyfriend shared his secrets with so easily?

"I...I..." Any explanation I could come up with flew out of my woozy head. "We were out at the tiki bar."

Luke frowned. "I know this. I am asking why you have come here tonight?"

His different accent plus his accusatory tone began to tick me off. The embarrassment of being caught off guard morphed into justified rage.

"And I'd like to know what you've done to my boyfriend. Scratch that. My *fiancé*. Because the way you're addressing me right now doesn't sound exactly friendly." The magic I'd tried to banish flared to life again with my extreme emotions. I clenched my hands into fists to hide my raw reaction.

"Fiancé?" his friend exclaimed with wide eyes. Rapid words in a different language exploded out of him, and Luke cringed a little.

"Cas, *aspetta, per favore*," Luke pleaded, holding up a hand to stop the tirade. "And speak in English so my betrothed can understand you." He moved to the side so the stranger could emerge fully from the secret passageway.

"Don't bother." Turning on my heels, I marched away with too many emotions mixing into a horrible cocktail of confusion.

"Rue, don't go." Luke followed behind me. He swore under his breath, and while I didn't understand the foreign words, I recognized cussing when I heard it.

I made it to the front door, wanting to escape, but he flashed in front of me and took my outstretched hand reaching for the doorknob into his.

"Forgive me, *cara*," Luke said, lifting my hand to his mouth and kissing my knuckles. "I wasn't expecting to see you tonight, and you caught me off guard."

Although honey dripped from his tone, I still didn't buy the sweetness. "You're the one who gave me a key and told me I could come by whenever. If I recall, you even hinted that you wanted me to surprise you from time to time."

Shame and another emotion I couldn't read flooded his face. "I know. And I did mean it. This house is just as much yours as is my heart."

"Don't try to distract me with sweet talk." I yanked my hand out of his grip. "I was trying to surprise you so that we could talk a few things out. Guess I'm the one who got surprised instead. I'll go, and you can be as *busy* as you like." I threw the words from his text back in his face and grabbed the doorknob.

"Luca," his friend called out from behind us. "You must introduce me to this charming lady you claim has agreed to marry you."

If I wasn't already so irritated, I might have found the newcomer's accent a little enticing.

With one eyebrow raised at my boyfriend, I asked, "Luca?" I gave up trying to flee and changed tack. I held out my hand and approached the stranger. "The name's Ruby Mae Jewell."

The handsome man accepted my greeting, but as soon as his skin touched mine, a little of my wild magic zapped him. He gasped and pulled back, shooting a suspicious glance at Luke.

"Oops," I recovered, squeezing my fingers together and willing any leftover power to dissipate. "Guess we got a spark from my feet rubbing against the carpet." I pointed at the intricate oriental rug underneath us.

"Ah, that must be it." Instead of shaking my hand again, he placed both of his behind his back and bowed in an old-fashioned salutation. "I am Cassio Rosati, and I apologize for the situation we find ourselves in. It is my fault that there is discord between you and your *fidenzato* for I showed up at his doorstep without a proper invitation."

I took in the man in front of me. His words sounded polite, but something about the furtive glances he kept casting in Luke's direction bothered me.

"Cassio," I repeated, testing his name on my tongue. "May I assume you knew Luke from his home town?"

He chuckled and relaxed a little. "*Sì*, Luca has been my friend for...how long has it been?" he challenged my boyfriend.

"Too long," joked my fiancé, but his tone

suggested anything but mirth. "And please call me Luke while you're here."

"As you wish, Luke," Cassio agreed with an exaggerated hard *K*. He addressed me again, "Luke and I have been the best of friends for many centuries, but it has been far too long since the last time we were together."

"I will not apologize for my choices again," Luke grumbled. "You can respect them, or you can leave."

Cassio held up his hands. "I am not starting another argument with you. I am merely explaining to this fine lady that despite our long friendship, it has been many years since I have seen you."

"By my design," Luke stated, his brow furrowing.

His friend responded in Italian, and the two exploded into a passionate argument, their arms and hands waving about in wild gesticulation.

Attempting to stop the two of them, I called out both of their names. When that failed, I placed my thumb and middle finger to my lips and blew a shrill whistle I usually reserved to call Bobby into the big house.

The sharp noise succeeded in interrupting the incessant tirade. "Okay, boys, that's enough."

Luke clenched his hands into fists and sighed. "You're right. This is getting us nowhere."

Cassio stared at me in disbelief. He sniffed, and a haughty expression settled on his face. "I find it interesting that you of all people would obey so quickly. She must be special for you to place her first above all else."

Annoyed and a little offended, I dropped my Southern manners like a hot potato. "Ahem, *she* is right here and wants to know exactly what the problem is between the two of you."

Luke approached from behind and placed his hands on my shoulders. "It's fine, Rue. Cas was just about to leave."

"You know that I cannot until I have discharged my duty," his friend replied. "You have been found, and unless you choose to run again, it is folly for you to put off your own obligations any longer."

"Run?" Panic replaced my indignation, and I turned in my fiancé's arms. "What's he talking about, Luke? And before you utter one word, you'd better stop speaking in riddles and lay everything out on the table with me."

Cassio smirked. "She does not even know who you really are, does she?" He shook his head in disgust. "*Signorina*, how can you agree to marry him if you don't even know who he truly is?"

Luke looked from me to the visitor several times

before his shoulders slumped and he let me go. "Fine, but I would like some privacy to explain myself."

His friend shook his head. "You know I cannot leave. Not until I have your official response. And as everything unfolds, I believe the significance of the order may be too much for you to refuse. Plus, I want to make sure you tell her *all* of the truth."

Defeated, Luke clicked on a side lamp and gestured for Cassio to enter the living room. Before I entered, my fiancé pulled me into him and hugged me close. He rocked me back and forth in the embrace, and despite my uncertainty in the situation I found us in, I hugged him back.

With a long sigh, he released me and held my hands in his. "I know you tend to get a little...fiery... when you don't like what you hear. Please have patience and listen to it all before you cast judgment on me." His fingers twisted the ring he'd used to propose. "And know that this symbolizes everything inside of me."

He lifted my left hand and placed it over his still heart, the absence of a beat reminding me how very different we were. For a brief second, all of my doubts gathered into one knot and formed a lump in my throat. I nodded in agreement, unable to say anything.

Luke kept hold of my hand, entwining his fingers through mine, and led me into the room to sit together on the stiff couch. Cassio occupied a high back chair opposite us, his eyes examining where Luke and I were connected. A heavy silence filled the room, and I counted my rapid heartbeats until somebody talked. When both men refused to speak, I took charge.

"Fine, let's start with a simple question." I squeezed his hand and shifted so I could see his eyes. "Why does Cassio keep calling you Luca?"

"It is my given name," my fiancé replied. "For years, I have used other monikers, but when I arrived here...I don't know. I liked hearing you call me something close."

"Luke Manson is a far cry from your true identity," Cassio scoffed. "I will never understand why someone with everything you possessed would choose to walk away from a life full of privilege. And responsibility."

His friend's admonishment irritated Luke, and he sneered at Cassio, saying something in Italian that gave me chills even though I didn't understand the words.

caught the specific words he used. "What do you mean *if*? The only two people who have a say in whether or not we tie the knot are sitting on this couch."

My fiancé opened his mouth to speak, but Cassio cut him off. "Yes, perhaps Luke Manson could marry at will, but Luca de Rossi cannot. Not without permission from his parents, and considering what your father has been busy negotiating, I doubt that a union between the two of you will last."

Before I could utter any protests, Luke blurred from his spot next to me and picked Cassio up by his shirt and slammed him against the wall behind them.

"You will not come into my house and insult my bride-to-be with tradition and expectations," he growled, spitting his words into Cassio's face. "Ruby Mae is the woman I choose to tie my life to, and you will treat her with the respect she deserves. Or you can leave. It is entirely your choice, *Mimmo*."

Cassio grasped one of Luke's hands in his and twisted his grip loose. They grappled with each other, blurring about the room with their violence until Luke flipped Cassio onto the wood-and-glass coffee table in front of me, shards and splinters exploding from the impact.

I pulled my knees up to avoid the catastrophe

and scrambled to my feet, balancing on the soft couch cushions. "Hey! You two knock it off!" Summoning a little power, I conjured small fireballs in both my hands. "Don't make me have to scorch your behinds."

Cassio's eyes widened, the flames reflecting off of them. He crab-crawled away, terrified. After a couple of Italian curses, he pointed at me. *"Una strega*, Luca! She is a witch!"

My fiancé stopped fighting with his friend and pointed at the fireballs. "It's a little much, don't you think?"

"Well, there were two crazy vampires beating on each other so much that you broke a coffee table." I gestured at the wreck around where he stood. "A girl's gotta do something to protect herself. Y'all are acting like two toddlers instead of grown men who know better."

Luke took careful steps around the broken glass and shredded wood. He offered a hand to his friend. "She's not wrong."

Cassio kept a wary glance on the fire I controlled. "No, she is not. I have been provoking you all night, so I guess I deserved it." He accepted Luke's help in hauling him off the floor. "But you should know, *signorina*, that we have always worked out our differences in this manner much to our mothers' disappointment."

Luke pulled him into a manly hug and kissed him on both cheeks. "Yes, my mother may never forgive us for destroying the fresco painted by Pinturicchio himself. When was that? 1470?"

Cassio chuckled. "No, the artist painted it in 1471. We destroyed it in 1527. If I recall, you were mad because I had won a bet with you and you refused to pay the price."

"You won *a* horse from my stable. Not my prized horse," Luke protested in jest. "You were trying to lay claim to my Bernardo on a technicality."

Cassio held up a finger. "No, you never specified which horse."

The two men's friendlier demeanors added to my general bafflement. However, their banter back and forth reminded me of some of the squabbles that happened with frequency in my family, so I extinguished the fire in my hands with a flourish, letting go of the magic. Centuries-old vampires, and it all boiled down to the same thing. Boys would be boys, and they definitely fought over their toys.

"At this point, I don't know which end is up with you two. But I will say this to you, Cassio." I sat on the back of the couch, unwilling to move too far for fear of broken glass. "I would like to get Luke's parents' blessing, but I don't much care about what his family thinks. Whether or not they approve makes no never mind, and I *will* marry him if and when we decide to do so." Wiggling my ring finger at him, I showed off the engagement ring.

Luke's friend gawked at the jewelry. "So, that's where it went. I always thought it was lost when she…" He trailed off, his brow furrowing in thought. "It is more than befitting, though. Your sister, of all people, would approve."

"Yes, Isabella would definitely like Ruby Mae." Luke winked at me.

Cassio touched his friend on the shoulder. "But I am sorry, old friend. You know how your parents will react when they find out."

"If I do not return with you, then how will they find out unless by your tongue, old friend?" Luke challenged. "And I would invoke the same trust I have had with you for so long as my chosen brother not to betray me in this matter."

Hurt spread over Cassio's face. "You insult me if you think I would reveal to them anything you would wish to remain between us. Has it not been I who has kept your new names and locations a secret all this time?"

"Then why now?" Luke bellowed, shaking off his friend's touch. "Why disturb my peace and with such a request?"

"Your mother and father wish for you to take your rightful place. They have waited longer than they intended, and decisions are being made in your absence that will affect you whether you want them to or not." Cassio gripped Luke's shoulders again and shook him a little. "It is time you stop running, my friend."

I couldn't keep up with their quick mood changes. Waving my hands to get their attention, I tried to make heads or tails with what I had. "So, let me get this straight. Cas here surprised you by visiting because you've been hiding from your family, changing location and names over however long."

"Yes," Luke confirmed while Cassio agreed in Italian.

"And I'm guessing he wants to bring you back with him because something big is about to go down with your family that he thinks you should be a part of," I continued, counting the second piece I'd picked up from their conversations.

Cassio nodded. "You have the right of it."

"But there's something up with Luke having to

ask his parents for permission to marry me if he does go back. And, based on your reaction, I'm guessing they would be less than pleased about him being engaged to me?" I asked with a finger pointed at my chest.

Luke's friend had the presence of mind to appear apologetic. "It is not my intent to insult you in any way, and I am afraid I have acted abominably since meeting you."

I narrowed my eyes at Cassio since he had been providing all the answers to the numerous questions I'd held onto for so long. "And what about me is so objectionable?" I pressed. "Is it that I'm American and do not descend from any royalty? At least, not that I know of, unless you include the royal pains in my butt the members of my family can be at times."

"No, your country of origin would not be a deterrent." Cassio chose his next words with greater care. "However, his parents would like for him to marry someone more…suitable."

His statement reminded me of Azalea's difficulties from her parents with her marriage to Harrison. "I'm not of the right class, right? Too common for royalty?"

"I don't care about such things, *cara*," Luke defended. "All I ever wanted in a partner was someone who loved me. Who sparked joy in my life and made me want to be better. I could not be luckier that I found you."

His romantic words warmed my heart, but I stayed seated on the back of his couch rather than rushing over to embrace him. "But there's something else that neither of you has said but you both know the answer to. Why wouldn't I be accepted as a potential wife for you?"

The two vampires exchanged more mysterious glances with each other. Cassio dropped his grip on Luke and backed away with a bow, allowing my fiancé to give me the answer that both seemed reluctant to convey.

Luke stepped over the ruins of his coffee table and scooped me up in his arms, carrying me to safer ground. He put me down with gentle ease.

He kissed my forehead, the tip of my nose, and planted a chaste one on my lips. "It's not you specifically. They would never accept me being with any witch. It is why I cannot return."

"It is not the only reason why you have not come back to Perdaggia." Cassio approached the two of us. "Isabella wouldn't want you to continue to suffer so needlessly."

"What does your sister have to do with everything?" I placed my hands on either side of Luke's face. "You have been avoiding talking about her ever since you gave me the ring. Whatever it is, tell me and let me share the burden."

Luke lifted my left hand in front of him and kissed the ring on my finger. "I cannot go back because of what I did."

I leaned in a little closer, willing him to finally tell me the whole truth. "What did you do? Whatever it is, it'll be okay. I won't let it haunt you for the rest of your life."

"There is nothing you can do, *cara*, for it has already been done so long ago." Luke lowered his head to avoid my gaze. "I killed my sister."

CHAPTER FOUR

Although Luke's words echoed in my head, I did not pull away from him. After we first committed to each other as more than just two people fooling around, I had to come to terms that parts of my vampire boyfriend's past were unsavory. But I tried to judge him not by what he had done but by what he did and who he was now with me.

"That can't be true." I looked to Cassio for clarification. "Is it?"

"She died because I refused to listen to her. I refused to support her when she needed me the most," Luke continued, pain radiating off of him in waves. Pink-tinted tears pooled in his eyes.

"I have said this to you before and I will say it

again because it bears repeating, especially in front of your betrothed," Cassio said, once again placing a kind hand on his friend's arm. "You were not the cause of her demise. I have said this time and time again, and yet you refuse to believe me."

"My mother and father do not agree," Luke said, dashing a finger under his eyes to catch the pink wetness. "And neither do I."

I yanked him against me and threw my arms around him. In all my frustrations with his keeping secrets from me, I never would have guessed the depths of his despair and the burden of blame he lived with daily.

After a few soothing moments, I released Luke and maneuvered until he couldn't escape my gaze. "Tell me what happened to her. Maybe I can give you a fresh perspective."

My fiancé tried to speak but failed in his abject guilt. He motioned to Cassio to tell the tale for him.

"Isabella possessed a very strong will. Nobody would refuse her anything. What she wanted, she usually got. And yet, she was the least spoiled girl I had ever known." A smile crept over Cassio's lips. "So giving. So kind. Always wanting to look after others and their needs first before her own."

"Sounds a lot like her brother," I said, trying to get Luke to ease up on himself.

Cassio raised an eyebrow at his friend. "I don't know. This one tends to brood a lot more than Isa did." He shoved Luke in jest. "Remember?"

A smile replaced my fiancé's grimace. "She would tease me and do things to try and make me smile. The game became how long we could both hold out. She almost always won."

Cassio joined Luke in light laughter until he mused, "Isabella was the best of us. But her headstrong ways got her into trouble she could not easily escape."

Luke cleared his throat and turned his haunted eyes to mine. "When she became of age, my parents presented suitor after suitor, wanting to marry her off. And back in those days, they focused on matches that would strengthen the family's power."

"So, other vampire royals," I guessed, trying to imagine what life would be like as a female having her life bartered and traded for position. "Let me guess. She wanted to marry for love instead, which upset Mommy and Daddy."

With a nod, Luke confirmed my suspicions. "It wasn't so much that she fell in love. My parents would have understood that since they were a love match. But it was about the person she chose."

"He was a witch," I finished for him, a knot of dread twisting in my stomach.

"She kept her lover a secret for far longer than I would have guessed," Cassio added. "The three of us shared everything with each other. But not *him*."

The cold way he spoke about Isabella's boyfriend concerned me, but I didn't want to derail the conversation to explore his personal issues.

"What happened when your parents found out?" I asked. "Because in my experience, secrets don't stay secrets for very long in a family."

Luke looked off to the side as if seeing the scene he described. "Mother chose her timing well when she confronted Isa with the fact that she knew. Told her that a temporary dalliance was okay but that she needed to think about her obligations as a de Rossi. That marriage and love did not have to exist together if she so wished."

After considering his words, I gaped at him in surprise. "You mean, your mom suggested she should marry to further your family's power but keep her witch boyfriend on the side?"

Luke shrugged. "She thought as any vampire

would. At some point, Isabella's love would perish where we would not."

His easy dismissal of the life of the witch that Isabella loved chilled me, and I shivered. I would return to that topic another time, but I needed to hear the rest of the story.

"How does all of this connect to Isabella's death?" I pushed.

Cassio volunteered more information. "Luke's father was not as understanding as his mother, and he demanded that Isabella give up the witch. He would not settle for anything less than her obedience in the matter."

"And my sister did what was in her nature. Maybe in both of our natures," Luke said with a little self-loathing. "She made plans to leave the family life and join her witch."

"But somehow, your parents figured it out and caught her before she left," Cassio added.

Luke stepped away from both me and his friend. He paced over to the window and stared out into the darkness. "Father wanted to force her. To bend her to his will. So, he placed her in the tower."

"Like Rapunzel? Locked away from the rest of the world?" I asked. "But she was a vampire.

Couldn't she just jump out of a window and not die?"

"Isabella was caught between what was expected of her and what she wanted." Cassio's eyes flashed to Luke. "I think she thought that if she waited long enough, her parents would accept her feelings for her lover."

"How long was she in the tower?" I asked in a quiet voice, already guessing the time to be long enough to cause a disaster.

Luke leaned his arm against the window. "By the time I came to talk sense into her, she had been isolated for over six months. No contact with anyone, shut away from all stimulation." He cocked his head to the side so he could see me. "The locals called the tower *Torre del Pianto*. It means Tower of Tears because the residents down below could hear her cries."

"That's terrible," I uttered, trying not to cry from sympathy for his sister.

Cassio closed the distance between them to stand beside Luke. He placed his arm around my fiancé. "You tried to get her to change her mind. You did your absolute best, from what you told me."

"But it wasn't good enough." Luke banged his fist against the frame of the window with a dull thud. "I will never forget her words to me, that I wouldn't understand why she couldn't give in until I had experienced the same kind of passionate love myself. Instead of being sympathetic, I said that her stubbornness would be her undoing. And that she should stop acting like a child. My final words to my sister were those of anger, not sympathy she so desperately needed from her brother."

Guilt dripped off of every word Luke uttered, and I wanted to be the one to console him. I approached and waited for Cassio to move out of the way.

Slipping under Luke's arm, I snuggled into him. "Did you go there trying to hurt her?"

"No." His deep voice reverberated against me.

I hugged him around his waist. "Did you say what you did out of concern for her? Did you want what you thought was best?"

His chest expanded against me. "Yes. But you haven't heard what happened next." Luke pulled me in close, and I counted myself lucky that he didn't try to run or push me away. "I was in the passage underneath the city, heading back home. By the time I emerged, she had already taken her life."

"How?" I whispered.

Cassio spoke from behind us. "Fire."

My body stiffened, and I swallowed hard. No wonder Luke's friend had been afraid when he witnessed my special brand of magic.

Luke leaned his head against the top of mine. "The witnesses at the time said that a fiery angel fell from the sky and disappeared when her feet hit the ground. But that's how the humans processed what really happened.

"After I left, Isabella was so distraught that she took the oil lamp from her room and broke it over herself. There is very little that can end a vampire's life, but fire is something we do not recover from very well if at all."

I tried to disentangle myself from him, but my fiancé held onto me fast. If fire was so detrimental to vampires, then what in blazes was Luke doing with me?

"Knowing my sister, she wanted to end things and yet she sacrificed herself in her last act." Luke drew in hard breaths to steady himself. "The exterior of the tower was made of thick stones, but the interior, including the many steps from the bottom to the top, was made of wood. Had the fire spread to the timber, it could have ignited the buildings next to it, and the whole city enclosed in the walls would have been consumed by flames."

I closed my eyes, trying not to imagine the one thing that made me who I was taking away a piece of Luke's life and heart. "How did she sacrifice herself?"

"Knowing what a fire in the tower might do, I think she jumped out the window. Of course, I wouldn't know because I wasn't there." He groaned low in his throat. "By the time her body reached the ground below, the fire spurred on by the oil from the lamp disintegrated her. And my sister was no more."

Immense sorrow bubbled up inside me, and I couldn't imagine how Luke suffered for so long on his own. "You did not kill your sister," I insisted. "It sounds like she made the choice on her own."

"I did not physically push her out the window, no. But I think my parents wanted someone to blame," my fiancé said.

"They have never said that," Cassio countered. "Not once."

Luke kissed the top of my head and turned us away from the window. "Sometimes words are not needed to know the truth." He lifted my chin with his fingers. "Isabella was right. I didn't understand until I met you."

So, falling for me meant that my boyfriend was reminded at all times of how his sister had felt all those years ago. What a terrible load to force on himself day after day.

Standing on my tippy toes, I brushed my lips against his. "Well, this has to stop. Right now."

"What?" Luke asked in confusion.

I brushed some hair out of my face and addressed his friend. "Cassio, you're here because you've been sent to bring Luke back home?"

"*Sì*. That was my purpose for coming," he admitted.

"Then that's settled." I glanced between the two of them. "You are going to go back to Italy and face your parents, and I'm coming with you."

LUKE PULLED the shirt I'd folded and placed into my suitcase back out. "You are not coming with me."

"I hear the words coming out of your mouth, but I also know that you were the one who paid to expedite my shiny new passport." Smacking his hand in mock scolding, I replaced the shirt back into the luggage. "It must be nice to have the means to grease the right hands to get what you want."

He shrugged off my comment. "Sometimes my money can be used for good purposes. But I think I prefer my simpler life here." Backing up, he took a running leap onto my bed, knocking over another stack of clothes ready to be packed. "You're sure I can't convince you to stay and elope?"

I stopped stuffing a pair of flats into the side of the suitcase and clapped my hands. "You mean, we can stay here, just the two of us?"

"Yeah." Ever since Cassio had left, a little of Luke's habit of assuming a Southern accent had returned. He switched on the charm to tempt me. "If you don't want to elope, I'll bet I can get us a marriage certificate in record time, and we can put together something with just you and your friends right here on your property."

"Mm-hmm." I crawled onto the bed next to him.

"We can get Ellie and Pops to coordinate with the Tiki crew to cater and have a grand ol' shindig." He caressed my cheek with the back of his fingers.

"Sounds just about perfect," I purred, getting close enough that my face hovered mere centimeters away from his. "Only one problem."

"What?" He closed his eyes, expecting a kiss from me.

I pushed his shoulders, making him fall back on my pillows. "That's just a different form of running away from the problem. It's time you faced things head-on. Learn from your sister and stand up for what you want in life."

Pursing my lips, I kept the last part of my plan to myself. Yes, I wanted to push my fiancé into facing his parents after so long and to declare his love for me in front of them. Getting their blessing would be great, but I didn't expect it. However, I did hope to delve deeper into how his sister died. Something about the story didn't sit quite right with me, and I could use the visit to my advantage to discover what had really happened up in that tower.

"Fine." Luke rolled out of the opposite side of the bed. "If I can't convince you not to go, then I should go pack. I'll pick you up first thing in the morning."

I flashed him my best smile. "I'll be ready and willing."

He circled around the end of the bed and yanked me against him. "You know, there is one advantage to taking you with me."

"What's that?"

His eyes brushed over my body. "I'll have you all to myself for several blissful hours trapped in the airplane with me."

My breath caught a little at his passionate suggestion. "Sounds like pure torture."

"And here's a taste of what's to come." His mouth

covered mine, and for the next few minutes, I forgot all about packing.

After I finished putting together everything except the last-minute toiletries, I headed up to the big house to eat dinner. Expecting to dine at the small table in the kitchen, my father surprised me with a full meal laid out on the formal dining room table.

Uncle Jo, Aunt Delia, and Dani Jo joined us, and we dug into the dishes sitting on various trivets and potholders. It didn't escape my notice how most of the food included my favorites. Ever since my decision to accompany Luke to Italy, Granny Jo had been doing her best to subtly convince me not to go.

"Good scald on the fried chicken as always, Granny," I complimented when she floated into view.

"I'll bet they can't fry in Italy like I can," she said, not giving up on her mission to make me not want to go.

I shoveled a mouthful of collards in my mouth to keep from laughing out loud. "No, the food won't be the same, but I'm a little excited to try new things. Luke says I won't believe the flavors, plus he's going to try to take me to his uncle's vineyard, too."

Aunt Delia and Dani Jo gushed over the opportunity to visit a different country, asking me all kinds of questions about the upcoming trip. I promised both of them I would take as many pictures as possible and save enough space in my suitcase for souvenirs.

"Aren't we glossin' right over some pretty important details?" Uncle Jo waved his fork in the air as he chewed and talked. "Like the fact that you're stepping into some sort of vampire soap opera? Or that your fiancé's parents have a thing against witches?"

My aunt smacked her husband's arm. "Now, don't go discouraging your niece. Ruby Mae is tough as nails, and she needs to try and work things out with her future in-laws."

Uncle Jo rubbed his arm like it hurt. "I seem to recall someone else who begged me not to visit her parents to ask their permission to marry her once upon a time."

Aunt Delia scowled at him. "I did no such thing."

My uncle stared up at the ceiling as if straining to remember, tapping the side of his head. "What was it my future bride said? Oh, yeah. That her parents would use up all their supply of goofer dust and use their root magic to run me out of town."

Dani Jo snickered at her parents, and I egged them on. "And what ended up happening?"

My aunt rolled her eyes. "He fooled them the same way he fooled me with his country-boy charms. And by eating everything my mama put in front of him."

"I also might have procured a little magical trinket her dad wanted." Uncle Jo held up his hand at the side of his mouth as if he were whispering some big secret. "A little bribery can go a long way."

I stopped munching on my bite, a sudden realization taking root. In all my excitement about getting out of my small town and experiencing another part of the world, I hadn't thought about what I would do to win over Luke's parents. And I was already starting from behind.

My father reached out to squeeze my shoulder. "I'm sure they'll love you, butter bean. And if they don't, well, then you'll have to try your best to convince them otherwise. I've never known you to back down from a challenge. Ever." He planted a peck on my cheek.

"Thanks, Dad," I murmured, grateful to have him metaphorically kiss my emotional boo-boo better.

After the meal finished, Dani came back to my place and helped me go through a last-minute checklist to be sure I didn't forget anything. Dad accompanied us because he wanted to be near me as long as possible.

"I truly am sorry for Luke's loss, but I can't help but feel that her love story is just so…" my cousin trailed off.

"Tragic?" I asked, stuffing another pair of clean undies into an empty space of the suitcase.

"No, romantic," gushed Dani. "She wanted to love the person she chose and wouldn't compromise."

I snapped my fingers in front of her face as she swooned. "And Isabella *died* for her love. I mean, what am I going to do if Luke's parents tell him he can't marry me? This could be a truly bad idea for me to go. Maybe Granny's right."

My cousin shoved the suitcase aside and patted the space on my bed next to her. I sat at her request, and she took my hands in hers. "You told me not too long ago that you thought there was something Luke was hiding that was holding him back from you. Well, now you get a chance to make him face all the demons from his past. And better yet, you get to stand right by his side to help him through it."

I frowned, considering her words. My reasons for going were noble, but the obstacles to get to the end goal would be bigger than I'd ever faced before.

"I'm glad I called Charli in Honeysuckle Hollow.

She connected me with one of the vampires there who educated me a little on expected etiquette." I regretted not writing down all of the instructions, but I felt like I got the basic gist. "I'll just act like a good Southern woman. Smile and be pleasant to everyone. Try to be kind and helpful at all times."

"And only say the bad things behind their backs," my cousin teased.

We giggled together, and I hugged her hard. "I wish I could take you with me, Dani Jo."

"Oh, I would go in two ticks of a heartbeat if I could." She rubbed my back. "But you can do it. Your daddy's right. None of us have ever seen you shy away from doing something you feel is right."

"Guess stubbornness runs in the family," I said, pulling my suitcase closer to inspect the contents one last time.

"Speaking of obstinate members of our bloodline," my father interrupted, causing my cousin and me to jump. "I just got a call from Jo. He says to bring you up to the big house one last time."

I whined in protest, trying to convince him I needed to stay on task. Since he kept insisting I should go back, I gave in and squeezed in between him and my cousin in his truck.

"I'll bet Granny wants to try one more time to

convince me not to go," I moaned as I climbed out of his vehicle.

My father chuckled. "You might want to hold onto your money for now."

As we walked up the steps onto the front porch, the scent of cigar smoke wafted in the air and one of the chairs creaked as it rocked. "Hey, Granddad," I said, greeting the ghost of my father's father and leaning down to scratch Slobby Bobby on his doggy head.

We entered into the foyer of the big house, and Uncle Jo called for us to come into the living room. Aunt Delia motioned for Dani to come sit by her on the couch, and my father and I stood as I faced my family.

"What?" I asked, crossing my arms in premature defense.

Uncle Jo pointed at the elephant coin necklace lying on the dark wood of the coffee table. "You know how this works, right?"

"Of course. It allows any of our dearly departed relatives to take a ride in it, so to speak." I looked to my father to clear up my confusion. "You know I've been using it for ages now."

"That's the point, butter bean." Dad nodded at the

object. "We'd like you to take it and wear it at all times while you're away."

I picked the coin up in my fingers, letting the chain dangle down. "I guess I can wear it underneath my clothes. It'll allow a little piece of home to be with me. Thanks."

"Maybe more than just a little piece," Uncle Jo interjected. "We want you to take a family member with you."

My thumb rubbed over the etched elephant. Flipping the token over, I read aloud the stamped phrase, "*Non ducor, duco.* I guess it's appropriate that it's in Latin considering I'll be in Italy." I raised my eyes to glance around the room. "But isn't it risky for me to take a family member in that kind of form so far away?"

"We've discussed that," Aunt Delia said, leaning close to her husband. "And we think it depends on who it is."

"Well, Granddad likes to ride along the most," I said, considering the choice. "He's probably the strongest by far."

"No, he's not." Granny Jo materialized beside me, wringing a dish towel in her hands.

I gaped at my ghostly great-grandmother. "Wait a minute. You're not suggesting that *you* want to go with me."

"I ain't suggestin' anything. I'm tellin' you that if any of us Jewells are gonna go with you for protection, then it might as well be me." She nodded her head for emphasis, and her whole body shimmered in and out of view.

Pointing at her spectral figure, I looked to the others to talk her out of it. "I appreciate the sentiment, and I'll be happy to wear the token. But I don't think it's worth the risk that I might lose her."

Uncle Jo raised his hand. "I once took Aunt Eustasia with me on the 127. She did just fine on the world's longest yard sale, which lasted three whole days plus travel time from here to Michigan, all the way down Highway 127 to Gadsden, Alabama, and back home. She did just fine."

"But at any moment you thought you might be losing her, you could come right back." I placed one hand on my hip while the other gesticulated at the window and the wide world beyond it. "I'm going to be across an entire ocean!"

Granny Jo huffed and hovered next to me, waiting for my panic to subside. "It's always been my choice to remain here, much like the other Jewells. But I feel it down to my rattlin' bones that I'll be just fine to go with you. Maybe even see about some of that food you've been talkin' my ears off that you wanna try. Couldn't hurt to learn some new recipes."

With the rest of my living family members encouraging me to accept the incredible gift, I tried to oblige with a little grace but couldn't help giving voice to my final concern. "But what if I lose you?"

"Funny, that's the same question I've been asking your daddy and uncle for a week now," she retorted. My ghostly great-grandmother lifted her hand up as if to cradle my cheek. A cold energy caressed my skin. "Child, let me do this and try to keep a watchful eye on you. Believe me, I'm much more expendable than your precious life."

Tears welled in my eyes. "Thank you, Granny," I whispered.

"You're more than welcome. I'm glad that's settled then. Before you leave in the morning, you stop on by and pick me up." She clapped her hands and rubbed them together. "Now, who wants some pecan pie?"

CHAPTER FIVE

L uke shook me awake, and when I tried to bat his hand away, he chuckled and kept insisting. "Rue, come on, *cara*. The plane will be landing soon, and the cabin crew wants us back in our seats.

Pushing the covers off of me, I yawned and stretched. "I don't know why I got so sleepy. It's pretty handy to have a bed on a plane."

"We left your place pretty early, plus you had both of our glasses of champagne when we boarded." He brushed a strand of my hair away from my face.

"What can I say, I was nervous. I've only flown a few times, and never on a private jet." The same hollow pit that had upset me when I first boarded returned.

Not once in our entire relationship had Luke made me feel like I wasn't equal to him. For the most part, he lived the simple life of a talented car mechanic. The only outward show that he possessed more money than one would assume was his penchant for expensive vintage cars.

It had been a recent discovery that when he remodeled his modest house, he'd dug out a secret basement and outfitted it with a way to house a considerable amount of goods he'd obtained over his many years of existence. The opulence of our ride back to his country of origin both impressed and frightened me.

The flight attendant waited for us to buckle into the plush leather seats of the cabin before offering us one last drink. "Is there anything else you'll be requiring, *Signor de Rossi?*" she asked in an accent that mixed a little Italian lilt with a British education.

"Will our means of transportation be ready for us upon our arrival?" Luke asked in a crisp tone unfamiliar to me.

The attractive woman nodded. "I believe all of the preparations are on schedule as requested. Please let me know if there is anything I can do for either of you."

As we descended, clouds danced in front of the window as scenes from the land below came into better focus. Luke crowded over me to point out the landmarks that defined the different areas.

"And there is our destination. *A Roma.*" The *R* rolled off his tongue.

I suppressed a girlish giggle, realizing I would have plenty of time to enjoy his attractive accent even more. "I thought we were going to your home town. Perdaggi?" I mangled the pronunciation.

"Perdaggia," he corrected, changing the hard *G* to sound like a *J*. "We could have routed there since there is a private airport just outside of the province, but I thought I would let you get your feet wet first. Plus, I'd love some time for just the two of us."

His statement earned him a very long, tender kiss. When I broke away, I gazed out the window. "Rome," I murmured, staring down at the sprawling city below. "Will we get a chance to see the Colosseum?"

"*Certo.* Of course. I couldn't bring you to the Eternal City without showing that to you." He settled his chin on my shoulder, gazing out the window with me. "Where else would you like to see?"

My cheeks heated, and I shrugged. "Honestly,

that's the only place I know for sure. Why don't I let you surprise me?"

His lips brushed from my shoulder up my neck and right by my ear, causing me to shiver with excitement. "It would be my absolute pleasure."

The plane descended, and I squeezed Luke's hand as it dipped and bounced.

The flight attendant unbuckled her seat belt and made her way to us. "*Mi dispiace*. There is a little turbulence as we get lower. We should land a little ahead of schedule."

"Thank you, Elena." Luke flashed her a smile that I knew only conveyed politeness on the surface.

The faint blush that bloomed on her cheeks annoyed me, but since she'd been so nice to me the entire flight, I let it go.

We landed with a soft bounce and taxied a little distance until the plane slowed down and steered toward a small hangar. Airport personnel waved their directions using orange lights and coordinated hand signals. Once we rolled to a stop inside, the roar of the jet engines died.

I looked to Luke to give me cues for what happened next. He relaxed in the seat, looking very different in a pair of khaki pants and a crisp burgundy button-down shirt. His sports jacket lay over the seat across from us.

With a critical eye, I examined my own choice of clothing and cringed. Wrinkles covered my favorite green sundress since I wore it while napping in the private plane's bed. The denim jacket I'd taken onboard in case I got cold had a couple of small holes from lots of use plus some fraying around the edges.

Feeling a little conspicuous, I pulled on the chain around my neck and held the token in my hand. It warmed at my touch, and I smiled, knowing my great-grandmother supported me no matter what I wore.

After some tense moments of waiting, the pilots turned the engines all the way off. Elena got off the phone at the front of the cabin and opened the door.

"I believe everything is ready for you," she declared, her perfectly pink lips grinning.

"After you, *cara*," Luke insisted, refusing to let me pick up my carry-on.

I threw my purse over my shoulder and clutched it as I reached the door.

Elena nodded her head at me. "*Bienvenuti a Roma.* Welcome to Rome, Miss Ruby."

Giving her my sincere thanks, I climbed down

the stairs with great care, heaving a sigh once my feet hit solid ground. I waited in nervous anticipation for Luke to join me. He grasped my hand in his and kissed my knuckles.

A man about the age and size that Deacon would be, if my cousin wasn't in his pig form, stepped away from a shiny black car and approached. As soon as Luke saw him, he let me go.

"Claudio!" he shouted, embracing the young man with delight and kissing him on both cheeks. They rambled on in Italian for a moment until my fiancé held up a hand and gestured for me to join them.

"Ruby Mae, this is Claudio Morandi. He and his uncle work for my family." Luke draped his arm over my shoulders. "And this is my...this is Ruby Mae Jewell."

I stuck out my hand to shake, ignoring my fiancé's choice not to reveal our relationship status. "Pleased to meet you."

The young man accepted my offer, shaking once before releasing me and bowing. "Any friend of Luca is more than welcome."

"Claudio, while it is just us, I would prefer if you called me Luke." A wrinkle creased my boyfriend's brow.

"Of course, as you wish." The young man bowed again. "Although it will be a hard habit to break."

"I have no doubt. But at least until I return home, I can dream a little longer." Luke ran his fingers through his hair, and I did my best to soothe him with an extra squeeze around his middle.

A couple of airport workers hurried over to place our luggage in the trunk of the car. Claudio busied himself making sure they had everything before we left.

I took the brief moment to check in with Luke. Throwing my arms around his neck, I scrutinized the look in his eyes. "Is everything okay?"

He sighed. "I'm sorry for not telling him about us. It was a knee-jerk reaction and very ungentlemanly. But we have just today to live where it's you and me. I want to make the most of it before, as you say in your part of the world, all hell breaks loose."

Claudio returned and ushered us to the open doors of the back seat. "If you please, I have already alerted the staff of your arrival. Based on the time of day, we should be there in about an hour."

Luke assisted me into the car, and I settled against the soft leather of the seat. He buckled the belt over me with a sly grin, knowing I hated being fussed over. When he finished, I shot him a mock annoyed glare, causing him to laugh. Some of my own tension eased away at the sound.

"*Andiamo!*" he declared as he sat down in the seat next to me.

I recalled the word during our brief Italian lesson on the jet. "That means *let's go*, right?"

"Very good." He nodded in approval. "And do you remember how to say *good day*?"

I struggled to remember the right phrase. "Bon Jovi?" I teased.

He chuckled. "Great band, but not close enough. It's *buon giorno*."

"Bon jorno," I butchered, sighing at my mistake. "How about I just say hey and howdy to everybody. It's probably what everyone would expect from a Southerner like me."

He grabbed my hand and held it in his. "That'll work. I want you to feel free to be yourself while you're here."

I grimaced, gazing out the window as we drove away from the airstrip. "It's going to be hard to feel comfortable knowing the little that I know about your family and how they feel about witches."

Luke's thumb rubbed circles on the skin of my hand. "It has been a long time. I don't think they would risk hurting relations with me on my first return."

I mulled over his chosen words with care. He didn't say with any clarity what position they would take once they found out I was a witch. Nor did he reassure me of what his plans were if his parents did come out directly against me and our impending wedding. I touched the spot where the token lay against me, hoping time would give me more answers.

Once we got closer to the city, the traffic built up around us. "Holy hexes, everyone is going so fast. And it's like they don't even see the lines on the road." I flinched away from the car that grazed by us.

Claudio laughed from the driver's seat. "If you think this is bad, wait until we get to the middle of the city."

Despite riding in a luxurious car, my nerves jangled the more the traffic grew. Luke checked his phone and typed out a few messages like nothing was happening, but I cowered and suppressed squeals of alarm every time a car came close or a scooter buzzed right past my window.

Luke unbuckled his belt and scooted closer to me. "Try not to focus on the vehicles. Start looking at what's surrounding us."

Not sure if I could calm down, I did as he suggested and gasped at the architecture towering above us.

"Think about all the history that exists in this tiny section of the country. The Romans established an empire right here, but they were not the first to settle here. The Etruscans, the Sabines, they lived here many millenniums ago. It is the oldest occupied city in all of Europe, and it's right out there for you to see."

Luke did his job of distracting me with great ease, pointing out specific landmarks or buildings and giving me some basic history. He talked of all the historical figures who clawed their way into power but never kept it for very long.

"And I suppose you were there when Caesar was in charge," I teased, bumping him with my shoulder.

"Ancestors of my family were alive during those times, but no, I was born during a different era," he replied, missing my joke. As soon as he caught on, he tickled my ribs. "I may be old, but I'm not ancient."

We cuddled together as he continued to explain the Italian way of living and how he missed the fast pace of it. "You will see when we walk around. It's both fast and slow at the same time, like a heartbeat can be. Full of vitality and richness, for this city is alive."

By the time we made it to wherever Claudio took us, I was ready to ignore the bit of exhaustion hitting me and go exploring. I expected to be ushered into an opulent lobby of a luxurious hotel but as soon as we arrived indoors, Luke placed his hand on the small of my back and escorted me to the elevators. Claudio stayed behind to take care of our things.

Luke pressed the button next to a smaller set of doors and smiled at the other guests. When the bell dinged, he gestured for me to enter before him. As the doors slid closed, he retrieved his wallet from his back pocket and pulled out a card, waving it in front of a sensor. The engine whirred to life and the elevator moved.

"Wow, it's almost like it knows you," I marveled.

"In a way, it does. My family pays for a private room to be available to us at all times." My fiancé fidgeted next to me, and I took his hand in mine.

"Are you getting nervous about this trip?" I asked.

"A little," he admitted. "I've stayed away for a very good reason, but you have given me a better one to return." He brushed his lips over our entwined fingers.

The bell dinged again, and we exited directly into a sprawling space.

"Sweet tea and spells, is this like a penthouse?" I took tentative steps into an entryway bigger than my entire cottage. The soles of my flats clicked on the shiny marble covering the floors.

"We're on the top floor," Luke said, walking past me to flick a switch on a far wall. The curtains pulled away from floor-to-ceiling windows and light flooded in. "Claudio will bring up our things and arrange them in our room. Come out here to the balcony, there's something I want you to see."

Trying not to catch flies with my gaping mouth, I closed the distance between us and stepped outside into the warm sun. Church bells pealed and echoed off of buildings, welcoming me to the city. Off in the distance, I spotted large buildings that must have some huge significance. Below us, people shuffled down both sides of the street like ants moving from place to place, their voices rising in the air in a constant chatty murmur.

A giddy giggle burst out of me, and I covered my mouth to capture it. "This is so amazing. I can't believe I'm here." I gripped the metal of the railing to ground myself.

Luke stepped closer, covering my back with his

body. He brushed my hair out of the way so he could plant a kiss on my neck. "Do you want to rest and go out later or would you like to go see what we can find right now?"

"I took a nap on the plane. Let's go do this!" I exclaimed, practically jumping up and down like a little girl. "Wait, should I change into something more comfortable? Picking up my feet, I pointed at my flats.

"You won't have to walk very far if you'll allow me to take the mode of transportation I want." His eyes twinkled in challenge.

I slung my purse across my body. "Let's see what you've got."

We made it back downstairs in the private elevator and stepped outside. Luke talked to one of the bellboys who yelled into a walkie-talkie. After mere moments, a valet pushed a shiny scooter in front of us. Two helmets were looped over the handlebars.

"You've got to be kidding. Didn't you see the crazy traffic out there?" I shrieked as Luke slipped some bills to the hotel staff.

My fiancé took the white helmet off and handed it to me. "Trust me. I have excellent reflexes."

I opened my mouth to argue but remembered

who and what he was. If anybody here had the skills to keep us alive, surely a very old vampire did.

Shoving the helmet over my hair, I accepted his challenge with wordless determination. He helped me buckle the strap underneath my chin and mounted the scooter.

I suddenly became very aware I was wearing a dress and thought about going back upstairs to change. At that moment, a couple younger than us flew past us, the girl's dress riding higher up her thigh than mine fell. She yelled something at the boy in loud Italian, and I smiled at Fate's direct dare.

Being careful to tuck the skirt of my sundress tight under my body so it didn't flow about too wildly, I wrapped my arms around Luke, who balanced the scooter while I got settled.

"I used to own a Vespa like this. They're incredibly efficient for navigating busy city roads," Luke's voice echoed through speakers in the helmet.

"Wow, I figured we wouldn't be able to talk until we stopped," I said.

"The microphones and speakers will allow me to continue telling you about things as we pass them. Just try not to scream when a vehicle comes close to us," he chuckled. "I promise I will get you where we're going in one piece. By tonight, you'll be begging me to let you drive."

"Doubtful," I replied, squeezing him a little tighter.

I soon discovered that a scooter cut through a lot of the congestion easier than a car. Only a few times did I close my eyes and take deep breaths to keep from squealing when other scooters got close enough that they almost touched my leg.

Luke drove me to different sites, parking the scooter out of the way and giving me more information than any tour guide could possibly know. He pushed his way to the front of an enormous fountain with carvings to make it look like a rock landing leading up to a white building with frames that held intricate statues of figures inside.

"This is the Trevi Fountain, and it is pretty young in comparison to a lot of other sites in the city. I think it was finished in the 1760s. That building is the Palazzo Poli, and the main statue is Titan, son of Poseidon and Amphitrite."

"Ah, so it goes with the water theme," I teased. "I think I've seen this in some old black-and-white film Granny made me watch with her." At the mention of her name, the token heated against my skin.

"Yes, it's been featured in many films, and you

can thank one of them for the next thing we're about to do." Luke fished around in his pocket until he pulled out a coin. "Here. Hold this in your right hand and turn around to face me."

"But then I can't see the fountain," I said in confusion.

He grinned. "It'll be there right behind you. Trust me."

I did as instructed and waited, watching others in the crowd doing the same thing while somebody took pictures of them.

"Now, I want you to come up with something that you really want." Luke's smooth voice captured my attention, and the rest of the noise surrounding us faded. "When you know what your wish is, keep that desire in your heart and close your eyes. Then toss the coin over your left shoulder."

I transferred the coin into my left hand to make it easier, and he corrected me. "Toss the coin from your right hand over your left shoulder. That is the custom."

There was a good chance the money wouldn't make it into the fountain, but I did as he asked. Closing my eyes, I tried to come up with the best wish I could.

I wanted Luke's homecoming to go well. And for

his parents to accept our engagement and me despite my magical background. But most of all, I hoped to find out what really happened to Isabella so that I could help my fiancé release his guilt and find peace after all these years.

"What are you wishing for that is making you look so serious?" Luke asked.

I shook my head and shushed him. Repeating my wish, I sealed it by kissing the coin, hoping my list wasn't so big that the fountain couldn't make it come true. After a countdown from three to one, I tossed the coin over my left shoulder and opened my eyes.

"Did it go in the water or did it hit someone?" I asked with a cringe.

Luke chuckled as he looked at the pictures he'd taken on his phone. "You did it perfectly. I've got the video to prove it."

We rode the scooter further into the city and stopped at the edge of a square, or *piazza* as I was learning. Wide steps led from the street all the way up to another level of buildings. Loads of people walked up and down while others picnicked while they sat on the stone stairs.

"This is the Spanish Steps. They were built pretty close to the same time as the fountain." He turned me a few degrees and pointed up at one of the buildings flanking the steps near the bottom. "That is where the famous poet John Keats came when he was sick and unfortunately passed away. It is now a museum with a huge collection of memorabilia and manuscripts having to deal with his contemporaries like Percy Bysshe Shelley."

I scrunched up my face. "I hate to admit it, but I never paid that close attention in English class. And I never really understood poetry. I guess that doesn't make me sound very cultured."

"Well, there are lots of things you do know and are an expert in that others aren't. Just because we all have differences doesn't mean we can't get along." Luke hugged me to ease my insecurities. "Besides, I'll bet you've heard of the novel *Frankenstein*."

"I've seen the movie. Guy with bolts coming out of his neck," I said.

He kissed the top of my head. "That was Hollywood's version. The book is far better, but my point was that Shelley's wife, Mary, wrote that book. They say it is the first science fiction novel."

I stuck a fist in the air. "Yay, girl power!"

Luke and I took some amazing pictures while posing on the stairs to send back home. We walked past the much more modest fountain in the middle of the square, and he directed me into a noisy cafe across from the Spanish Steps.

My heart raced at the loud din and chaos inside. A crowd of people shouted orders, and Luke kept a tight hold of me so I didn't get lost in the shuffle. After placing an order at the till, he brought the receipt, placing it and a coin on top of the glass display in front of the servers working the hefty coffee machines.

In a few short minutes, Luke retrieved the goods. He handed me a tiny cup not even a quarter of the size of my normal coffee mug.

"That's a macchiato," he shouted. "It's an espresso with some hot steamed milk."

Taking two packets of sugar, he dumped them both in, and the white pile floated for a second before sinking into the dark liquid. Luke handed me a minuscule spoon to stir my drink.

I lifted the warm porcelain to my mouth, but he stopped me. "Blow on it first. It'll be pretty hot."

Following his directions and watching how he drank his, I took my first sip. The sizzling liquid almost burned my tongue, but the strong flavor tasted like no coffee I'd ever had before. Its thick richness coated my mouth, and I savored it in small nips until it was gone. Using the spoon, I dug out the sugary sludge at the bottom flavored by the espresso and licked the little spoon clean.

Fresh energy zapped through my veins that reminded me of the electrifying jolt I felt after finding an incredible bargain. I stopped myself from jumping up and down by grabbing onto his arm.

"What's next on the agenda?" I asked, tugging on him.

Luke's eyes sparkled with amusement. "Well, I have called in some favors, and if you don't mind, I'd like to do a little shopping."

Too excited from my experience so far plus a little buzzed from the espresso, I agreed. Instead of heading back to the scooter, he wrapped my arm through his and escorted me down a nearby street.

"Via Dei Condotti," I read from the sign.

"*Brava,*" he complimented. "Your pronunciation was not so bad this time. Perhaps it's breathing in the Roman air."

"Or maybe it's the hot guy taking me around town," I shot back at him.

The crowds lessened as we walked further down the street. Tourists stood in front of store windows and posed. A tall woman with fashionable sunglasses and a tight dress that fit her body like it was made for her huffed as she maneuvered around a couple of student-aged kids.

When she came into full view, I noticed the extreme height of her stilettos that contributed to the illusion of her grandeur. A man opened the door for her, and she slid inside, away from the onlookers.

Luke led me around the people taking photos, and I glanced up at the sign for the store. "Gucci? That's a pretty fancy brand." I read the sign over the store across the street, recognizing it as well. "These are all pretty expensive stores."

The feelings of inadequacy that nibbled at my joy of the day grew a little more. Part of my business in my family's trade included knowing quality goods and their value. Every single store down this street carried a lot of clothing and goods worth far more than I possessed.

"Here we are." Luke turned to enter into the Valentino shop. He waited for a young man to open the door for us.

My curiosity got the better of me, and I allowed my fiancé to guide me inside. Even the air seemed clearer and all of the general din from outside disappeared once the door closed. I got lost in the beautiful pieces of clothing displayed on elegant mannequins.

Bright jewel-toned tops were tucked into crisp cream pants. A little black dress hugged the plastic model's curves with perfection. The only clothes I'd ever seen that rivaled the craftsmanship were those of Robin Westwood. Thinking about her old store and her promise to help me find or make my wedding dress made me a little homesick for a brief moment.

Luke joined me as I admired a dark blue dress. "That would look amazing on you. I can have them add that for you to try on."

I scoffed. "It's all very pretty, but there's nothing in here that I can afford."

"But I can," he replied. Sensing my reluctance, he put his hands on both my shoulders and turned me around. "There's nobody else in here. The store is all yours to choose from."

A lump formed in my throat, and I did my best to swallow it. It took me a couple of tries before I could find my voice. "That's very generous, but I don't need anything from here."

"Would you like to try another store?" he asked, concern wrinkling his brow. "Is there another brand you prefer?"

Heat rose in my cheeks as I noticed a store employee listening to us talking. Plastering a weak smile on, I strolled a little farther away from nosy ears.

My fingers floated over a rack of different hues of pink. "It's such a nice gesture to want to buy me something, but you've done so much for me already."

"I wanted to spoil you. Make this trip really special," Luke said, his bottom lip curling into the slightest of pouts.

Tugging on the protruding lip, I lightly tapped his nose. "You've already done that. I like you playing tour guide to my tourist. Plus, you refuse to let me pay for anything."

"That's no different than back at your home when you get us food or drinks at the Tiki," my fiancé countered.

I snorted. "It's way different. First, there's an entire ocean of a gap between the cost. Second, most of the time I get that stuff for free because Harrison owes me."

Luke took one step back and frowned. "This isn't going the way I planned. I just wanted you to have some nice things. That way, when we get to Perdaggia…" His voice trailed off.

My eyes widened in comprehension. "Oh, I get it now. Let me finish that sentence for you. That way, when we get to your place, Mommy and Daddy will be impressed. And you won't risk being embarrassed by my cheap clothes and country manners."

His silence spoke loud enough for me. Flustered, I stormed toward the door to leave, shoving past the employee who tried to open the door for me.

Outside in the sunlight, the foreign world around me seemed even stranger. I couldn't remember which way we'd come from, and since Luke had been guiding all of our activities from the second we left the plane, I didn't even know what hotel to get directions to.

For the first time in my life, I felt truly lost.

CHAPTER SIX

Needing to get out of the posh district before the tears that threatened to fall made a spectacle, I chose to turn right and stomped away. A strong hand on my arm stopped my progress.

"Ruby Mae, wait," Luke insisted. "I didn't mean anything—"

"Yes, you did!" I shouted, turning on him and poking a finger into his chest.

A few people near us snickered and pointed at our public tiff. I dragged him by the hand around the corner and into a narrow alleyway.

"You know, I've had this ache inside me ever since boarding that private jet." I stepped away from Luke's reach, wanting to finish what I had to say without him distracting me. "To be honest, I think it's been there for a while now, but I've been too afraid to talk to you about it."

Luke's brows furrowed, but he stayed quiet, giving me the space to keep talking.

"All the things you've kept from me. The life you've had. Your family." I lifted my hand and showed him the ring on my finger. "Your sister. You didn't share any of this with me. And now that we're here, I feel this deep chasm stretching between us more and more."

My fiancé had the good sense to appear remorseful. "That is not how I want you to feel."

I closed my eyes and took a deep breath before opening them to face the hard truth. "Maybe it was foolish of me to accept your proposal when there are too many differences between us."

Luke moved in quick vampire fashion to hold me against his chest. "Oh, *cara*. It breaks my heart to know I've hurt you like this. I don't know how to convince you that nobody"— he leaned back so I could see the truth in his eyes—"Nobody but *you* has ever captured my heart and seen me for who I am."

A stray tear escaped my eye. "But I'm realizing I might not really know you at all."

He wiped the salty drop with the tip of his finger.

"Yes, you do. In some messed-up way, I thought I could protect myself and you by keeping my past hidden. Maybe I was too enamored of the way you strip me bare. Too selfish to give up wanting to feel like I was everything you needed and wanted."

I placed a hand over his dormant heart. "I do love you. But I wonder if the Luke I love is the one who lives a simpler life as a mechanic. Not Luca, the crown vampire prince who is way out of my league."

Luke captured my lips with his to stop more doubt from tumbling out of my mouth. In the moments where we existed as just the two of us, the love we felt for each other shut out the rest of the world. But that kind of existence couldn't be sustained forever, even with a vampire.

A sob rose in my throat, and I ended our kiss. I pulled on the chain around my neck and pulled out the elephant token, folding my fingers around it to find the strength to finish the tough conversation.

"If you need me to be someone other than who I am, then maybe I should go home." I squeezed my fingers a little tighter, the edge of the medallion cutting into my palm. "Because designer clothes won't change the real me."

"I don't want them to." Luke swore under his breath and ran his fingers through his hair. "Rue, I am so sorry that I have been an instrument to cause you pain on any level. It was never my intention for you to be hurt. In fact, my justification for keeping my past away from you was because I didn't want it to stain our relationship. And yet it has anyway."

Luke dropped down on his knees in front of me, and I startled backwards away from him. Taking my left hand in both of his, he pulled me closer.

"Please believe me when I say to you that I am the worst of men and a terrible fiancé," he admitted, kissing the ring on my finger. "When I gave you this, I meant it as my solemn oath that I would take care of you for as long as you would have me. And I have failed."

I glanced around to make sure nobody else witnessed his self-deprecating confession. It may have been my intent to get him to see my side of things, but I never meant for him to negate what he was to me.

"Get up," I pleaded, tugging on him. "The last thing I need is for you to grovel."

He did as I asked but kept ahold of my hand. "Tell me what I can do to make things better."

I let out a long sigh. "First, stop saying you failed. If we're going to be man and wife, then we're going to screw up from time to time. I accept your apology, but don't drown in the guilt."

"But I cannot live with the fact that our trip here has made you feel worse," he said.

I rolled my eyes. "I may have been being a tad more dramatic than I should have been. Don't get me wrong, I'm mad as a kicked hornet's nest about you hiding things from me, but we're not going to get anywhere if we keep trying to go backwards."

Luke frowned as he tried to understand my meaning.

I took off my ring, and his face dropped. However, I handed it to him and held out my left hand with my fingers wiggling. "Now, when you put it back where it belongs, let's make a promise to each other."

"I would be happy to pledge any troth you require," he said with anticipation.

Raising my eyebrow at his archaic phrasing, I thought about what kind of promise we needed. "From here on out, we talk to each other about everything. Every fear, every joy. Everything." I raised a finger in the air. "And you will answer any and all questions I have about your past, especially the ones that come up from visiting your home town."

Luke brushed his lips over my fingers. "You will never have to hear about my life from others' tales. Is that it?"

"No." I squeezed the elephant token in my other hand. "Being together, especially in a marriage, is a lot tougher. Granny always told me the best advice she could give is not to go to bed angry. But since you sometimes skip sleep altogether, I think our motto needs to be that good or bad, we work through our problems. And we don't give up until we find a way to the other side."

Luke counted up my points and repeated them one by one until he gained my approval. With a trembling hand, he slipped the ring back into place and planted a chaste kiss over it.

"Now, about those clothes," I added.

Luke waved me off. "It was a stupid idea of mine."

"No, if you truly believe that it might help how your parents react to me, then I don't mind a few pieces. I'd rather start on the right foot with them," I said, biting my lip at the thought of meeting the future in-laws.

"Would you like to go back or pick another place?"

My fiancé acted as if I might leave him at any moment, and perhaps I had instilled that fear in him.

I wrapped my arm through his again. "Here's the thing. I'm not a girl who loves to shop. And I would much rather spend my time sightseeing than trying on expensive items that I'll be afraid to touch in the first place."

"Then how do you propose we go about things?" Luke asked.

"Well, since you seem to be a man of means, which makes no never mind to me, by the way," I added.

He bumped me with his hip. "And I love you for that."

"Then maybe you could have some pieces sent up to your room so I could try them on in private?" I suggested. "And we can try to squeeze in a few more places now?"

He stopped our progress back on *Via Dei Condotti* and kissed me for all to see. A few shrill whistles echoed in the air and two young men clapped for us.

We made our way back to the Vespa, and I hopped on like a pro. Weaving through the traffic, Luke got me to the next destination fast.

I stared up through the hole at the top of the Pantheon and listened in on a nearby guide explaining the history in English to a small group.

Yellow and maroon squares and circles lay amongst the veined white marble of the floor.

"This has been standing here for almost two thousand years," Luke whispered to me, leading me away from the group. He gave me a rundown of its vast history, and I nodded as I tried to soak in the years. Although I still battled with the overwhelming feeling of how young and inexperienced I was, especially compared to my fiancé, I no longer feared our differences. If it got to be too much for me to handle, I would uphold my part of the promise and tell him.

We took a break in the square outside the Pantheon, eating gelato from the store across from the historic site. Sitting on the steps of the monument in the middle of the square, I took in the bustling of people around us while indulging in the tasty treat.

"I can't believe how many flavors they had. And they let me try them all," I marveled, licking some of the strawberry that mixed with the lemon dribbling down the cone. "Little Ruby Mae would be jealous of me now. I always wanted multiple scoops when I was a kid."

"Gelato is good for you. Plus, you chose two of the healthiest flavors," he said, watching me with intense scrutiny as my tongue sought out more yumminess. "If you like *limone*, I should take you down to the Amalfi coast where they make the aperitivo limoncello. We'll try some after dinner maybe."

"What flavors did you get?" I asked, eyeing his choices.

"Chocolate and Fig. You should try some." Luke held out the cone to me, and I leaned over and bit right down the middle.

"Mm, I wouldn't have known it would be such a tasty combo just by looking at it." I wiped my mouth with one of the many napkins we'd grabbed.

After our sweet treat, we roamed the ruins of the Forum, and my imagination ran rampant with images of people in togas trying to conduct business. I stood in line and waited for Luke to take a picture of me standing in the place where Caesar had supposedly been stabbed to death by all his betrayers. At least it was another tourist, and not me, who yelled out the famous line, *"Et tu, Brute,"* with dramatic license.

The air chilled a bit on the ride to the Colosseum. By the time we parked the scooter and walked to the famous building, the setting sun cast orange light against the monument. The last straggling tourists paid to take pictures with locals dressed up as

Romans and gladiators, but Luke steered me away from them.

When we got to the main entrance, I pouted. "Oh no. It's already closed for the day."

My fiancé smirked. "Haven't you been paying attention? It's my turn to impress you with my special skills." He wiggled his fingers in front of him in a bad imitation of me wielding my magic.

Luke circled to a different entrance where a shorter, squat man with a bald head and a mustache waited against the fencing that protected the outer walls.

"*Buona sera, Professore,*" Luke called out, garnering the attention of the stranger. They continued their pleasantries until it came time for introductions. "Ruby, this is my friend Vito Lanciani. He is a professor of antiquities, and tonight, he will give us a private tour."

My insecurities from earlier forgotten, I blessed my man with means enough to get me into a historical site I'd only seen in my sad, beat-up textbook in Mr. Hathaway's history class in high school.

The outside of the structure was impressive enough, but the city had spent a lot of money constructing platforms that allowed the visitor to see just how immense the entire operation had been.

I could almost hear the roar of the crowd from the circular theater when I stood on the wooden surface raised in the middle of the arena.

Underneath my feet existed several different floors, and I couldn't believe that they used to bring in animals and other spectacles to watch. The professor gave each piece of information in such a way that I could picture it all. The excitement and the violence. The bloodshed and the deaths. No matter how much history existed on my family's land, it couldn't touch where my feet stood at that moment.

We had to leave once the evening got too dark for it to be safe for us to be inside the structure. The professor escorted us out, and when we exited, I thanked him profusely, pumping his hand up and down.

"It has been my pleasure, Miss Ruby," he said, his cheeks reddening under my enthusiasm. "Please, if you ever return *a Roma*, you call me and let me teach you more about my fair city."

Luke expressed his gratitude and kissed his friend on both cheeks before saying goodbye. He led me in the opposite direction of our scooter.

"Somebody is going to pick it up for us." He tugged on my hand. "I thought we could walk a little and then I could take you to a little wine bar I'm fond of. When you're ready, there's this tiny little ristorante far away from the tourist areas."

Luke's sincere sweetness amused me. He was trying so hard to make up for everything, and I agreed to his plan in a heartbeat. Confronting the big ol' elephant standing between us had deflated the stress I'd been holding onto for a while. In this new-to-me yet very old country, we had a chance to renew our relationship and walk together down a better, clearer path.

"Lead the way," I told him, allowing hope for our future to blossom inside me.

With us finally on the same page, I couldn't see how anything could get in our way.

CHAPTER SEVEN

I t turned out that *limoncello* was a mighty tasty after-dinner liquor. Also, drinking too much of the lemony drink could cause an incredible tipsiness and a little memory loss.

Stumbling out of the bed Luke had placed me in at some point, I made it to the table next to the kitchen area of the penthouse and collapsed into a chair.

"*Buon giorno, principessa*," Luke crooned from across the table. "I trust you slept well last night from all the noise you made."

I held up a middle finger at him. "If you're implying that I snore, I will divorce you right now, even though we're not even married yet."

A plate of something that smelled yummy landed

in front of me, and I risked opening one eye to check it out. A variety of pastries waited for me to choose which one I wanted. Despite the slight hangover, my stomach growled.

"Why did you let me drink so much?" I complained, taking a bite of the first golden, flaky offering. A little chocolate filling made me smile.

Luke chuckled. "It wasn't my fault. Alessandro wanted to please you, and you kept consuming every last drop he poured you."

I groaned as I recalled the tangy taste of the limoncello. "I don't know what I was thinking. Although, that meal was incredible. Tell me the names of everything I had."

Luke put down his phone and recalled the entire meal. "We started with the classic appetizer of *insalata di caprese*."

"Ooh, right. The mozzarella cheese was unlike anything I've ever had. And it tasted perfect with the fresh tomato and basil leaves." I licked my lips. "I'll have to try and get my hands on some olive oil from here to bring back for Granny to use."

"Wait until I take you to my uncle's vineyard. He'll give us some of his own pressing," Luke said. "And then you tried some of my *bucatini all'amatriciana* while you greedily ate all of your gnocchi. We split the roast chicken, and you swore you were too full for anything else."

I shaded my eyes with my hand while finishing the first pastry. "That's when the limoncello came out."

Claudio brought me a small cup of steaming espresso with a dash of milk on top. Luke pushed the sugar bowl towards me, and I scooped in two heaps, enjoying that second where the crystals floated on top before sinking. Even the sound of the spoon stirring bothered my head.

"Drink your macchiato. It'll help," Luke assured me.

It took two shots of espresso and another pastry to make me feel partially human again. "What does our day look like today?" I asked.

"Our departure has been delayed a little so that Claudio can help set up the clothes I'm having sent over," he said, checking his phone. "And if you don't mind, there is a Ferrari for sale that I wish to see in person to check on its condition."

I remembered the brand of car that his friend Cassio drove to his house back in Cedar Point. "Is this something you're looking to restore?"

"Yes. It's a 1957 335 Sport model that doesn't run but has been kept in a garage for decades." Luke held up a picture on his phone of a sleek two-seater red sports car. "One that was in perfect condition sold at auction for over thirty-two million euros."

I choked a little at the price tag. "Is that what you're thinking of spending?"

"No, it'll sell for far less. With a little work, she'd be a nice investment piece," he said in his business tone.

While I knew about his addiction to finding old cars and fixing them up, I had no clue the kind of money involved in his habit.

"Does the amount scare you?" Luke asked, watching me with care. "Should I not have told you?"

"No, it's your life. It's your passion, from everything I've observed." I tried to distract myself by looking at the sad state of my nails.

"But once we're married, what's mine will be yours, *cara*."

The room spun at the revelation I hadn't considered, and I gripped the table to stay upright. "It can't be."

"Of course it can. You'll be able to invest what you want into your family's business. Maybe expand to other locations." My fiancé leaned forward with excitement. "Maybe take your search for special items on the road. I'll bet there are more than a few magical objects sitting around European houses. Or even South America. Maybe China or Japan."

The air became harder to breathe, and I struggled not to squeak my shock. I always knew Luke had amassed some wealth, especially after he showed me his secret horde underneath his house. But it didn't occur to me for one second that any of his wealth might be mine if we married.

"That's…a lot to process," I admitted.

"I take it as a good sign that you're still sitting at the table and not running out of the hotel, screaming," my fiancé said with hope.

I smirked. "The thought had occurred to me." My hand patted the rat's nest of hair I'd pulled into a messy bun. "But I figured the locals didn't need to see this much of the real me."

"I think you look quite fetching, all sleepy and disheveled," Luke complimented.

"And I think your vocabulary has gotten fancier now that we're back on your home turf," I teased back. "It's a little confusing, but I also kind of like it. Especially when you throw in all the Italian."

He lifted a saucy eyebrow at me. "*Verimente?*"

"Ooh, you're trying to make sure we stay inside the hotel today, aren't you?" I flirted.

A string of foreign words fell from his lips, and I

so. Plus, time for negotiations and to set up transport back to my house." Luke calculated his time. "I'd say maybe a couple of hours."

"That would give me time to get somewhat presentable," I muttered under my breath.

"I should be back in time to see you choose some of the clothing pieces, and then I can help you pack." He pushed his chair back and stood. "We can get on the road during *riposo*, so the traffic will be a little lighter."

"Why?" I asked.

"Oh, it's the time of day where people go home to eat lunch and rest a little," Luke explained. "Everything opens back up after four in the afternoon."

"Like an enforced nap time," I said in awe. "That actually sounds amazing."

He waggled a finger at me. "No napping for you. You'll want to take in the beauty of the countryside as we drive into Umbria. And if I time it right, you'll get to see *Castello di Rossi* in all its glory."

I called my cousin once I was alone and filled her in on everything. Hearing her voice gave me comfort I didn't know I was craving. Once she found out about my discomfort with Luke and his money, she admonished me, reminding me that I was just as ready to share what I had with him. Why wouldn't I want it to be a two-way street?

True to his word, Luke set up for the staff at the hotel spa to come up to his penthouse. The long massage did help rub away some of my stress. The nail technicians had set up a station outside on the balcony, and I sat in a comfy chair drinking bubbly prosecco and getting all my nails cut, shaped, and polished while still enjoying the ambience of Rome.

Against my protests, Luke arranged with Claudio to take all of my choices, and a few extra outfits that caused a rather visceral reaction from my fiancé, with him back to Perdaggia along with our luggage. I regretted leaving the hotel so soon, but seeing our mode of transportation for the rest of the day cheered me right up.

A little black car waited for us at the entrance. Its sleek lines earned a low whistle from me. "She's a beauty," I sighed.

"Then she's the perfect match for you." Luke dangled the keys. "Want to drive her?"

I shrieked in fear. "Are you kidding? With the way the crazies drive around here, we'd crash for sure."

Luke opened the door for me, and I slid into the passenger seat with leather as soft as butter. When my fiancé joined me behind the wheel of the sweet car, he handed me a box tied with a bow.

"You've given me more than enough," I chastised.

"Think of this as more of a gift of utility than of generosity then," he said, wiggling it in front of me.

I thanked him as I accepted the gift. Pulling the strands of ribbon off, I opened the box and tore through the tissue paper. "Is this a scarf?" I asked, retrieving a dark green square of silk decorated with an intricate pattern.

Luke pointed at his head. "I thought you might want to protect your hair. When we pull off of the *autostrada*, I intend to put the top down so we can enjoy the view properly."

In no time, he drove us from the middle of the busy city onto the highway. I did my best to grit my teeth and bear the fast pace as the speedometer crept higher and higher. When we exited, Luke parked the car and dropped the top. Making sure my scarf was secure, he resumed the drive in a more leisurely manner.

Every twist and turn of the two-lane road brought another picturesque scene into view. More than once, I begged him to pull over so I could snap as many pictures as possible to remember the roaming beauty of the land less than two hours north of Rome.

The sun set in the sky as the road curved and wound its way toward a walled city that rose in front of us. Parking lots full of cars lined the sides as we got closer to the two-story gap in the wall.

"Because the roads are so thin and mostly cobble-stone, they limit how many vehicles can enter and drive through the city," Luke explained as we approached the entrance. "They make the buses and other tourists park outside and walk in."

As we drove closer, a few people yelled at us or held up their hands to get us to stop. My fiancé ignored them and kept driving until he reached a man in uniform who stood in our way.

The guard spoke to Luke in fast Italian, and my fiancé retrieved his wallet from the pocket of his sports coat draped over my lap to keep me warm during our drive. Whatever he showed to the guard did the trick, and our car was allowed through.

"We'll take it slow, but keep your eyes open for the surprise," he teased. "You'll know it when you see it."

Luke navigated the streets with ease and patience. Several times, we had to wait for tourists to move out of the way so we could drive by. The busy center of the town gave way to a driveway that seemed more private.

He pointed to my right. "Keep your eyes trained on that spot just over that hill."

We drove a little farther until we crested a hill. Crowds of people dotted the nearby landscape, many with professional cameras snapping the image that captured their attention. My breath caught in my throat and my mouth opened.

A large stone castle sat on the hillside, but it was the facade of it that everyone admired. The last rays of the day's sun reflected off the stone in a manner that made it blaze a bright red.

"The name Castello di Rossi means the castle that belongs to the di Rossi family. But it has a bit of a double meaning that many have noted over the centuries," Luke explained.

"Double meaning?" I asked, still captivated by the bright color of the building that made it otherworldly as we drove closer.

"Sì. Many call it the Red Castle, which matches well because my surname actually means red." He slowed down and pulled over so I could take in the full effect. "But since it was built during a time of much violence and death, it also earned a moniker befitting it."

I stopped staring at his ancestral home and faced him. "What name was that?"

The car rolled back onto the narrow road, and Luke drove us to the entrance to the castle. The color of his home deepened the closer we arrived.

As we drove through the gate to enter the grounds, Luke answered my question. *"Castello di Sangue."*

Even though I couldn't translate the words, something about his tone made me shiver. "And what does that mean?"

My fiancé grinned, and I mistook his expression for happiness. It took me a moment to notice his protruding fangs on display.

"In English, it means Castle of Blood."

CHAPTER EIGHT

I don't know what I expected when I found out Luke's family occupied an actual, real live castle. The only vision of what one might be came from movies or television. Oh, and that one time I ate at Medieval Times for one of Deacon's birthdays.

No trumpets announced our arrival once Luke brought us inside. In fact, he avoided the front entrance altogether.

"Isabella, Cassio, and I tried to map all of the secret passageways once," he said as he ran his hand over the rough stone exterior. "The hard thing to know is which ones will lead you directly to rooms you want to avoid. I remember once, Isa and I found this one passage and followed it, only to exit into our parents' private chambers."

I thought about the one time I'd gotten scared during a thunderstorm at night and had busted into my parents' bedroom. My mom had shrieked at me to go away, and I was too young to catch onto why she would send her scared child back to her room. It wasn't long after that when she left us forever. I never told Dad I blamed myself for losing her.

"Aha! Here's the touchstone." Luke placed his palm over one particular rock in the wall. When he pulled it away, a little blood smeared on his pale skin.

He licked his hand clean and the tiny puncture wound disappeared. "The mechanism requires a little sacrifice so the place can recognize friend or foe."

I lifted my eyebrow at him. "That sounds an awful lot like spellcraft. Unless vampires gained a level of magic we've all been unaware of."

The second I uttered the word "magic," a line in the shape of a door appeared in the wall, becoming more solid by the second. With a loud *kerthunk* and a click, the block of stones opened, revealing a dark passage.

Luke gestured for me to enter first, and I snorted.

"As if." I peeked my head in and heard the scuttling of some unseen creature. With a shiver, I refused again. "There's a whole lot of nope in there."

"My apologies. In such close proximity to my home, I forgot that you don't possess the vampiric ability to see in the dark." My fiancé held out his hand. "If you'll trust me, I promise to get you through to the other side in perfect health."

I adjusted my purse to sling it across my body and accepted his offer. Taking reluctant steps behind him, I followed into the dark chasm. Once we crossed the threshold, the door closed on its own with a crunch of stone and gravel.

"Would it offend you if I cast an orb of light?" I whispered. "I literally can't see where I'm going."

An eerie silence followed my question, and I wondered if Luke answered by shaking his head. Which I'd never know.

"It may be too risky to cast a spell on the castle grounds," he replied. "Since I haven't been here in ages, I don't know what security measures they've added. And I'd prefer to get inside without too much notice."

We hadn't even gone a foot inside the castle and already the first issue of me being a witch reared its ugly head. "But if vampires didn't create your little magical secret passageway, then who did?" I hissed. "It had to have been witches."

"Our family wasn't always averse to your kind," Luke said, tugging on my hand to pull me forward.

My stomach twisted at his unintentional line drawn in the sand between vampires and witches. "So, they're happy to continue using the fruits of our power but won't entertain that their children might fall in love with someone not of their *kind*," I pushed to make my point. The last word echoed off the walls.

Drips of water and other various creepy noises kept me on edge, and I yelped when my foot stepped into a puddle.

Luke stopped our progress. "Listen, would it offend your female empowerment sensibilities if I were to pick you up and carry you the rest of the way? At the rate we're going, it'll be tomorrow before we get there."

I wanted to tell him I could handle it, but when I opened my mouth to answer something scurried over my foot. "Nope, nope, nope. No offense. None at all. Go ahead and pick me up," I declared loud and fast, hopping from one foot to the next to try and minimize the chances of something else touching me.

Luke's amused chuckle reverberated off the walls, and he scooped me into his arms. His lips brushed my forehead. "It'll be much faster this way."

A light wind blew against my face as Luke sped through the corridors in record time. Despite not being able to see where we headed, I could still sense our movement, and I cuddled into his chest, closing my eyes and waiting for the journey to end.

My body jerked a little when he put on the brakes and slowed down to stand in front of another doorway. Light blazed around the edges of the barrier, providing a little illumination for me to see the immediate ground in front of us.

Expecting him to put me down, I tapped on his shoulder. He lay a finger against my lips to warn me from saying anything too loudly.

"What's wrong?" I uttered in the quietest whisper I could. "What's on the other side?"

Luke remained as still as a statue. "My room."

His answer befuddled me, and I wiggled in his grip. "Isn't that where you wanted to go?"

My fiancé's chest expanded and contracted when he sighed. "I guess I was trying to avoid what comes next."

"What do you mean?"

With my eyes partially adjusted, I noticed him

nod in the direction in front of us. "The second I go in there, I can no longer pretend I'm just Luke Manson, a mechanic who works with a pretty relaxed boss and has a gorgeous and feisty girlfriend."

I tightened my grip around his neck. "You'll still have me no matter what."

He planted a quick peck on my lips. "I know, and I love you for reassuring me."

It took me a second to catch onto his hesitance. "Luke, you're going to have to face your family at some point. It might as well be sooner rather than later. Plus, I'd really like to stand on solid ground where I don't have to risk stepping in something icky or having something take a bite out of me."

His body stilled under mine, and I worried I'd pushed him too far, too fast.

"You're right," he agreed after a long silence. Shifting my body to hold me in his left arm, he reached out and yanked on something.

With a click, the door gave way. Bright light flooded the darkness, and I blinked my eyes to adjust. Luke placed me down on solid stone, and it took me a moment to compose myself. When I stopped adjusting my clothes and my purse, I looked up and gawked at the scene unfolding in front of me.

"Most of my whole cottage could fit in this room, Luke," I exclaimed, turning in circles to take it all in. "This belonged to just you?"

Every which direction I turned, I saw items that looked like they belonged in some movie. Intricate tapestries hung from the walls. A shiny suit of armor complete with a sword and shield stood at guard in one of the corners. All of the dark wooden furniture of the room matched, and I imagined the hands that carved every curve and decoration into the grain. A large ornamented mirror hung over the dresser. My head pinged back and forth from admiring everything to calculating the worth of it all in my head.

"It's uh…" I started, still too bewildered to come up with the right words.

"Exactly how I left it," Luke stated as he surveyed his old place. "Except I left the bed unmade when I departed."

In all of my open-mouthed gaping, I hadn't even taken in the sight of the largest bed I'd ever seen. Wooden posts stained a dark reddish-brown rose to the ceiling in carved spirals on all four corners. A canopy of thick black velvet hung across with a gold fringe all around its edges.

A mountain of pillows laid on top of a thick comforter. A large emblem of some sort was embroidered into the fabric, and whoever had made the bed took care to position the symbol in the exact middle of the expansive berth.

"You could fit a whole army on that mattress," I exclaimed, shooting my fiancé a suspicious glance. "You didn't though, did you?"

My joke achieved my goal, and Luke stopped frowning and gave into his genuine laughter. "No, no army has camped in my bed."

Three loud knocks on the door echoed throughout the chamber, and I froze in place. Luke's smile faded, and he stood up a little straighter.

"Enter!" he called out in a formal tone.

The wooden door creaked open, and a man in a fitted suit entered the room. "Master Luca, it is nice to see you back on the premises." He bowed as he addressed my fiancé.

"Enzo. I would ask how you knew we had arrived, but you've always had access to eyes and ears all over the castle." Luke kept a straight face. "Have you informed my parents yet?"

The newcomer placed his hands behind his back. "I thought you might want a little time to yourself to adjust. After all, it has been a while since you have stepped foot inside these walls."

The corners of Luke's mouth twitched, and he

burst out into a laugh. With long strides, he closed the distance between him and the man in the suit. "It's good to see you, old friend."

They greeted each other as old friends, kissing both cheeks and hugging. A sense of awkward intrusion washed over me, and I tried to hide behind one of the bedposts.

"There is no use trying to hide from Enzo." Luke gestured for me to reveal myself. "He truly does know and see all."

Although I had encouraged my fiancé to face his past, I didn't know the best way to deal with my potential future. The token warmed against my skin, clearing away my fear. I pulled up my proverbial big-girl panties and flashed my best smile.

"Hey, how you doin'? I'm Ruby Mae," I crowed with a little extra oomph in my Southern manners, offering the man my right hand.

He accepted with a firm yet gentle touch, bowing deep until I could see the bald spot shining towards the back of his gray hair. "It is a pleasure to meet you, miss."

"Enzo has been working with the family for as long as I can remember," Luke explained, delighted to see me meet an old friend.

I failed at my first attempt of a curtsy, managing

a weak wobble in response. "Are you a vampire as well?"

Enzo let go of me and placed his hand behind his back again. "No, miss. But when one of my bloodline is chosen to serve, we are given means to elongate our normal lifespan."

Something about his explanation triggered a memory. "Oh, Claudio is related to you, isn't he?"

A beaming smile brightened his aloof expression. "You've met my nephew. He is young in his service to the family and still in training. However, I believe he has progressed nicely. I trust he took care of you well on your brief sojourn in Rome?"

"Very," I said, finding it easy to speak the truth.

"That is extremely good to hear." He relaxed his rigid stance. "With Master Luca's return to the home, there will be much to do over the next week or so. My nephew will have many opportunities to prove himself worthy of taking over for me."

Luke's smile disappeared. "I was hoping this trip would not be extended for too long. And that we could do away with any unnecessary...chaos."

Enzo reached out and gripped my fiancé's shoulder. "My friend, how could you expect otherwise when you have been away for over a century? Not only that, but I have heard that your father intends to make a demand on your life that you will need to prepare for."

"No!" Luke pulled out of the man's grip. "I did not come home to be saddled with a responsibility I never wanted."

"Nonetheless, you will have to face what you have been putting off for so long." Enzo took a step closer but kept his hands to himself. "Everyone's choices hold their own consequences."

Luke looked like he wanted to punch something, but he ran his hand down his face instead. "I know this will not be easy on many levels." He half-grinned at me. "At least I'll have you with me at all times."

Enzo cleared his throat. "Actually, Claudio has been instructed to set Miss Ruby up in a room down the hall. He has already taken her things there."

"Why can she not stay with me?" my fiancé asked. "I recall a time when my father and mother said nothing when you found the contessa in here."

Enzo chuckled. "And with nary a stitch of clothing on, if memory serves."

I cleared my throat, reminding the two men of my presence. Enzo's eyes widened as if he'd been caught with his hand in the cookie jar.

"My deepest apologies for breaking protocol, Miss Ruby." He bowed again.

"Oh, stop kowtowing to me. I'm not anybody special," I waved him off. "But I'd prefer not to hear about past conquests, especially nekkid ones."

Luke clicked his tongue. "The contessa was *not* a conquest. I suspected my sister's hand in the predicament I found myself in."

"Isabella always had a wicked sense of humor," Enzo admitted. His head tilted to the side. "May I ask a question of the two of you?"

Luke gave a curt nod. "You may."

"Will you be announcing your engagement at tonight's reception?" he asked.

My breath caught in my throat and I coughed a couple of times. "How did you—" I stopped myself from finishing the question the second I caught Enzo looking at the ring. "Never mind. But there's going to be a reception tonight?"

Luke closed his eyes and uttered a curse under his breath. "Of course my parents would plan something tonight." He pinched the bridge of his nose. "Informal or formal?"

"Based on the preparations so far, I would recommend evening attire," Enzo suggested. "We will be outside on the patio."

Uncertain of the actual answer to Luke's question, I looked to him for guidance.

"Wear one of the long dresses," he said. "They should do just fine."

Just fine. As if that would go a long way to impressing his mother or father.

"And as for my question?" Enzo pushed.

Luke covered my left hand with both of his and leaned his forehead against mine. "Tonight will be a spectacle, knowing my parents as I do. Perhaps we should postpone springing the engagement on them until tomorrow. When it is just the family."

I fidgeted in discomfort. "So, you'd like my first encounter with your family to be one wrapped up in deception?"

He grimaced. "I know it doesn't sound like a good idea."

"I'd really rather not start on a bad foot," I pleaded, fear stirring up my empty stomach. "Maybe it's better to get it over with all at once. You know, if you announce our engagement in front of a lot of people, your parents will have a harder time denying it."

Enzo's eyebrows lifted, and he nodded once in approval. "Your lady has made an excellent point. A public announcement would give you an advantage."

"In a game I have no wish to play," Luke complained. He ran his fingers through his hair and stalked away from me. "Gah, why can't things ever be easy with this family?"

I followed him and threw my arms around his body, leaning my head between his shoulder blades. "Because family means fighting for one another. Even if that also means fighting against each other."

Luke relaxed under my embrace. "But I don't want to fight. I don't want anything but to live my life."

I pressed my face against his back and giggled. "That's the first time I've ever heard you sound like a whiny teenager rather than a grown-up. A very old grown-up to boot."

He scoffed, taking my hand and whirling me around in some fancy dance move until he caught me by my hip. "And yet under this roof, I feel less like myself and more like a naughty child returning home to receive his punishment."

"If that's how you approach the situation, then that's how your parents will see you," I said, hoping to get my message through despite my accidental stomp on his foot. "It would be better to adjust your sails and change their expectations of you."

Luke looked over my shoulder at his old friend. "Do you understand what she means?"

"I think this intelligent young woman is saying

that you should present yourself as you wish to be seen. Be on the offensive from the start rather than the defensive," Enzo reinterpreted.

I stopped dancing to attempt another curtsy. "Thank you for the compliment."

"It was well-earned, miss," Enzo said. He pulled on a chain that led into a pocket of his waistcoat and retrieved a pocket watch. "I must apologize, but perhaps I should escort Miss Ruby to her chambers to give her time to get ready."

After bolstering Luke up, I'd used up my reserve of confidence. The sudden prospect of leaving my fiancé's side panicked me.

"What are you going to wear?" I asked Luke.

"Oh, one of my fitted suits. When you figure out which dress you'll choose, let me know and I'll wear a tie to match." He addressed his friend, "I assume my dressing room has been replenished and updated?"

"With the latest fashion, Master Luca," Enzo replied. He bowed again and gestured toward the door. "Miss Ruby, if you'll allow me, I'll be happy to escort you to your quarters."

Luke asked for a moment of privacy. When Enzo left the room, my fiancé swept me into his arms and kissed me with so much passion that my ears rang.

A little dizzy from our intimate moment, I flashed him a goofy smile. "What was that for?"

"For everything you've done for me before. For being here with me now." His charming smile dazzled me. "And for loving me forever."

"Big talk coming from a vampire." I twisted the ring on my finger. "You sure you're ready for this?"

Luke winked at me. "In the words you like to use so often, bring it on!"

Enzo's and my footsteps bounced off the walls as we walked further and further away from Luke's chambers.

"I'm guessing Luke's mother picked what room I would stay in," I said with a knowing smirk.

"You are very astute, miss," Enzo said with a chuckle. "How did you guess the truth?"

I snorted. "Because my father went out of his way to make sure Luke didn't spend the night with me when we first dated."

"And things have changed now?" the kind man asked.

"Oh, yes," I exclaimed. "My whole family treats him as if he's already one of us." In my head, I pictured a portrait of Luke hanging next to mine on the wall of Jewell ancestors in the foyer of the big house.

Enzo stopped in his tracks, and it took me a second to notice his absence beside me. I turned to face him.

"It warms my heart to know that after all the time he spent alone, he found someone." He placed a hand over his heart. "And I am beginning to appreciate that the person he chose is you."

Touching my heated cheek with my fingers, I uttered my thanks. With quick steps, I hurried down the corridor until a clearing of the throat stopped me.

"If you would, miss," Enzo said, standing by an open door. "This will be your private quarters during your sojourn at Castello di Rossi."

"Thank you." I brushed past him into the lit space but only made it a foot inside the door. "All of this is for me?" I squeaked.

The size of the room did not compare to Luke's, but the living room and dining room of the family homestead combined would make up the square footage. The furniture and decorations had a more delicate touch to them, and fresh flowers filled several vases placed throughout the space.

One of the fancy dressers had a gold and brown marbled top with gold-painted ornamentation plastered all over the rich wood with an intricate inlay design over the entire surface.

Pulling out one of the drawers to test its make, I bent down to inspect the piece. "The design, I think, is French. Based on the notches on the inside, I'd say handmade rather than manufactured. And since we're in a castle, I would bet it's an original, but I'm not exactly sure from which century."

"That would be eighteenth century, miss. And you have a wonderful eye." Enzo ushered me further into the room.

"It's the family business," I said with pride. "We deal in a lot of antiques, although I would imagine I've only seen replicas and not the real thing."

"Then maybe when you have a moment to yourself, you might allow me to take you on a tour to show you some of the really good stuff," he offered. "The family has lived here so long that they have forgotten to appreciate the quality of the pieces they've acquired over so many years."

"They've forgotten what makes a house a home," I said. "It's the choices in people *and* the furniture and decorations."

"Precisely." Enzo pointed at an adjoining room. "The lavatory is through there. And your closet will be the next door over."

I snorted. "What, I don't get a dressing room?"

"If you would prefer I find better accommodations for you—"

"No, no!" I interrupted, a little embarrassed. "It was a joke. This will be more than enough for me."

He offered me a smile. "Then I will leave you to it. Tonight's event should start in about an hour. I hope that will give you enough time to prepare."

The knot in my stomach twisted into the size of a boulder. "I'll be ready," I managed in a weak voice.

Enzo turned to leave but paused. He approached me and took my hand in his. "Remember what you told Master Luca. Present yourself as you wish to be seen and you will have the advantage." With yet another bow, he left me alone.

I pulled my purse off my shoulder and looked for a place to put it. All of the furniture seemed too nice, and I'd hate for my first act inside the castle to be one that caused any scratches on the fancy pristine wood.

Choosing the door that opened into the closet, I found another room too large to believe. My suitcase sat against the far wall, and when I checked it, I found it empty of its contents. On one side of the closet, my clothes hung from a short rack with the few shoes I packed lying underneath.

On the opposite wall, all of the clothes Luke and I had picked out together in Rome hung in a color-coordinated row. Except there were pieces there I'd never seen. Shoes I had never tried on rested on a built-in rack off to the side.

Feeling a little overwhelmed, I backed out of the room of a closet, my hands gripping over my stomach. "How in the world did I ever think I was going to survive this?" I moaned out loud.

"By holding your head up high, trying your best not to stand out too much, and living by the motto that you'll have to fake it till you make it," a smooth female voice answered me.

I jumped, startled by the intrusion. "Holy hexes, you scared me."

The regal woman smiled, her fangs glistening. "You will really need to work on your peripheral vision. We vampires can move about without making noise, and it's a good rule of thumb not to be caught unawares by any of us."

Knowing she could sense my pounding heartbeat, I took a few deep breaths to calm down. The extra moment gave me a second to figure out who I might be talking to, but with so little information to go on, I had no clue.

"I'm sorry, where are my manners." I wiped my

clammy hand on my dress and stuck it out. "I'm Ruby Mae."

She shook hands with me with a light grip. "I am used to such salutations, but you must refrain from doing the same with the lady of the manor. No need to stand out more than you already will."

I narrowed my eyes at her. "Who are you?"

"My apologies. I thought you might recognize my voice since we spoke on the phone together." With a slight bob of her head in a show of respect, she addressed me again. "I am Lady Eveline de la Roche. I have traveled all the way from Honeysuckle Hollow at the behest of your friend Charli to help you."

CHAPTER NINE

Lady Eveline laced the corset of my dress a little tighter and I gasped.

"Good fashion comes at a price sometimes," she said, tugging a little harder.

I struggled to breathe. "But if it kills me, will it be worth it?"

"Well, let's see." She escorted me out of the closet and planted me in front of another ostentatious mirror. "I think the dark purple was the right choice. It accents the color of your hair. And the cut of the dress shows off your comely figure well."

I stared at the woman glancing back at me with wide eyes and a bow of a mouth twisted into the shape of an *O*. She didn't appear like any version of me I'd ever seen. The side slit up the left leg went so high that I blushed.

"I don't know if I can pull this off," I admitted.

"You most certainly can, and you must," Lady Eveline insisted, carrying a pair of stilettos to me. "These should be perfect."

Although I usually wore flats to dress up in and sneakers or cowboy boots on an everyday basis, I knew how to carry myself in heels. However, I was pretty sure I'd never worn a pair that would probably cost more than two months' worth of Ellie burgers. If I sat, I was unsure whether or not I could stand back up again in the tight outfit, so I appreciated my new best friend allowing me to use her to keep myself upright while I slipped on the heels.

I wobbled a bit when I stood but found my footing enough to take a few paces back and forth.

"I'll almost match Luke's height now," I beamed. "But I don't think I can wear them forever. I hope whatever's planned won't take hours."

Lady Eveline continued to fuss over me, straightening the fall of my skirt and trying to correct my posture. "Damiana and I are old acquaintances. No doubt she's planned this soiree in order to intimidate you a bit."

I smirked. "You mean, gain the home court advantage."

The vampire woman smiled enough to show fang. "Precisely. I thought it best for me to be there to help smooth your introduction with her."

"That is so nice of you," I gushed, wanting to reach out and hold her hand. But something about her demeanor told me she'd prefer to stay less familiar.

Lady Eveline took a step back to inspect her work. "Almost there. I think you should keep your hair wild like it is rather than putting it up." She tapped her mouth as she scrutinized my appearance. "It makes you look a little dangerous."

"That doesn't sound particularly good when I'm trying to downplay my true nature," I worried.

"No, it's exactly how you should present yourself. Don't hide. Be upfront and embrace who you are." Lady Eveline frowned as she fussed with some strands of hair that refused to be tamed on any level. "Damiana's focus will mainly be on her son, but if you stand up to her by his side, she will see you as a force to be reckoned with."

"Which might be a temporary fix while others observe us. However, behind closed doors, I wonder what tricks she might use to try and get rid of this witch?" No amount of fine clothes would change that possible outcome.

Lady Eveline reached out a cold hand to touch my bare shoulder in a gesture I doubted she did very often. "I live in a town amongst some of the better beings on this planet, and many of my friends are witches. Let her see your true self, and you will have the best chance at showing her why her son picked you out of all the women in the world."

When I got back home, I'd have to find something special to give to Charli for encouraging her friend to come here to support me.

The vampire pointed at her neck. "I think the whole look would be better without that necklace."

Tugging on the chain, I pulled out the coin hidden just under the edge of the dress. "I'm not supposed to take it off."

"But a bare décolletage would be far more fetching. And also show Damiana and Lorenzo that you have no fear of their vampiric nature," she explained.

I held the token by my fingers, staring at it in indecision. On the one hand, I could use the presence of my ghostly great-grandmother to help bolster me. But it would be nice to find another way to confound Luke's parents' expectations of me.

"One moment," Lady Eveline said, staring at the metal. "May I have a closer look?"

I slipped the necklace over my head and settled the token into her palm. She let the gold chain slip through her fingers and dangle while she turned the medallion over.

"This is in remarkable condition. Almost like it is brand new. Wherever did you get it?" she asked.

A part of me wanted to keep my family secrets, but since Charli had vouched for the vampire, I put my trust in her. "It's been handed down for generations."

"I see." Her lips pursed a bit as she examined it. "Perhaps it would be good to let Damiana see this on you at some point."

"Why?" I asked, my fingers itching to take the token back.

As if sensing my unease, Lady Eveline handed the heirloom to me. "Because of what carrying a coin such as this a long, long time ago meant. If she recognizes it, the memory may help you earn her esteem."

"I'll be honest, I don't know how far back in my lineage it goes. All I know is that my first ancestor who settled in the United States carried it with him from England." My thumb rubbed over the relief of the elephant.

"Its origins may not matter. Only the symbolism," she said.

With a little irritation at the games I had to play adding up, I tried not to sulk. "So, should I wear it or not?"

She considered my question by looking at my ensemble. "I think not for tonight. But wear it the rest of the time you are here in plain sight until both Lorenzo and Damiana take notice."

With a pang of regret, I settled the necklace onto the smooth surface of the fancy dresser. "Is that it?"

Lady Eveline walked around me. "Nearly there. Here, you should use these."

She unhooked the dangling earrings from her ears and handed them to me. The crystals twinkled in the light.

"Tell me these aren't diamonds," I choked out, knowing the answer.

"Of course. Since the evening festivities are outside, they will provide a nice surprise whenever the wind blows your hair back." The kind woman waited for me to put on her earrings and clasped her hands together. "There. I'd say you are more than ready."

I strode back to the full-length mirror and checked out the new Ruby. Turning a little to the left and right, I couldn't help but love my new look.

"So, this is what a little money can do," I joked. Catching Lady Eveline's attention in the reflection, I bowed my head in gratitude. "Thank you so much for your help."

"You're more than welcome, my dear. There's just one more thing to do," she said.

"What's that?"

With a wide fanged grin, she responded, "Now, we have to teach you how to curtsy."

WHEN ENZO HAD SAID the word "patio," I pictured a small backyard with maybe a few tiki torches for lighting. The outdoor space Luke escorted me onto was the size of a football field. It took up one whole side of the castle and extended onto a balcony that overlooked the hillside. Tall cast-iron torches blazed to cast a soft glow into the evening sky.

A fresh breeze blew across me, and I shivered, but not because I was cold. I surveyed the entire scene, taking in the many people milling about who appeared far more comfortable in this setting than I felt.

Luke pulled me closer to him. "Would you like my coat?"

I shook my head, determined to maintain the facade that Lady Eveline had so carefully constructed.

"You look amazing tonight," he growled into my ear, sending a different kind of shiver down my body.

"Thank you," I replied, gazing back at him without having to look up. The height equality gave me a new appreciation for my sky-high stilettos.

He nuzzled into my neck. "Almost good enough to eat," he whispered, running his teeth against my sensitive skin.

Raising my shoulder to cut off his access, I squeezed his arm. "I don't think this is the appropriate place for such an open display of affection," I scolded in a low voice, noticing several eyes watching us.

He emitted a dramatic sigh. "I suppose you're right, but I'd have far more fun taking you back to my room and—"

"Luca!" an elegant woman shrieked from across a long distance. She tittered his name several times and flitted over to us, her heels barely touching the ground.

Luke groaned. "Brace yourself," he muttered.

The stranger approached clapping her hands, her eyes trained on my fiancé. She grasped his arm, yanking him out of my hold, and tugged him closer to her. Pressing her impressive breasts against his chest, she stood on tiptoe and kissed him on both cheeks more than once. She assaulted both our ears with high-pitched Italian spoken so fast, I doubted whether or not she could be understood.

After a few failed attempts to pull away, Luke gripped her wrists to pull her claws out of him and push the annoying woman away from him with a little force.

She pouted a little, an expression I knew she had perfected since childhood. Scolding in more Italian, she spoke loud enough to create a scene.

Luke wrapped his arm around my waist. "In English, please, Amara," he insisted. "So that my guest can understand."

Her eyes blazed with ice, but she forced herself to gaze at me for the first time. "*Mi dispiace*. I am sorry you find me so rude."

I clenched my hand behind Luke's back into a fist

at her backhanded apology that placed the blame on me rather than herself.

"Oh, it's all right." I threw my head back, feeling the borrowed diamond chandelier earrings brush against my skin. "I just don't want Luke to have to translate all night for me. I'm sure he has better things to do."

Amara's eyes inspected every inch of me. Finding nothing to complain about, her little mouth quirked into a half grin. "Your dress is lovely. I am sure I admired it when I went shopping before. It is one of last year's collections, is it not?" She batted her eyelashes at me as if she hadn't just hurled a disgusting insult at me.

Cassio approached behind her, shaking his head and rolling his eyes in a dramatic fashion so Luke and I could see him. He clicked his tongue in disapproval. "Amara, tonight is for frivolities and to welcome Luke back home. To insult his guest is to cause an affront to the family itself."

The petite woman's lip jutted out even more. "I was complimenting her dress."

"Is that what you were doing?" Cassio challenged, raising one eyebrow. "Then let me add my personal compliments. Ruby Mae, I find you most ravishing tonight." He bowed his head in respect, a gesture he had not offered to Amara.

Luke gazed at me, his eyes burning with lust. "My sentiments exactly."

A little huff came out of Amara's mouth. "Yes, well." She failed to hide her disdain for me, sneering. "I hope you enjoy your stay here." Turning on her heels, she found someone else to pay her some attention.

Cassio grimaced. "I wish I could say you won't have to deal with her much, but unfortunately, I heard from a very reliable source that your parents have invited her to stay."

Luke cursed under his breath. "For how long?"

His friend shrugged. "I didn't hear the rest of the conversation. But since she holds favor with your mother, I would assume for the entire time you are here."

"Perfect," I exclaimed, knowing what Cassio was too polite to say. "They're trying to set you up with a more suitable prospect."

Luke let go of me and maneuvered to my other side, grabbing my left hand in his. "Then we will have to convince them that they are barking at the wrong bush."

I gazed at him in puzzlement. "Are you trying to say barking up the wrong tree?"

He snapped his fingers. "Yes, that."

"Although if the dog is Slobby Bobby, it would be more like drooling all over the roots of the tree," I joked, needing the moment of levity to steady my jangled nerves.

A server with a tray of glasses passed by, and Cassio stopped them. He passed two crystal goblets full of dark red liquid to Luke and me and took one for himself.

Holding up the glass, Luke's friend proposed a toast. "Here's to survival."

"And to love conquering all," my fiancé added, clinking his glass against mine.

The two vampires drank without reserve, and I stared at the liquid in the crystal. When Luke noticed I had not joined them, he chuckled.

"It's red wine," he whispered into my ear. "Remember, you're in Italy. *Il vino* has a higher place in our esteem than blood. Try it."

At his bidding, I lifted the glass to my lips. Wine was not my drink of choice, and I wouldn't know good hooch from mediocre. But anything would taste better than the Three Buck Chuck we used to get from the convenience store back when we were in high school.

"Mm," I uttered, licking my lips in appreciation of the first sip. "It tastes…fruity. Although I guess that's a dumb statement since wine is made from grapes."

Luke swallowed his mouthful. "No, wine can be very complex. Saying it has a fruity taste is a place to start. Now, try some more and give it your best guess as to what kind of fruit."

Wanting to please him, I took another sip. The flavor felt familiar, and I searched my memories for the right one. "I think I taste…blackberries? And maybe something else…something earthier."

My guess earned me a warm smile from both men. Cassio complimented me in Italian, and Luke kissed my cheek.

"*Brava*," he beamed. "My uncle will adore teaching you about his wine."

"Are you taking her to the vineyard in Montefalco?" Cassio asked.

Luke nodded in affirmation. "If things get a little too heated here, I can whisk her away to get a little breather."

"With what I witnessed, I hope that anything too fiery won't get out of control," his friend warned, glancing at my hands that had wielded the fireballs at Luke's house.

I finished another swallow of the wine, a warm buzz flowing through my veins. "Don't worry, I promise I will be on my best behavior."

Another server walked by with a tray, but it held more drinks rather than food.

"Is there anything to eat around here?" I asked, my stomach rumbling a little at my sudden realization of my lack of sustenance due to nerves.

Cassio grimaced. "I was hoping you wouldn't notice or would have already eaten."

"Tell me my parents have considered *all* of their guests when planning tonight," Luke growled.

"I believe your betrothed may be the only one here who needs to eat," Cassio said.

A little fuzzy from the fast consumption of wine and a very empty stomach, I gasped in realization. "They don't intend for *me* to be the meal for everyone here, do they?"

Both men scoffed. Luke smooched the top of my head. "No, everybody here will be old enough that they have full control of their appetites."

"Although I would not put anything past Amara," Cassio snorted. "She does not seem to like you very much."

I patted Luke's behind, a little too emboldened from the wine. "That's because she has her sights set on my honey bunny. But she has no idea who she's tanglin' with if she thinks she can push me aside so easily."

Cassio tilted his head in observation and narrowed his eyes. "Did you know your accent just became a little stronger when you said that?"

I shrugged. "Granny says it always happens when I get too sassy for my britches."

Luke's friend frowned. "What are britches?"

"Something I'm not wearin'," I said, speaking before my brain caught up. "Because it might ruin the line of the dress." I turned around so the two boys could see my point.

"Never mind about that," Luke interrupted, glowering at his friend's amusement and taking my empty glass from me. "Come on, Rue, perhaps it would be better if I introduced you to my parents now rather than waiting. Then after that, I'll take you to the kitchens and make sure you get something in your stomach."

I winked at my handsome man. "Sounds like a plan."

Cassio wished us luck, and Luke wrapped my arm around his as he guided us through the different groups of guests. He greeted several with friendly banter but kept us moving forward toward an area with the most attendees crowded around.

Through the throng of bodies, I caught sight of the most beautiful woman dressed in black with brilliant white jewels sparkling all over her. Her outfit created the effect of stars twinkling against a dark sky. But it was the flash of dark red from the choker around her neck that caught my eye.

Even from a distance, I recognized the same ruby amulet that Luke wore underneath his shirt. His mother and father wore theirs on full display for all to see.

Luke's mother spoke to everyone with ease and seemed relaxed until she caught sight of her son heading in her direction. She kept her gaze trained on me but tugged on the arm of the man standing next to her, whispering to him. With his parents' attention focused on us, the other guests took notice and began whispering and watching as we approached.

I snatched another full glass of wine from a passing server who hadn't noticed all the hubbub, and took a couple of full swallows of drink for courage.

"Do you think that wise?" Luke whispered to me.

The warm buzz that chased away my nerves gave me my answer. "I think it's necessary."

Lady Eveline arrived at my elbow and took the glass away. "Courage does not come from the bottom of a bottle," she admonished. "Keep your chin up, allow them to do most of the talking, answer when spoken to but do your best not to give away more than what is asked."

My fiancé faltered in his steps. "Who is your friend?"

Maybe he'd been right about the wine. My manners had been muddied by the red drink. "This is Lady Eveline de...I forget the rest."

"My full name is not important. I live in Honeysuckle Hollow with Charli Goodwin." She nodded her respect.

"Ah, I see," Luke uttered, squeezing my hand resting on his arm. "Your friend made sure we had someone in our corner. Very smart, for I am afraid our support here may be a bit thin."

He brought us to a stop at the edge of the crowd surrounding his parents. With very few words, the two in charge instructed the guests to back away and clear a path for us. All conversation stopped as everyone prepared to ogle at the spectacle.

"Here we go," I muttered under my breath,

hoping my heart wouldn't jump out of my chest and land in a squishy, bloody mass in front of the pretty lady's feet.

Luke let go of me and straightened to his full height, bending his head and bowing a little at the waist. Lady Eveline dipped next to me.

Trying to remember the quick lesson, I placed my left foot behind my right and bent at the knee, keeping my hands to my side. I feared I would tip over, but despite my slight inebriated state, I managed to rise again without incident.

As soon as we showed our respect, the regal man and woman in front of us did the same, although their intense focus weighed heavy on me.

Luke stepped forward and bowed again. "Mother. Father."

I held my breath and waited for someone to break the heavy silence.

Although she kept a watchful eye on me and glanced at Lady Eveline in puzzlement, Luke's mother broke first. She opened her arms and plastered a wide smile on her face.

"My beloved son," she crooned, speaking in perfect English. "At last, you have finally returned."

CHAPTER TEN

Luke closed the distance between him and his parents. Much kissing of cheeks ensued, and I stood with Lady Eveline, watching the reunion in fascination like a spectator. I touched the spot where the family's token would have been if I hadn't taken it off, missing Granny's presence.

After a short discussion in Italian in low voices between the three of them, Luke said something that upset his parents. His father frowned, but his mother touched her husband on his arm and nodded in my direction.

Luke held out his arm for me to join him, and I strode to his side, linking my fingers through his for strength and comfort.

"Mother, Father, I would like to introduce you to Ruby Mae Jewell." He smiled at me. "She is…"

I waited for him to say the word that would spark an immediate reaction from his parents.

He paused and swallowed hard. A wrinkle formed between his eyebrows. "She is my special friend."

An ache rose in my heart like a kudzu vine, wrapping itself around the organ. "Hey," I said, doing my best to ignore the pain from his denial and relying on all my Southern charms to cover up my disappointment.

When neither of the parents extended me a hand in welcome, I freaked out. Unsure of what to do, I wobbled into another curtsy.

"As you are not under our rule here," his father declared, touching the impressive ruby laying against his chest, the gold of the chain and elaborate design of the setting glittering with richness. "You do not have to show such displays of respect." He glared down at me with thinly veiled contempt.

His mother regarded me for an extra beat and let out a sigh. "Do not be impertinent to the poor girl, Lorenzo," she chastised her husband. "Her gesture was well done. Let me be the first to officially welcome you to our home, Miss Ruby. And Eveline,

I am more than surprised to find you here as well. I do not recall extending an invite as far as your domain."

My new friend stepped forward, her stilettos clicking on the stone ground. "Damiana, I did not know we needed formal invitations to visit with one another." Lady Eveline embraced Luke's mother and kissed her on both cheeks. "It has been a long time."

"It has," Damiana exclaimed. "And I would be glad of your company if I did not suspect its timing and your familiarity with my son and his guest."

Lady Eveline glanced back at me. "Ah, yes. Ruby Mae and I met through a mutual acquaintance, and since I had business on the continent, I thought why not stop by? Being here allows me to see you and to vouch for this charming young lady at the same time."

Luke stiffened at her words, and I looked between the four vampires.

"Do you do so in an official capacity?" his father asked in a stern tone.

Lady Eveline considered his question before sighing. "Yes, if I must, Lorenzo. Although I rather think you should be the ones to extend your reassurances to the woman that your son brings to your home."

"I don't understand," I blurted. "What reassurances?"

Luke squeezed my hand. "Your friend has vouched for you."

"What does that mean?" I hissed under my breath at him.

"It means that per our edicts, we must ensure that no harm will befall you during your stay with us," his mother explained. "And were you not so quick to jump to conclusions, Eveline, you might have witnessed our generosity. However, I do apologize if this introduction is not going as smoothly as one would hope."

Maybe the lack of food weakened my barriers or perhaps the wine clouded my senses. But in that moment, I wanted to smooth things over and put everyone at ease.

"I promise I'm housebroken," I joked. Nobody laughed, and Luke shifted in awkward embarrassment next to me.

Lady Eveline shot me an annoyed look and lifted her eyebrows to remind me of all the advice she'd offered. I pursed my lips tight to keep anything else from spilling out.

Luke's mother bowed her head to me. "You are welcome here, and as my son explained, we will not tolerate any harm to you while you remain our guest."

"Thank you." My voice shook as I spoke.

More awkward stillness followed our exchange. The longer it stretched, the more I wanted to hide.

"Do you have anything you would like to say to us?" Luke's father asked.

"Such as what?" My fiancé's voice sounded hard and wary.

"Lorenzo," his mother warned. "Now is not the time for confrontation. We held this reception in hopes to welcome our son back into the fold."

"Which we would not be needing to do were he to assume the duties he knows await him." The gruff expression on Luke's father's face made my knees weak, and I expended a lot of energy to keep them from knocking underneath the purple material of my dress.

Lady Eveline sniffed and spoke in a more colloquial fashion. "I recall a certain vampire in his younger years taking off and traveling the world, all in the name of a woman he refused to give up."

Luke's father grunted. "No need to bring up the past, Eveline."

"And yet, with so much history behind us, we tend to get far too wrapped up in it all the same," my one vampire supporter declared. "Your son is home. He has chosen his partner well. Is there not plenty to celebrate in the here and now?"

Luke's mother considered her friend's words with a grin. "Perhaps your presence here in this moment is beneficial to us all." She addressed me directly. "Forgive us if we seem...stilted in our hospitality. Our son's absence has been hard on us."

I recognized a guilt trip when I saw it, and I squeezed Luke's hand in support. "If it gives you any relief, he has a wonderful life back home. Many friends who are loyal because he is such a good man."

Luke's cheeks turned a light shade of pink, the equivalent to a vampire's blush.

"That is good to hear, that you have not been lonely in your time away," his father said. "Although we would know such things from you if you had not expended the effort to hide away from your responsibilities."

Luke gritted his teeth. "I can see we will not be making any progress in our relationship. It was foolish of me to think that the years away would soften your hearts and your demands."

"Your female speaks of home as if you were not standing in it right now," his father continued. "No other place should have that name where you are concerned."

Luke pulled his hand out of my embrace and stepped forward. "I am sure you have heard of the English saying that home is where the heart is." He pointed back at me. "Where Ruby Mae exists, that is my home."

Although his words should have made my heart skip a beat, the brewing confrontation between father and son terrified me. A breeze picked up and blew some of my hair in front of my face. With my fingers, I pushed the strands behind my ear.

Damiana stopped smiling and blurred to standing in front of me, yanking my hand away from my head. "Tell me this is a replica."

"It is real, Mother," Luke said in a steady voice. "I had hoped to tell you in private rather than in front of so many onlookers, but I have asked Ruby Mae to marry me."

Gasps and murmurs exploded around us. A shrill female voice I recognized from earlier cried out, "No!"

Luke's mother's bottom lip trembled, and she dashed a pink tear away. "I thought this ring was lost. I did not know you had it." She let go of my hand. "Forgive me," she said again. "All the time in the world does not dampen the loss of a beloved child. If my son has given you this, then you must mean a lot to him."

"Damiana, you cannot possibly mean to allow—"

"I mean to welcome this child as the woman our son has chosen to introduce to us as his betrothed," she insisted.

A throat cleared from behind me, and a tiny bird-like figure stepped forward. "Did I hear right? Our Luca is engaged to be married?" Amara asked her question without acknowledging my presence. She tapped the side of her crystal glass with a long fingernail in impatient annoyance, and the light sound of each *tink* bore into my head.

"Amara, not now," Lorenzo growled, still angry with his progeny. "We will speak more of this later."

"As you wish." The younger vampire turned to face Luke. "I suppose we should toast your impending nuptials." She raised her glass with too much force, and the wine splashed all over the front of my new dress.

Her smirk did not match her words when she begged for forgiveness for her clumsiness. A little too keyed up from the entire encounter and light-headed from a lack of food and too many sips of wine, I tried to fix the situation.

"It's no problem," I said, summoning some of my magic to my fingers and casting an easy spell to lift the liquid out of the fabric. "My great-grandmother taught me that at an early age since I loved to play a little too much in mud puddles."

The droplets of wine rose away from the dress and hovered in the air. Amara scuttled away with a dramatic shriek, but Luke's mother watched the liquid as each droplet faded into mist and dissipated into nothingness.

"*Strega!*" his mother hissed, backing away as if I had done something to hurt her. With one hand clutching her neck and covering the ruby amulet, she wagged a finger at me and shrieked, "You are a witch!"

Lady Eveline nodded once in approval. "Yes, she is one, Damiana—"

"You knew!" The woman of the castle turned on her friend. "You knew of this…this…"

"Abomination," Luke's father finished, a disappointed frown aimed at his son.

My friend from back home interceded on my behalf. "There is no need to insult her thus, Lorenzo. She can no more deny her heritage than you can."

"I am not asking her to renounce her magic," the

181

man spit out in anger. "But she should not be here. And well you know this, Luca."

My fiancé's mother dashed her hand across her cheek to wipe away the pink trail of tears. "How could you bring her here?" she accused. "After what we went through with your sister. Do you hold such disregard for us that you would do something this outrageous?"

Luke opened his mouth to reply, but his father stepped in front of him as if he didn't exist. He barked out something to his guests in Italian. Everyone stood still as statues, unable to comprehend the magnitude of the request.

"All of you! Leave! Now!" Lorenzo bellowed.

"Father," Luke protested.

"No!" His father cut him off. "I will not tolerate such impudence in my home. Come, Damiana. Let us no longer participate in this tragedy and depart." He held out his hand, glaring at me.

His wife hustled to her husband's side, her face contorted in anguish. I placed a hand over my heart in sympathy. Standing between Luke and his parents, I didn't know what my place in this world was. But I did understand why my fiancé had refused to return for so long.

Lady Eveline spoke, knowing that her friends

could hear her with their vampiric ears. "What about Ruby Mae's safety?"

Luke's parents stopped midstride. His father turned back to face us. "Our rules dictate that I cannot force you to leave," he addressed me. "Your life will be protected as long as you remain under our roof. Which, I can honestly say, I hope will not be for too long." Fueled by anger and disappointment, he escorted his wife into the interior of the castle.

"Well," Lady Eveline said, joining me by my side. "That went about how I would have expected."

"It was the disaster I always knew it would be," Luke muttered.

I reached out to console him through touch, but he flinched away. His eyes stayed glued to the door through which his parents had departed.

Rubbing the temples of my throbbing head, I tried to ignore the swirl of emotions that churned my empty stomach. "So much for approaching things with confidence." A sob caught in my throat, and I covered my mouth to capture it. "They absolutely hate me," I moaned in a shaky whisper.

My sorrow snapped Luke out of his indignant mood, and he placed an arm around my shoulders. "I should have broached the subject with them before tonight. It came as an unnecessary shock. They need time to get to know you as I do."

"You will both have some mending to do," Lady Eveline admitted. She sipped on a glass of wine she'd found somewhere.

"You'll be able to help, won't you?" I pleaded.

The one vampire left standing with us dropped her gaze. "Alas, I have affairs that I must attend to, so I will be leaving in the morning."

"Oh." A fat tear rolled down my cheek at the thought of losing her valuable support.

I stood on the outdoor terrace in a foreign country with few friends. As strong as I was, I couldn't help the overwhelming sense of wanting to return home.

Luke turned me to face him. "We have not lost the war." He wiped another drop from my face. "The first shots have been fired. We will give them the rest of the night to soak in the new reality that they will have to accept you as my wife or deal with my exile for good."

"Threats will not serve you well," Lady Eveline warned.

"It is not a threat," Luke said with firm determination. "It is what will happen if my parents continue their attack."

More sobs burst out of me. "I don't want you fighting over me. I'm not worth it."

"Oh, *cara*." Luke swept me into a tight embrace, rocking me back and forth. "Do not ever discount yourself like that again. You are my every treasure. And if they give you a chance, my parents will come to know your value to me as well."

His words offered me a little comfort, and I chuckled when he produced a handkerchief from some inner pocket of his jacket. Accepting it, I cleaned off my face the best I could with no mirror.

"I will leave the two of you alone to nurse your wounds," Lady Eveline said. "Despite how things may have seemed, you did well tonight being yourself. My advice to you from here on out is to continue to do so with pride." Her heels clicked on the stones as she entered the castle.

Left alone, I didn't know what to say to Luke about the whole situation. The fires in the cast-iron torches danced in the night air, and I watched them burn, wondering if the true nature of my powers would complicate matters even more.

Luke rapped a knuckle softly against my head. "I can hear the wheels turning. Try not to worry too much."

I hugged him close and leaned my head into his shoulder. "I screwed things up, didn't I?"

"No, the fault is my own." My fiancé's deep voice reverberated through me. "But you know what the best thing is?"

"What?" I asked, my voice muffled against his expensive shirt.

"We'll fix it together. You and me." He pulled back so I could see him. "That's all that matters, Ruby Mae Jewell. Now, let's go find you something to eat."

He escorted me inside the castle walls, and I couldn't help but feel more like a prisoner being marched to my doom than a fairy tale princess finding her happily ever after.

CHAPTER ELEVEN

Once inside, I expected to be inundated with questions from the numerous guests. But the second we crossed over the threshold, we didn't see one person hovering about for the latest gossip. The pit in my stomach grew as I realized just how quickly everyone obeyed Luke's parents and to what extent.

Rapid footsteps echoed down a nearby hallway, and Enzo appeared in front of us. His grim expression did nothing to ease my nerves.

Luke's grip around my waist tightened. "If you're acting as a messenger for my parents, don't bother," he barked.

"My apologies, Master Luca, but you know my

commitment to my duties," Enzo replied with a slight bow of his head.

My fiancé stiffened next to me. "I do, and therefore, you can tell Mother and Father that anything they wish to say to me, they can say in front of Ruby Mae or not at all."

I pulled out of his hold to face him. "Honey, maybe you should speak to them. They were caught by surprise tonight in front of guests. Cut them a little slack."

Luke's eyebrows lifted toward his hairline. "You are taking their side?"

"No-o-o, not exactly," I uttered. "But I saw how your mother was making an effort before I screwed up. I think you should give them a chance to talk to you in private."

"You were not the one to cause offense tonight," Luke growled. "First, they provided no food despite knowing your status as a non-vampire. And then their reaction to you was an abomination."

My stomach growled again in solidarity with the no food comment. Enzo frowned at my discomfort. "I will be sure to have somebody send a meal to your room as soon as I finish here. That is an egregious oversight, and I take full responsibility for it."

"No, you shall not," countered Luke. "That is one

of many offenses for which my parents owe both of us an apology. And if talking to them now will move us forward, then perhaps confronting both of them would be prudent."

"I believe that would be the best course of action for now, Master Luca," Enzo agreed. "If you were to attend to them in their quarters, I will make sure Miss Ruby is escorted back to her room." He rushed off to find some help.

Luke cupped my cheek with his hand. "Will you be okay?"

I leaned into his touch. "Will you?"

He sighed, his thumb caressing my skin. "Despite what happened tonight, they are my only family. And there are things to be said. Bridges to be mended on both sides."

"You sound very wise for your old age," I teased, wanting to ease his tension.

Luke took a step closer and kissed my forehead. "No, I've just learned a lot being with you and your family."

My heart warmed, and I wrapped my arms around him. "You know, they consider you a part of us, too."

"I know." He planted a kiss on my forehead. "It is my desire to have the kind of relationship with my parents that you do with your family that spurs me on right now."

Enzo returned with a young man in tow. He gave instructions in rapid Italian and then turned to me. "Gino will escort you to your quarters, and I have arranged for some food to be brought there."

"Thank you, sir," I replied.

Luke let me go with reluctance. "I will come see you after I am finished." He joined Enzo to go to his parents' room. Turning and walking backwards, he held up a finger of warning. "Don't go wandering around on your own."

I pointed at my chest. "Does that sound like something I'd do?"

He chuckled. "Absolutely."

"Good luck." I waved goodbye at him and followed the timid young man Enzo had brought to me through the confusing corridors.

The staff member opened the door to the one room I recognized, and I entered with relief. Before I could thank him, he disappeared. The heavy wood closed with a slight clunk, and I was left alone in the silence of the strange room.

Holding onto the edge of the decorative dresser, I balanced while taking off the high heels. With a groan of relief, I flexed my toes on the thick oriental carpet under my feet.

Taking off the borrowed earrings, I reflected on the night. Nothing had gone the way I'd hoped, and it hurt to think about how I'd messed up my first impressions with my potential in-laws. I set Lady Eveline's diamonds on the surface of the dresser and picked up the elephant token. I slipped the chain over my head, happy to have a piece of my family with me again.

"Hey, Granny," I crooned in a quiet voice. "You may not believe this, but I missed you so much." My fingers stroked the surface of the metal, and I grinned when it heated to my touch.

Heaving a sigh of relief, I winced as the tightness of the corset cut into my sides. I struggled and contorted my arms to reach the ties to release me from my bondage with no luck. I would need to be careful to wear clothes that didn't require help to put on or take off in the near future.

A heavy knock on the door startled me, and I stopped my focused fidgeting to answer. A different young man entered the room carrying a tray. The plates and utensils rattled as he walked over to a small table by one of the windows. Setting it down, he removed the silver covers to reveal two small plates of food.

"Thank you," I gushed, my mouth watering before I even sat down to take a bite.

At the last second, I remembered my dress predicament and turned to ask for some help but found myself alone again. After everything that had happened, I wanted nothing more than to get out of the confining outfit, change into comfy clothes that I'd brought with me, and hunker down for the rest of the night.

I rushed over to pull open the recently closed door. "Excuse me, but I could use some help," I said as I entered the empty hallway. Even though the food deliverer had just left my room, there was nobody in sight no matter which way I turned.

"Dang blast it!" I cursed loud enough for my words to bounce off the walls.

Covering my mouth, I moved forward, hoping to find someone to give me a little assistance. If I could communicate enough for them to untie the corset, I could figure out a way to loosen it enough to get it off.

My bare feet plodded over the long, carpeted runner lining the floor of the corridor. Although I worried I might get lost, I heard enough noise up ahead that I hoped I'd find the source eventually. Reaching a crossroads of corridors, I strutted into the middle and glanced down each one, straining to hear anything that would give me a clue as to which way I should go.

The metal of the token heated enough for me to feel it even though it hung against the purple fabric of the dress. The second I touched it with my fingers, a sudden noise like a light giggle echoed from the darkened hallway to my left.

"I should go back to my room," I said out loud to myself, not believing my words for a second.

Another tittering giggle answered me, beckoning from further down the unlit corridor. The elephant token pulsed against my palm, and I made my choice.

Glancing around to see if I was truly alone, I risked a little magic and conjured a light orb. There was no carpet rolled down the stone floor of this hallway. Making sure to cast illumination to see where I stepped, I ventured on with caution. The coldness of the stone underneath my feet chilled me, and I gripped the token tighter, absorbing its little bit of warmth.

The pitter-pat of an animal scuttling across the floor near me stopped me in my tracks. Bringing the ball of light closer, I searched my perimeter and found a mouse with its beady eyes sitting on its haunches, staring at me.

"Shoo," I called out, waving my hand at it. "Get away from me."

It squeaked in response and ran right at me. Yelping, I jumped over its little body and landed on the other side. My legs couldn't carry me fast enough away from the vermin.

My heart raced, and I exhaled in pants until I laughed. Thank goodness nobody saw my cowardly escape from such a tiny creature. Since I made it even further down the darkened corridor, I might as well keep going.

The further I progressed, the colder it became until chills broke over my entire body. I could swear I saw the moisture of my breath in the air.

"Curiosity may kill a cat, but it's freezing me," I said through my chattering teeth. "I should go back."

Instead of another giggle, a faint female voice called out, and I perked up. Whoever it was couldn't be that far away. Determined to catch her, I hustled a little faster until I came to a dead end.

A dark wooden door blocked my path, and I turned around to see if I'd missed any other hallways where the voice could have come from. Pushing my light orb closer to the door, I noticed small sparkles coming from the grain. I took a closer look and found a deliberate carving in the wood resembling vines with tiny delicate flowers. Jewels of different colors were inlaid into the design to accentuate the blossoms.

"Whoa," I exclaimed, unable to resist touching one of the sparkling gems.

The second my hand touched the door, a loud click reverberated. It opened, giving way with a long, loud creak.

I stood in disbelief, half wanting to go inside and half wanting to take off in the opposite direction. The more rational part of my brain warned me that the demise of the young woman in horror movies started just like this.

A light floral scent wafted out of the room. It wrapped itself around me, and I drew it in with deep breaths. Something that smelled so fair couldn't be that foul, right? Ignoring my rational side, I pushed the door open further and stepped through the threshold.

As soon as I stood far enough inside, the door slammed behind me with a thud and flames flickered to life in all of the candles in the room.

"That's not in the least bit creepy," I said, regretting my decision.

I gripped the door handle and attempted to pull it open. The heavy thing refused to budge despite my best efforts.

"Grits and ghosts," I exclaimed. "Now, what am I supposed to do?"

"What kind of trouble have you gotten yourself into now, Ruby Mae?" a familiar voice scolded.

With a terrified screech, I startled, and my light orb snuffed out. Turning around, I found my ghostly great-grandmother staring back at me with her hands on her hips.

"Granny, you made me jump out of my skin," I complained, touching the token. "What are you doing?"

"There's a lot of energy in this room," she said, floating around. "Enough that I could take a break from that dang blasted coin, even though I've been trying to get out since you put me back on. Didn't we tell you to keep that thing on you at all times?"

I opened my mouth to explain why I'd chosen not to wear the chain with the dress but closed it fast. No amount of explanation in favor of fashion over family would get me anywhere.

"Trust me, I wish I hadn't. But that still doesn't

explain why I can see you now." I strode closer to her, so glad to see one of my beloved family members. Too bad she couldn't give me a much-needed hug.

"I'm not rightly sure myself," Granny Jo replied. "There's something about this room that called to me."

"Or someone," I said. "I heard a giggle and a girl's voice."

"Young or old?" my great-grandmother asked.

I shrugged, unsure. "I followed the noise until I discovered this room."

"Then we should figure out whose room it is," Granny suggested.

"Do you think you can help?" I asked. "I mean, won't it drain you to be too far away from the token?"

She considered my question while bobbing in the air. "I can't explain it, but I think I'll be fine." Snapping her fingers, she lit up. "I know. It's like you plugged me into the wall or something. I feel full of energy."

As if needing to prove herself to me, she floated backwards further and further away. I held my breath, ready to rush to her if her incorporeal figure shimmered out of existence. But her spectral form stayed as strong as it did in our family home without wavering once.

"Okay, then. You take that side, and I'll look over here." Trusting my great-grandmother's judgment, I turned to snoop through what I could find.

I could hear drawers opening and closing behind me, but I inspected a table sitting in front of a long velvet curtain. Sitting down in the chair in front of it, I glanced at the contents lying in front of me. A feather quill sat on top of some old papers with an inkwell nearby. I lifted the top and found its contents dry, and I shivered, remembering the last time I found such instruments.

Picking up a small object that reminded me of a chess piece, I scrutinized it from all angles in the light of a candle. I sent a little power to strengthen the candle's flame to see by and found an inscription on the circular bottom of the item.

"I think I know what this is," I uttered, rustling through the other items on top of the table until I found what I wanted.

Holding onto the end of the colored stick, I thrust the other side into the flame of the candle until it glistened and melted. I let the thick substance drip onto one of the papers until it formed a small blob. Placing the other object on top, I pressed it into the melted wax until it left an indentation.

"Granny, look at this," I called out, staring at the mark.

"This room definitely belonged to a female. And the clothing I could find is not from any century I'm familiar with," she said when she joined me.

I held up the wax seal. "Do you see the letter at the center of the flower?"

She squinted through her ghost glasses. "Not really."

Tracing the outlines in the wax, I showed her my discovery. "That's an *I*. I'm pretty sure that stands for Isabella."

The second I uttered the name, the faint sound of a woman crying echoed around the chamber. My great-grandmother and I turned in all directions to follow it, and the flames of all the candles in the room elongated and flickered larger. I noticed Granny Jo's figure became brighter and more solid in her agitation rather than her usual fading in and out.

"Grits and ghosts, indeed," I muttered, watching the candlelight return to normal. "I wonder if she's still here. Maybe that's why you can materialize in this room. Because there's already someone haunting it."

I'd only told my family a little about Luke's sister, not wanting to betray too much of my fiancé's private business. But Granny understood enough about young love and tragic death from her experience in the world plus her secret love for romance novels.

"We ghosts stick around for lots of reasons," Granny Jo said in a quiet voice, "but if anybody deserves to haunt this place, Luke's sister had plenty of things to hold her here."

"Do you think you could talk to Isabella?" I asked, curious if my great-grandmother's ways of dealing with the dearly departed in our family home would work here.

Granny Jo floated toward the middle of the room. "Won't know the answer unless I try. What was her full name?"

I shuffled through some of the paper on top of the desk but didn't find anything with her name on it. "I know Luke has a long name, but I've only heard her called Isabella. Isabella de Rossi."

My ghostly great-grandmother closed her eyes and held out her hands, hovering over the stone floor. She repeated the sister's name a few times, calling to her. "Isabella, if you're here, come talk to us."

A cool breeze picked up in the room and whirled around us with growing energy, the scent of flowers growing stronger. A voice rode the wind, but I couldn't understand the words.

"We just want to talk, Isabella," I added, turning my head to keep my hair out of my face.

The voice grew a little louder, and I battled between excitement and dread as the air thickened with a strange presence.

"I'm in love with your brother. With Luca," I cried out, wanting her to try to connect with me.

The faint voice repeated her brother's name. "Luca," it said in a mix between a whisper and a low moan.

Granny floated closer, hovering between me and the presence we both felt in the room. "I don't know about this. Something doesn't feel quite right."

"Lu-u-u-u-c-a," Isabella's spirit dragged out in a grating tone that raised the hairs on my arms.

The air shimmered in front of us, and a ball of glowing energy grew out of nowhere. The wind picked up, scattering papers around the room. Instead of being blown out, the flames on the candles ignited into high blazes.

"She's going to destroy the room with us in it!" Granny yelled. "Do something."

I reached out with my magic to control the candles, but they burned even higher instead of extinguishing. Whatever we had summoned here had been waiting for a long time to manifest, and its power had more energy than I could contain by myself.

"Look!" Granny Jo pointed at something scampering close to the glowing ball.

The little mouse from before scurried into the middle of the vortex. One minute, I debated trying to save its little furry butt and the next, I watched as its entire being changed in size and morphed into a brown-haired woman.

She raised her hands in the air and shouted commands I couldn't understand. The voice on the wind changed into a pained shriek, and the glow disappeared in ghostly flames that consumed it.

When I turned to say something to my great-grandmother, I no longer saw her next to me. A quick touch to the token reassured me of her presence.

"Who are you?" I asked the woman who bore no resemblance to a mouse in size or actions.

Satisfied that the presence of Isabella de Rossi

was gone, she gave me her full attention. "We have no time for explanations. If you are who I think you are, then we must get you back to your room with much haste. Follow me."

Instead of leaving through the door, she walked over to a bare spot on the wall and raised her hand in front of it. Much like when Luke had sequestered us into the castle, the stone gave way to a dark passage inside the wall. She gestured for me to follow her, not giving me any other choice.

Once inside the passageway, she cast her own light orb to help us see. "I assume you are Master Luca's companion? The one who created the commotion in front of his parents?"

I nodded in affirmation even though she couldn't see me as she led me forward. "I'm Ruby Mae Jewell."

"And I am Fiametta," she said, pronouncing her name with a hard *T*. "You may call me Fia."

"You're a witch," I observed.

"Like you," she confirmed. "Although I have been successful at hiding my true nature while working here."

"You were the mouse that approached me in the hall, weren't you?" I asked, shying away from a filmy spider web hanging from the enclosed ceiling.

"Sì, I was trying to stop you from disturbing the

spirit and answering the siren's call." The young woman stopped at a fork in the passage to make sure I followed her. "It is this way," she said, directing me to the right.

"Why?" I asked, hurrying to keep up with her quick pace. "What is wrong with going to Isabella's room?"

Fiametta stopped abruptly and I almost ran into her. She directed her orb of light to hover above us. "The dead vampire daughter's ghost has been quiet for a long while. But now with the return of her beloved brother, she is stirred to life again." She glanced at the metal medallion hanging around my neck. "None of us know what will happen were she to awaken fully."

"Us?" I asked in utter confusion.

"There is no time for more talk. We must return you to your room." Fia resumed her rapid strides. "When Master Luca arrived in your chambers and found it empty with the meal untouched, he went a little...what is the word?"

My stomach sank. "He freaked out."

"Yes, that sounds right. He has tasked many of us to search for you, and I feared for the outcome were you not to be found in perfect condition." She slowed down, holding her hand over the stone of the wall. "The opening should be here...ah, yes." Symbols glowed inside the stone. "The door will open if there is nobody on the other side."

We waited while the spell she cast stayed activated. When the stone gave way, the new witch tugged on my arm. "Come with me."

The second I passed through the doorway, the stone settled back into place. The red carpet underneath my feet seemed familiar, and I recognized the antique amphora vases resting on a table in the hall near my room.

"*Aspetta, Fiametta!*" Claudio ran in our direction. He spoke to the young woman with passionate consternation. Unhappy with her responses, he addressed me. "Wherever you have been, you must reassure Master Luca of your well-being. Come."

"Claudio," Fiametta protested.

He responded to her in harsh tones. "Wait for me in our usual place." When he saw how distressed she was, he softened a little and said something else in Italian.

"Thank you, Fia," I managed before the young woman left. "I would love to talk to you again soon."

"Watch for me in the morning." She raised her eyebrows, conveying some hidden message, and I hoped I could decipher it before the next afternoon.

Claudio marched me down the hall and knocked on the door of my quarters. Luke's gruff voice answered, and the young man let me in.

My fiancé rushed over to me in a vampiric blur, crushing me against his chest. "Where have you been?"

"I wanted to find someone to help me unlace my corset so I could take this blasted dress off." Sticking as close to the truth as possible would allow me to assess the damage. "I got lost."

He mumbled words I couldn't understand and sighed. "I was ready to fight my parents, sure that they had found a way to get rid of you."

I grimaced. "I take it your talk with them was less than stellar, huh?"

He ran his fingers through his hair, mussing it up. "Their anger runs deep with my perceived abandonment of the family duties." Luke turned me around to face away from him, and I felt a tug on the laces of the corset.

"Did you manage to say the things you wanted to? Did they listen to you at all?" The bodice of the dress stopped digging into my sides, and I drew in a deep breath of relief.

Luke continued to fuss over the laces while he spoke. "After my father stopped yelling at me, I did manage to get in a few important points. But nobody was ready to apologize yet."

Holding the loosened dress up with my arm, I faced Luke again. "This isn't going to be the simple in-and-out trip you wanted it to be, is it?"

"No," he breathed out. "And now, my mother is insisting if you must stay then she is allowed to spend time with you."

"That sounds…" *Terrifying,* I thought to myself. "Promising."

Luke didn't add anything other than a noncommittal grunt. "And now that we have accomplished the task that took you out of the room and left you wandering the castle hallways, would you like to tell me what you were up to?"

I gaped at him and batted my eyelashes in mock innocence but groaned in acceptance when he responded with stony silence. "All right, I'll tell you. Just let me change into something more comfy and eat a little something first."

Escaping into the closet, I scrambled to find where whoever had unpacked my luggage had stashed the clothes I'd brought. Pulling open the drawers of the large custom-built island in the middle of the space, I found what I wanted. In record time, I changed into something that made me feel a little more like myself.

"That's better," I exclaimed with relief, exiting the closet and pulling my hair back into a messy bun. "Sorry if this wasn't exactly the sexy ensemble you were hoping for."

Luke grinned at me. "You look good to me no matter what you wear. Dressed to kill in an evening gown or relaxing in your sleeping attire, I'll take Ruby Mae Jewell any which way she comes."

He wrapped me in his arms, and I snuggled into his chest, no longer on equal footing from wearing the high heels.

"This feels much better," I said, taking in his familiar scent through a deep breath. "Safer."

"I hope to keep you thus," Luke replied, rubbing my back. "But if you leave without my knowledge, then that might become a challenge."

I squeezed my face in embarrassment. "I didn't mean to make you worry. Like I said, I did get lost." Pulling out of his grasp, I followed the scent of food and picked up the plate of cold pasta. I sent a little heat through my hands to warm it up.

"Someone would have seen you sooner if you were truly lost," Luke observed, watching me with careful eyes. "Tell me what you found."

I slurped on a lone noodle and sucked it in my mouth. "Promise me you won't get too mad."

He crossed his arms. "I make no promises until I hear what you were up to."

After taking two more quick bites to satisfy my empty stomach, I set the plate down. "Fine. But you might want to sit down for this."

He raised an eyebrow. "Why?"

"Because I'm pretty sure I made contact with your sister tonight."

CHAPTER TWELVE

L uke and I talked into the early morning hours. He grilled me over every little detail from the moment I left the room to when Fiametta brought me back. At some point, I fell asleep in his arms, and a young regal woman who looked like my fiancé haunted my dreams. It felt like I could speak to her, but because we were from two different times and places, we couldn't understand each other.

I woke up startled and alone. Light streamed through a crack in the curtains covering the window. Yawning, I took a page from Dolly's song, tumbling out of bed and stumbling to the bathroom. A quick hot shower refreshed me and washed away some of the not-so-nice memories from the night before. As the streams of water pounded against me, I recalled the more important details and wondered where Luke had escaped to.

After the shower, I chose some of my own clothes rather than any of the expensive ones Luke had purchased in Rome. Last night's fiasco left me a little wary, and putting on something familiar and comfortable provided me a little shield of protection from whatever the day ahead might hold.

A knock interrupted my first thoughts about food. Hoping to find Luke on the other side, I bounded over and opened the door to find Claudio instead.

"*Buon giorno.* I trust you slept well after your... adventure last night?" The young man's question made me a little suspicious as to how much he actually knew.

"I'm surprised I feel as rested as I do. It took me a while to finally get to sleep," I admitted, wanting to poke at him a little to play a hunch. "How is Fiametta this morning?"

Claudio's friendly expression changed into something more neutral. "I am not sure what you are asking."

Men. How dense could they be? "I'm asking how the woman you found me with last night is doing. I'm pretty sure the way the two of you spoke to each other was more than just collegial because you work in the same place."

He swallowed hard, and I recognized I'd put him in an awkward position. "I just wanted to make sure she was safe after I returned you to your room."

"Fia was my hero last night, helping me find my way back," I said. "If you see her, please give her my thanks again."

My use of her nickname eased a little of his tension. "I will be sure to do that."

I changed the subject to help the poor boy out. "What time is it?"

"It is after ten in the morning, Miss Ruby. Master Luca instructed the staff to allow you to sleep late. However, he has sent me here to invite you to join him on the terrace." He stood with his arms behind his back, waiting for my reply.

"Sounds amazing. Let me find my sandals and I'll go with you," I chirped.

"No need, miss. It's just through here." Claudio walked past me and pulled open the curtains to reveal a set of double glass doors.

With a little tug, they opened, and a fresh

breeze blew inside while sunlight streamed into my room. A first glance showed me a long terrace that stretched beyond just the length of my room. I padded out onto the porch in my worn-out bunny slippers I brought just because, and found my fiancé bantering in friendly conversation with Cassio at a table underneath a shady umbrella.

"Good morning," I greeted Luke, kissing his cheek. "Why didn't you wake me?"

"Your sleep seemed a bit fitful as I watched you, and as there's nothing particular on your schedule for today, I thought it best to let you sleep late." He got up and pulled the seat out next to him for me to sit down and join them.

Cassio waited for me to get settled before speaking. "I am sorry last night did not go as well as you'd hoped. I thought for sure your parents' joy for your return would outweigh their judgment."

"My springing magic on them like I did made things worse," I groaned. "So, don't feel too bad."

Cassio's eyebrows lifted. "I was too far away to see what had caused the outburst. You revealed yourself directly to his parents?"

"Amara spilled wine all over Ruby Mae's dress," Luke explained.

His friend scoffed. "An accident, I am sure. But how did a spilled drink cause such a commotion?"

I grimaced and shrugged my shoulders. "Because I wanted to show that the wine didn't spoil anything. So, I made it disappear."

"Then Amara got exactly what she wanted in the first place," Cassio noted.

Not understanding what he meant, I looked to Luke for an explanation. My fiancé frowned as he caught on to his friend's meaning. "She wanted you to be embarrassed in front of my parents. Negate you as a possible match for me. But she didn't know her deeds would work to such an extent."

"Oh, Luke, I am so sorry." My heart thumped in my chest, guilt filling me up.

My fiancé reached out to take my hand. "No, I was not placing blame on you. That lies squarely with my parents at the moment."

"And Amara," added Cassio. "She has always been a bit spoiled and thought of only herself. And if she is staying here for the duration of your visit, you will need to watch her with care from here on out." His chair scraped on the stone floor. "Well, I will let the two of you have some time together. Ruby, I hope you get to explore a little and find some enjoyment. *Ciao.*"

Once alone, I teased Luke about letting me sleep in. He joked about how he knew firsthand what I could be like in the mornings.

"Although I confess, I risked Claudio's life to wake you up because I sorely missed your company," he said.

"Aw, that's so sweet." I slid my hand across the small table to hold his. "But I think you're full of crap."

His eyes widened in surprise, but he chuckled. "And why is that?"

"Two things." I held up my fingers to count. "One, I think you want me around as a bit of a shield to your parents since they clearly don't like me. And two, I'm betting you want to talk more about...my explorations last night."

A server brought out a tray and served the dishes onto the table. The choices of pastry reminded me of the breakfast I had in Rome.

"That's a...oh, in high school, they were these premade ice cream cones." I leaned back in the chair. "Ooh, those were called Cornettos. That's a *cornetto*. Can't lie, kinda hoping it's a chocolate one."

The young woman smiled. "*Sì*, there is one chocolate and one cream. And I was told you prefer a macchiato. Enjoy." She disappeared inside.

I scooped sugar into the espresso like I had been taught and stirred. "There's not much more to add than what I told you last night." Taking a bite of the pastry, I relished the chocolate filling inside.

Luke tapped his thumb on the edge of the table in thought. "I won't even ask if you really saw a ghost due to my own experiences with your family." He flashed a glance at the chain around my neck. "But how can you be sure it was my sister?"

"That's just it. I can't other than what my gut tells me," I said, finishing the first pastry.

"I wish you had been able to communicate with it. Her." He leaned forward and took off his sunglasses. "There are so many things I wish..." He trailed off without finishing his thought, but I was pretty sure I knew some of what he would say.

I pushed the plate away from me and scooted my chair closer to his. "We've agreed not to lie to each other, so there's something I want to tell you. But I need you to listen to everything first before you say anything."

"I'll try," he said, unable to contain his concern.

Taking in a deep breath, I prepared myself to reveal my mission. "I think you blame yourself for your sister's death, but based on what you've told me, you didn't actually do anything to her."

When my fiancé opened his mouth to protest, I held up a finger to stop him and continue. "Part of my coming here with you was to meet your parents. I think it's only fair that they get to know who you intend to marry. Even if they decide not to like me. What you do with that reaction is entirely up to you, in my opinion."

I paused for a moment, letting my words soak in. We'd spent most of the night talking about the possibility of the spirit I'd made contact with being his sister. Luke had remained pretty tight-lipped about his talk with his parents, which gave me enough of a clue to how it went.

"The other reason why I came," I said, a little uneasy to reveal my true plan, "is to try and figure out the how and why of it all. You have your theories, but nobody who is still around after all this time knows the true story of what happened."

Unable to contain himself, Luke blurted, "But how do you think you'll be able to investigate Isabella's demise now? It happened several centuries ago."

I drained my espresso cup, tipping it up to let the sugary sludge slide into my mouth. "I haven't quite figured that part out yet."

The click of high heels interrupted us, and a sense of dread settled over me. Luke frowned at the sight of whoever approached, and I couldn't bring myself to confirm my suspicions as to who had joined us.

"Luca," his mother uttered in a tone that was less than pleased with finding us together.

She circled around the table so she could face us with Lady Eveline taking her place beside Luke's mother. The sight of my supporter lessened some of the tension clenching my stomach.

Luke stood up and dipped his head in courtesy. "Mother. Lady Eveline."

I scrambled to follow his lead and stood as well. "Good morning, Mrs. de Rossi," I managed, unhappy that a slight quiver in my voice gave away my nerves. "I am happy to see you again, Lady Eveline."

"Likewise, my dear," the friendlier vampire replied. "I delayed my departure so Damiana and I could have a talk, friend to friend."

Luke sat back down and gestured at the other chairs. "Would you like to sit down with us?"

His mother refused, her mouth twisting into a bow of disapproval. "That will not be necessary as I do not intend to stay for long. There is something that needs to be said."

I lowered myself into my chair with shaky legs.

There was not enough espresso in the world to bolster me for whatever Luke's mom had to say.

Damiana shifted her stance enough to face me and cleared her throat. "Last night, my behavior towards you was appalling. It is never our intent to make any of our guests uncomfortable in any way. I apologize." Sunlight glittered off the ruby secured around her neck as she tipped her head with the smallest of gestures.

Her apology caught me a little off guard, but my Southern upbringing saved the day. "Thank you, Mrs. de Rossi. And I apologize for surprising you in front of your guests."

Luke reached out to grasp my hand in his, squeezing it under the table. We had talked a little the night before about our missteps that contributed to the situation. At least now, his mother could see I wasn't completely without manners.

Damiana gasped a little in surprise, but then quickly recovered. "I will admit, finding out about your true nature has complicated things. But I accept your apology and recognize you did not mean to cause any harm."

My nerves calmed down only the slightest of smidges, but I appreciated the first civil words with my future mother-in-law. With a little more awareness, I realized I must look a mess in my own clothes compared to her fashionable outfit.

"Ruby Mae, perhaps now would be a good time for me to retrieve what I lent you yesterday," Lady Eveline said, her eyebrows raising with double meaning.

I scooted the chair back and sprang out of it with eagerness. "Yes, of course."

Once inside, I hustled over to pick up the diamond earrings. Lady Eveline tugged on my arm to usher me further away from the open door to the terrace. Once inside, she spoke with purpose.

"It took a great amount of my influence to convince Damiana to see reason when it comes to your presence," she said in a low voice. "However, word has spread amongst the staff about your little sojourn outside of your room last night."

"What are they saying?" I asked, worried that my plans to figure out Isabella's death might come to a very abrupt end.

Lady Eveline shook her head. "Nothing more than how it was an inconvenience of their time to find you." She scrutinized my reaction. "However, I suspect there was more to it than becoming lost inside this place."

I bit my lip, contemplating how much to reveal.

"Let's just say that there are some things I'd like to look into, and if I succeed, it might bring about a lot of healing for Luke's entire family." I held back my concern that finding out more about Isabella's death could also do more damage than good.

Lady Eveline nodded in resignation. "You remind me a lot of Charli, so I will only say this. You must take great care not to give Damiana or Lorenzo any ammunition. You are already on the losing side of the battle."

I leaned on the dresser for support, a sudden wave of exhaustion and worry hitting me. "I wish you could stay."

"Based on what I witnessed outside, you will do just fine on your own." The vampire lady slipped the earrings into her pocket as if they weren't made of precious stones. "I wish you all the luck in the world."

I thanked Lady Eveline as we returned outside to find Luke arguing with his mother. The temporary progress of peace I thought we had made was being obliterated with their loud voices.

"Enough!" Luke yelled, pacing away from the table. "Why can't you accept that I will not be parted from Ruby Mae. If you want a relationship with me, then you will need to forge one with her."

As much as I wanted to rush to my fiancé's side to comfort him, I knew this moment with his mother was a make-it-or-break-it one. With clenched fists, I stood my ground.

"Mrs. de Rossi, I realize that you have been deprived of your son's presence for a long time," I began.

"Too long," she agreed, her control slipping and her voice quavering with sadness.

"And that my accompanying him here has upset you," I continued. "But if you were willing to try to get to know both of us, then I think it would go a long way to making things better."

Luke's mother sneered at me. "Who are you to imply that I do not know my own son?"

Ooh, how a cornered dog will bite. Her reaction clued me in to her own insecurities, so I risked poking her a little. "You know who he was, but you do not know the man he is now. The life that he's lived, the choices he has made...you've been missing that."

She sniffed. "I've had my ways of hearing bits and pieces."

"But you don't *know* him. Who he is, and why in the world he would choose me out of all people," I added, goading her curiosity.

Damiana's eyebrow lifted in disdain. "Now, that is something I would like to know more about." Her expensive shoes clicked on the terrace as she maneuvered to be able to see Luke and me at the same time. "Perhaps you have a point."

Luke rejoined us. "Thank you, Mother."

"Do not thank me yet," she said, doing her best to keep the upper hand. "I accept that we do need to make efforts to listen more to each other. However, I cannot reconcile your attachment to a witch. You know what happened with your sister."

"I know that you and Father have blamed me for her demise for all this time. And I've carried the burden of that guilt with me ever since. But then I met Ruby." He held out his arm, waiting for me to join him. The second I did, he wrapped his arm around my shoulders. "And I understood for the first time what my sister may have been feeling. How unfair we were to treat her as if she had done something wrong other than to fall in love."

Shock and sadness filled the face of Luke's mother. "We did not blame you for her death, Luca."

"That's not how I remember things, Mother," my fiancé replied. "Nor how it felt. How could I stay when my mere presence would upset you?"

Damiana opened her mouth to say something,

but closed it, remaining silent for a few tense moments. With a sigh, some of her anger melted away. "Then it is our fault that our grief drove you away. So, perhaps the punishment of your absence was justified, even if it lasted for too long a time."

My heart ached for the broken family. So much hurt and distrust because they had not hashed out their issues before.

Although I could stay to support Luke, he needed to take advantage of the slight opening to really talk to his mother. "I am going to see Lady Eveline off, and then I might go exploring."

Damiana's expression softened when she addressed me. "If you need any transportation, please alert Enzo. He will be sure to take care of you."

"Thank you." I glanced with sympathy at Luke. "I'll be back before suppertime."

"Be careful," he uttered, mouthing a quick "Thank you" to me.

I blew him a kiss and returned to my room with Lady Eveline. She departed and left me to find some shoes and grab my purse.

I didn't know how long I would have for my secret mission, but if discovering more about

Isabella and her death would help, then I needed to get to work as fast as possible.

Leaving my room with determination, I stomped down the hall in search of a certain mouse of a witch to find out the best place to start.

CHAPTER THIRTEEN

Not being able to speak Italian was turning into a major inconvenience. Although most of the staff that worked in the castle treated me with respect, several that I approached would repeat the same phrase, which I figured meant they didn't understand me, and would leave. I resorted to asking for Fiametta by name, but even then, I couldn't understand any of them who tried to reply.

In frustration, I traipsed through different rooms until I found an open doorway leading to a luscious garden. Stepping outside into the daylight, I closed my eyes and soaked in the sun's rays. A small homesick part of me knew it was the same sun that beamed down on my family and friends back on the Crystal Coast. I spent a few minutes wandering around, smelling brilliant flowers and listening to bees buzzing from one blossom to the next.

A tiny brown bunny with a pink nose hopped into view. It sat on its haunches and stared at me, its ears twitching this way and that.

"Fiametta?" I whispered, looking around to see if anybody else heard me. "Is that you?"

The bunny cocked its furry head to the side, watching me. I took a couple steps towards it, and it bounded off.

"Wait!" I cried out. "Don't go!" Chasing after its fluffy tail, I did my best not to trample on flowers as I followed it off the gravel pathway.

"*Che cosa*? What are you doing?" a familiar woman's voice echoed over the garden.

I stood up straight and stared at her. "Fia? But I thought…" I pointed in the direction the bunny had scampered. "Never mind." With my cheeks heating in embarrassment, I made my way back to her, hoping she hadn't witnessed my little mistake.

"I heard you were asking for me," she said, wiping her hands on her apron.

"I was," I admitted. "And I may have thought you were trying to see me…in a whole different form."

She snickered. "You thought I would hop on over to talk to you?"

Well, crap on a cracker. She had seen me. "After how you found me last night, I don't think I'm totally crazy. Even if I looked it."

"What can I help you with?" Fia asked.

I checked our perimeter again and moved a little closer to her. "I wanted to ask you some questions about last night. You seem to know a lot about," I whispered in a quieter voice, "who we might have encountered in that very special room."

Her smile dropped. "This is not the place to talk. Since you are with Master Luca, you should know about his family and their sense of hearing."

I winced. It didn't occur to me that even if I couldn't see anybody near us, it didn't mean somebody couldn't listen in. Not in a household of vampires.

"I am not done with work yet, but if I tell my boss that you specifically require my assistance, I am sure I will be permitted to accompany you should you want to go somewhere." She lifted her eyebrows to underscore her meaning.

I caught on quickly. "Oh, right." I spoke in a louder, awkward tone. "Fiametta, would you be able to take me into town and show me around?"

"Very convincing," she snorted. "Give me a few minutes, and I will meet you at the back entrance."

I thought about all the corridors and rooms. "Where is that?"

Fia chuckled. "Okay, stay here, and I will come to you."

Her feet crunched on the gravel as she returned inside, and I took a stroll through the manicured garden. Someone had cultivated each grouping of flowers into elaborate patterns of colors.

Someone else joined me in the garden, and I stopped my admiration and looked up, expecting to find Fiametta. Instead, Amara strode with perfect steps despite her insanely high heels.

She said something to me as she approached, and even though I couldn't understand the words, her condescending tone was easy enough to interpret.

"Oh, I forgot you don't speak Italian," she uttered, not an ounce of apology on her flawless face. Her eyes roamed over my body as she judged my outfit. "Are you feeling well today?"

Holding my head up high despite my slight discomfort, I looked her straight in the eyes. "Yes, I am, thank you for asking."

"I only inquire after your health due to your appearance." Amara frowned as if concerned. "You look as if you have just woken up and have not had the time to properly dress for the day."

Well, bless her cold, dead, non-beating heart. If she wanted to play games, I knew a trick or two myself.

Putting on my best and brightest smile, I laid my accent on thick. "Oh, honey, you have no idea. Luke and I stayed up all night together, and...well, since my manners don't allow me to divulge what goes on between a man and his fiancé behind closed doors, I'll let you do the imagining." I winked at her with petty pleasure.

My little ploy to get her to think about my relationship with Luke did the trick. The snide woman's face paled even further.

She coughed a little, pressing her hand to her chest. "Yes...well..."

"Amara," Cassio called out on his way to rescue to me. "What a pleasant surprise to see you today." He greeted her like an old friend, kissing both of her cheeks. "And Ruby, may I say that in the light of the sun, your hair is even more stunning. There are women across the world who would pay handsomely for hair blessed with that lovely shade."

I primped my locks in jest. "And all it took for me was a little luck in the gene pool." Neither of them needed to know that while I got my hair color from my mother, there was nothing else I'd claim from that abandoning witch.

"How sad for you that the passage of time will make it all fade away." Despite the dreadful message of her statement, the awful woman grinned with glee, her fangs gleaming in the sun.

"You are truly incorrigible, Amara. Retract your fangs and let us join our friends for lunch in town," Cassio instructed, flashing me a sympathetic roll of the eyes.

"Oh, will Luca be joining us?" she asked, being sure to watch me for a reaction.

"I am sure he has better companions to spend his time with," Cassio answered for me. "You are welcome to join us, Ruby. If you have not spent any time in Perdaggia, we could show you around after eating."

"Perhaps you can volunteer your time in such a mundane venture," Amara sniffed. "I think it will rain this afternoon."

"Aw, and we wouldn't want you to float, now, would we?" I joked.

She frowned. "I thought the phrase was melting in the rain."

"That's sugar. Sugar melts. There are other things

that float when they are in the water," I said as sweet as pie.

Cassio snorted and did nothing to hide his amused comprehension. Amara narrowed her eyes at me. "I do not understand why Luca would choose someone like you. I hope you get drenched."

Since both of them already knew about my status as a witch, I didn't see the harm in my response. Summoning a little of my fire energy down my arm, I walked over to a nearby fountain and reached under the cascades of water. The heat from my magic evaporated the drops before they could touch me.

"I don't get wet," I bragged, twisting my arm this way and that for good measure. "I burn."

Amara swore in Italian. "Come. Let us leave." She stomped away with less grace than before.

Cassio let her put some distance between us before he addressed me. "You cannot let her get to you like that. She knows how to rattle her victims and has had centuries of practice."

"I know, I know," I grumbled, guilt replacing my temporary triumph. "And now she has firsthand knowledge of my powers."

"Oh, to be sure, others will have that knowledge

very soon," Cassio said, backing away from me. "Be more careful, Ruby Mae."

Fiametta appeared at the door from the castle and paused when she caught sight of Luke's friend leaving me. She dropped her head and curtsied to him as he passed. Hurrying over to me, she grabbed my arm and rushed me away. I tried to talk to her, but she stayed quiet until we reached her small, dark green car.

She unlocked the door for me with her key and did the same on her side. Although the interior of the vehicle barely fit the two of us, I didn't mind being cramped as long as I got some answers.

"I saw what you did." Fia gritted as she drove us down the road, leaving the grounds of the castle. "And you don't know who else might have seen your foolish display."

I winced. "I know. I let my ego get the best of me. No, I let Amara rile me up to do something stupid."

Fiametta grunted. "Yes, she is a nasty woman. Always rude to the staff. Many are afraid of dealing with her."

"I can understand. But you're right," I said, guilt swirling in my stomach.

Fia drove us down a curvy road that led away from Perdaggia and out a different exit of the walled city. Once we were on the other side, she blew out a long sigh.

"If Amara pushed you to act as you did, then I am not so sure I would have done anything different than you. I am sorry for my irritation," she said.

We were running away from the possible consequences of my actions, and I wouldn't know until I returned just how much I'd screwed up. The image of Luke's disappointment on his face haunted my imagination.

"No, my daddy raised me to be smarter than that. And if Granny Jo ever manifests again, I'm sure I'll get an earful." I drew out the token from underneath my shirt and rubbed it.

Fia's eyes flashed to the metal in my fingers, but she didn't ask about it. "There have been many times I wanted to react with magic openly at the castle. But the risk would have been too great."

"Why are you there? I don't quite understand how everything works. If Luke's family has run the place for as long as I think they have, then why hasn't anyone exposed them for what they are? And how could anyone who did know actually work for them?" Questions that had been piling up for a while came tumbling out of my mouth.

Fia chuckled. "That is a lot all at once. As far as

how it works, the de Rossi family is revered in Perdaggia because they saved the town from destruction. The family made sure that the residents have survived every hardship that befell the world outside the city walls. But inside the old barrier, they have kept everyone fed and safe for centuries. That kind of protection generates a lot of loyalty."

"So much that nobody questions why the two at the top of the food chain never age?" I challenged, thinking about Luke's parents.

"There is, of course, talk and the occasional small uprising of outrage from random zealots," Fiametta admitted. "But the de Rossi's generosity, although genuine, has been used to enforce compliance and secrecy. Also, the family is skilled at changing their appearances over time to match the years passing."

It still boggled my mind that anyone who suspected they were vampires would accept that without question. Then again, if I knew my family survived for many generations due to a generous benefactor, I might not want to rock the boat too much either.

"What about those who work for them? You're a witch. Are the rest vampires?" I asked.

The car slowed to a stop at an intersection. The sign ahead of us gave the names of towns, but the arrows pointing the direction to get there went both ways. Like the de Rossi household, it didn't make any sense at all.

Fia turned right and continued. "No, most of the staff are regular mortals. Achieving the opportunity to work in the castle is a great honor. The pay is the best in the region. The benefits are amazing. And we have to sign a very serious contract that includes severe consequences if any of us talk about what we see or hear."

"In other words, they would ruin your world if you tried to attack theirs," I clarified.

"Sì. But it is how it has worked for many centuries, and that is how I was able to procure the job." She slowed again and turned left onto a gravel road. "My place is just down here."

"I'm surprised you don't live in town," I said.

Fia scoffed. "I prefer to distance myself a bit and to keep my privacy."

Tall, thin cypress trees lined the driveway, and we crested a hill to find a modest home made of cream stone. Fiametta parked her car next to it, and we both got out. Old scraggly trees dotted the hilled landscape, but the view was spectacular.

A cool wind picked up, and I glanced at the darkening sky ahead of me. Amara might have been right about rain coming. I'd bet anything watching a storm from this vantage point would be beautiful. I got so caught up in taking it all in that I didn't hear her call my name to follow her inside.

"This location is amazing," I gushed as I entered.

The word that sprung into my head the second I saw the interior of her place was *cozy*. The space may have been small, but every piece of furniture and decoration fit perfectly.

Fia called out for me through another door, and I followed into a tidy kitchen with herbs hanging from the ceiling, a large fireplace, some modern appliances, and a sturdy table in the middle.

"This is the heart of my home," she admitted with a smile. "I spend most of my time in here."

I gazed out the large window at the scenery. "I can understand why."

She pulled out a chair. "Here, you sit. I will make you something to eat." She retrieved a nearby apron and donned it.

"Oh, don't go to any trouble," I said, but my stomach rumbled in protest.

Fia giggled. "It is my pleasure. And I can tell you why I work at the castle while I cook."

She poured me a glass of dark red wine to sip while I listened and watched. For the first time since

I'd arrived in Italy, I felt comfortable. The location might have changed, but this was no different than sitting in the big house watching Granny do her thing.

"My choice to work for the de Rossi family was made for me long ago although I did not know it until my *nonna* passed away a few years ago." Fiametta chopped some vegetables while she spoke.

"I'm sorry for your loss," I uttered, touching the token around my neck.

"It was tough. This was her house that she and my grandfather built." She nodded out the window. "They planted every one of those olive trees themselves, and I remember coming to help harvest the olives every year. And when my parents died, she took me in and raised me."

"Did she know what you were? That you were a witch?" I asked.

"Oh, yes. She was one herself, and she taught me how to harness my magic as well as all my cooking skills. It is her bloodline that flows through me and connects the past to my present." She lit a fire on her gas burner and heated up a skillet. "I come from a lost line of the *Benandanti*."

The name itself sounded so exotic. "Who are they?"

"History remembers them as evil people who were accused of various forms of witchcraft. Many of the family lines were destroyed during the great European witch hunts." She uncorked an unlabeled bottle and poured some oil into the heated pan.

"Your magic allows you to change into an animal?" I asked, remembering the night in Isabella's room.

She smiled as she threw some garlic into the pan. The distinct aroma filled the room. "Yes, my *nonna* thought I was especially skilled at it. A mouse is my preferred choice I think because that's what she used to change into the most. But I can manifest into other small forms as well."

I thought about my cousin Deacon and his problems. Maybe Fia could help him figure out how to change back into his human form? The pan sizzled as Fia added more ingredients, bringing me back to the here and now. We had more pressing issues to discuss.

"I don't understand how your past chose your present," I said, wanting to make all the connections.

Fia stirred the contents in the pan and then opened her refrigerator and pulled out a container. She drew out what looked like noodles and added them in.

"Ah, but what follows will delight you the most. Do you know why Isabella de Rossi died?" she asked, tossing the ingredients in the skillet with skilled flicks of her wrist.

"She fell in love with a witch and refused to give up her lover," I said, giving the short version of what Luke had told me.

"Precisely." Fia turned off the burner and retrieved two shallow bowls from a shelf. "I am descended from that witch. Paulo Gasparotto is my ancestor and he was Isabella's fiancé."

She poured the contents of the pan into the two bowls and busied herself finishing the dishes with sprinkled herbs and grated cheese. Setting my plate in front of me, she poured more wine in my glass and set a plate with a hunk of bread in between us as she sat down at the table.

I leaned over and drew in the delicious scent. "This smells so good. What's in it?" I asked.

Fiametta beamed with pride. "It is a family recipe. Nothing fancy."

"Don't sell yourself short. There are expensive restaurants who wish they had a dish like this." I raised my glass to toast her. "Where I'm from, we use food to show our love and care for each other. Thank you for the meal."

Fia's cheeks reddened, and she clinked her glass against mine. "*Grazie*. Now, please eat."

I swirled some of the fresh pasta onto the end of my fork and inserted it into my mouth. "Holy hexes, that is like nothing I've ever eaten before," I groaned. "It tastes very earthy."

Her eyebrows raised in appreciation. "Very good. I've used some fresh mushrooms I foraged this past weekend as well as some fresh onions and garlic."

"That's it?" I asked, incredulous that so few ingredients could create something that tasty.

Fiametta ate some of her own dish and nodded. "Good food does not need complications. And fresh is always best. If you are here over the next weekend, I could take you into the forest to hunt for mushrooms. It can be a fun game. Which ones are edible. Which ones might kill you."

I stopped chewing. "I'm assuming you used some good ones."

Her eyes widened, and she dropped her fork, clutching her throat. Just when I thought I felt a scratchiness in mine, she laughed at her own joke.

"I am well trained in which mushrooms are safe," she assured me, continuing to eat. "These are amanita caesarea, or Caesar's mushrooms. We call them *ovoli*. But there are deadly varieties. You do not want to make a mistake and use *ovoli delle mortali*. There are many in the same species that can cause sickness or death."

"Sounds like a dangerous hobby," I said, digging into my pasta again.

Fia shrugged. "It makes it a fun challenge. But I know which mushrooms are like gold and which ones to avoid well enough." She tore off a hunk of bread and paused. "Would you like to see something else that will amaze you?"

"Sure." I busied myself with finishing my lunch, washing it down with the simple but good wine.

I heard the sound of a heavy piece of furniture being moved and scraping on the stone floor. Something fell, and a muffled Italian expletive echoed in the small house. Fia returned a little breathless, holding a small box and placing it in front of me. She set a notebook down nearby on the table.

Pushing my plate away and draining the rest of the wine, I readied myself for what was inside the wooden container. A pair of hearts intertwined on the worn surface. Someone had carved letters inside the hearts.

My fingers traced the carving. "*P* and *J*?" I asked.

"No, that's an *I*. Paolo and Isabella." Fia scooted her chair closer to sit next to me. "My grandmother said this box has been handed down throughout the generations. Open it."

She didn't have to ask me more than once, and I unlatched the simple hook holding it closed and pulled the lid open. The interior was lined with soft red velvet, the years having worn a few holes in it. I picked up a dried flower and twirled it in my hand. A pale ribbon wrapped around some cut hair. Other random items filled the space, but I saw nothing of great worth.

"These must be mementos of their time together," I said, starting to place them back inside.

Fia stopped me. "But there is a false bottom. There's a velvet tag right there. Tug on it."

I did as she instructed, and the bottom gave way and moved. Pulling it out, I glanced at the contents it had hidden. Yellowed parchment bundled together with twine lay inside. The paper on top contained a red wax seal with an emblem stamped into it that I recognized.

"These are from Isabella," I exclaimed.

Thunder rumbled through the air, and the light in the kitchen darkened as a storm approached. Fia flicked on the light above us and retrieved the folded papers from their hiding place.

"Yes, this is Isabella de Rossi's correspondence

with Paolo Gasparotto." She untied the bundle. "Nonna told me tales of their great love and how it was denied by her family. It sounded unreal to me until she showed me this treasure trove of history and I deciphered through her own words."

Fiametta unfolded the letter on top and pointed at the words scribbled in ink. "It took me ages to interpret everything she wrote. First, I had to navigate her own handwriting. Then, I had to work through her language as it is slightly different than modern-day Italian."

"It is?" I asked, staring at the lines of words that all seemed foreign to me.

"Oh, yes." She glanced at me with sincerity. "Having one language for the whole country is fairly new. Each region had its own dialect that has, for the most part, been lost or changed over time. It took me almost a year, but I wrote down my best translation."

Fia handed me the letter while she picked up her notebook. Something about holding the actual thoughts and feelings of Isabella struck me. A deep well of sadness rose up inside of me, and I twisted the ring on my left hand to stop the slight tingling I felt from it.

"Of course, I wrote my own translation into Italian, so I will do my best to interpret into English," she said with a little grimace. "Many of the letters sound more romantic, very typical of young love. It is not until we reach the later letters where it gets intriguing."

"That would probably be when the two of them started facing complications," I said.

"Sì. Listen." Fia followed the lines in her notebook with her finger as she read. "Mm, here it is. She says she thinks someone has found out about them and she is afraid her family will find out. And in another one she admits to telling her brother and his best friend about Paolo because of how much she trusts both of them. But she expresses great sadness because neither support her relationship like she thought they would."

My stomach clenched in worry. Why would Luke oppose his sister being with a witch if he chose me? Then I remembered his own words, and that he didn't understand her love until he met me. Still, I didn't like this version of Luke from the past.

Fiametta turned the page in her notebook. "Another letter states how worried she is for the two of them and encourages Paolo that if they want to marry, they must do so soon."

"Do you only have her letters and not his?" I asked.

Fia nodded. "She must have kept his somewhere. You are going to wish we had them when I read you this next part." She returned to her own translation. "This comes from one of the last letters. Isabella writes that someone has threatened her to break things off."

"Does she say who?" I pressed, trying to look over her shoulder despite not being able to read the language.

"No, she does not use any name. But he must have in his letter back to her, because in her next letter, she tells him that to threaten the life of the person will bring about Paolo's demise." Fia dropped the notebook into her lap. "Whoever it was must have had a lot of connections within the family for her to be that scared. See here, she writes that this person is very dear to her. She thinks she can speak reason to whomever it is."

My breath caught in my throat. "You don't suppose she meant her brother?" From everything my fiancé had told me, he loved his sister with everything he had.

Fia pursed her lips, but her refusal to answer the question said enough. She opened her notebook again. "This was her final letter. Isabella writes to Paolo and says she will escape her life and start a new one with him. She is willing to give up every-thing she has to be his wife and live a simpler life. Her last words are for him to be ready."

A flash of lightning lit up the room from outside of the window, and thunder crackled, shaking the house. I jumped a little, my nerves jangled and on edge from the contents of the letters. And the new questions they inspired.

Fiametta replaced the actual letters inside the box and fixed the false bottom back into place. "We should drive back to the castle. If the rain becomes too bad, it will make the journey difficult."

I wanted to keep the letters but thought better of it. Even the translated words in her notebook wouldn't be helpful since I didn't know the language. Better for her to keep them all here than to bring them back to the castle.

The rain pounded down in steady streams, and the windshield wipers on Fia's car worked as hard as possible. She drove with great care as we made our way back.

"That is strange," she said, glancing in her rearview mirror.

"What?" I asked, wanting her to keep her eyes on

the road.

She kept looking in her mirror. "The headlights of the car behind us. They are getting closer at a rapid speed."

I turned my head to the lights glowing through the back window but couldn't see the actual car. "They are approaching fast."

"Whoever it is needs to slow down in this weather," Fia scolded.

The beams flashed on and off several times. "I think they're trying to signal for you to get out of their way," I said.

Fia gripped her steering wheel. "There is nowhere for me to go. They must go around if they want to pass." She watched them in her rearview mirror. "They are not slowing at all."

Our car sped up a little to keep whoever was behind us from hitting the bumper. They backed off a little, and then sped up again.

"I think they're trying to hit us," I exclaimed, bracing my arms against the top of the small car.

Fiametta muttered something under her breath. "Hold on. There's a place I can pull off up the road. We just have to make it."

She pressed the gas pedal harder to get her vehicle moving, but it couldn't outrun the one trying to come after us. The bumper on that car nudged ours, and we swerved a little, fishtailing on the wet road.

"Fia," I warned as the lights of the car approached again.

"A little farther," she insisted.

We both jolted in our seats as we got hit again. Instead of backing off, the car behind us accelerated, pushing Fia's vehicle forward.

"I am losing control," she admitted. "Hold on."

A curve in the road loomed up ahead, and I figured we'd fly off our course and crash. I called up a little of my magic to try and cast it at the driver of the other car.

"No, don't. You might hurt us instead," Fiametta insisted, her hands jerking the steering wheel to fight for control.

One more push from the car behind us, and we spun out of control. The wet world on the outside flashed in front of us again and again as we both screamed in horror. We whipped around until Fia's car slammed off the road. The tires slid on the hillside, slowing us down. The chassis of the vehicle tipped on its side, and in that one moment where we were on two wheels, I forgot about everything except Luke.

The car slammed back down on all four tires, the engine still running. Rain pelted the car, and our panting breaths fogged up the windows. I held my hand over my beating heart and glanced at Fia.

"Are you okay?" I asked.

She answered first in Italian, and then remembered to speak English. "Yes. I think so."

We paused to stare at each other and then burst into hysterical giggles. She reached across and hugged me, and I barely registered the pain in my muscles from all the adrenaline coursing through me.

"You handled that well," I said, complimenting her driving.

She thanked me, still catching her breath. "I think we got very lucky."

Another car approached and slowed down. A man got out in the pouring rain and came over to check on us. Fia tested the car and found it could still function. Thanking the kind person, she rolled up the window, and we got back on the road.

As we drove closer to Perdaggia, more questions formed in my head. "Why did someone try to run us off the road?"

Fia shrugged. "Lots of tourists rent cars and drive like maniacs around here."

"I could see someone maybe trying to pass us and going too fast. But whoever that was, they targeted us specifically." I paused, trying to figure it out. "Why us?"

Fiametta drove in contemplative silence for a while until we crossed into the walled city and drove up the private road to the castle.

The closer we got, the more convinced I became that I knew the reason. "I think we've stirred up ghosts of the past," I said.

Fia parked her car and sat back in her seat, her fingers drumming the steering wheel. "And someone wishes for us not to. I think you may be right. But you know what that means."

I clutched my purse in my lap. "Yep. It means we must be on the right path."

"Yes, but there are bigger concerns. We are being watched and followed." Her eyes widened as she looked at me.

Through the streams of rain pouring down the window of her car, I stared up at the facade of the medieval structure towering over us. Somewhere inside, someone knew the truth. The urgency to unravel the mystery increased, and I would have to find the delicate balance between being careful and discovering the answers before anyone else got hurt.

CHAPTER FOURTEEN

Claudio met us at a side entrance. He grabbed Fiametta and drew her aside, speaking to her in hushed rapid Italian. She interrupted him a couple of times, but he wouldn't stop fussing.

She held up her hand to get him to stop and addressed me. "You had better return to your room. It seems the tale of your display from the garden has complicated things for you."

I winced in anticipation. "I'll need a little help getting there. This place still confuses me." My fingers dug into my sore neck. "Are you going to be okay?" I asked.

Fia nodded. "Please send word to me if you feel

any worse. I can send up some cream to help any muscle aches."

Claudio renewed his tirade at my friend, but she brushed him off, insisting he help me back to my room. He did so, but his friendliness level dropped from ten to zero.

At the end of the hallway I recognized, he stopped. "Please, Miss Ruby, do not involve Fia anymore."

"She has her own reasons to work with me," I insisted, understanding his concern but needing to keep my connection to her.

"And she has ways to protect herself. I know," the young man admitted. "But I would rather she not cause any trouble, and ever since you have arrived, that is all that has occurred."

I wanted to deny his accusation but couldn't. "I understand. But the choice has to be hers." Even though I needed her help, I refused to force her.

Claudio heaved a heavy breath. "Yes, she has a mind of her own."

"Which is why you love her," I finished for him.

His mouth dropped open, but he did not utter a protest. "Sì. I do," he sighed.

I winked at him. "Then make sure she knows that, and she might take your concerns into consideration." I gazed down the hallway at the door to my room. "Claudio, just how angry is Master Luca?"

The young man frowned in contemplation. "I would not wish to be you at this moment."

Oh, sweet tea and spells. I glanced down the corridor in the opposite direction, weighing my options. Claudio chuckled at my reaction and urged me to face my fears, laying his hands on the top of my shoulders and guiding me in the right direction. His joke eased my worry that I had lost his favor, and I obeyed.

I reached for the handle to my door but flinched away at the last second. Even though it was the entrance to my own room, I knocked on the heavy wood instead.

Luke bellowed in Italian from the other side, and I swallowed hard, unlatching the door and entering. The man pacing in my room wore expensive clothes instead of stained coveralls. His jaw still held a bit of stubble but no grease or oil smudges. The smile he always wore when he saw me was missing, a deep scowl replacing it.

"Where have you been?" he growled the second he caught sight of me. "You can't just leave without telling me where you are going."

"I told you I might go exploring," I defended.

"When?" he shouted.

Although he might have reasons to be irritated with me, I wouldn't accept irrational anger. "On the terrace. When I was leaving you to talk to your mother."

It took him a few seconds to remember, but when he did, some of his frustrations deflated. "Oh."

"Yes, *oh*. And besides, Cassio saw me leaving with Fiametta in the garden. Didn't he tell you?" I asked.

He stopped in his tracks and slipped his hands inside his pockets. "No, he did not."

Maybe Luke's friend hadn't seen me leave with Fia, only that she came out to the garden to speak with me. Either way, I was surprised that he hadn't told Luke something with my fiancé fuming about me.

"Is there anything else you would like to share with me? Something that might have happened in the garden?" he pushed.

I took another step closer and held up my hands. "Before you say anything, let me just apologize. What I did was foolish, and even though Amara provoked me, I should not have taken her bait."

Luke frowned. "What could Amara have done to justify you threatening her with your magic?"

"What?" I shrieked, mortified at the false accusation. "Please tell me that's not what that...woman said. Or that you even spent a second believing that lie."

My fiancé cast his eyes down at the floor, unwilling to return my gaze. "It's what everybody believes. That you threatened her with your powers."

"And did you not push to find out how much truth there might be behind her story? Or ask your friend Cassio, who was there by the way, what really happened?" I shouted, my heartache matching the pain throbbing in my entire body from the car incident.

I waited for him to say anything in my defense, but only offending silence followed. "So, you did believe the worst of me."

He sighed. "Not really, no. I didn't think you did as she described." Approaching me, he tried to touch my arm, but I pulled out of his reach.

"Amara insulted me from the moment she saw me. Comments about my appearance or about how I didn't deserve you. Bringing up that you are both vampire and I'm not." Her words still stung. "I just wanted to show her that I had advantages she didn't. So, I may have displayed a little of my fire magic out of spite. To shut her up."

"She did the exact opposite of that," Luke scoffed,

respecting me by giving me space. "I will have a talk to Cassio about not divulging the truth if he truly witnessed it, although I don't know where he ran off to this afternoon."

I explained in detail exactly what happened in the garden, and after my full recount, he apologized in full to me.

"You're right. I shouldn't have believed anything that Amara said." He paced again. "And I understand why you reacted the way that you did, but it has caused the little bridge of peace I have been building with my parents to crumble."

"Is your mother terribly upset?" I asked, a little more remorseful.

Luke scowled. "I think it makes her even more wary of you than before. She sees your actions as a lack of respect to her."

I sank down on the edge of the bed. "Great. Just the opposite of how I wanted her to feel about me."

With slow steps, my fiancé proceeded towards me. He sat next to me and risked putting his arm around my shoulders. "I don't think my mother is a hopeless case. My father, on the other hand…"

I snorted. "He hates me, doesn't he?"

Luke chose his words carefully. "He…refuses to get to know you so that he might change his mind.

And he is trying to push Amara at me. As if that foul beast ever had a chance."

"Are you trying to get me to light this whole place up out of jealousy?" I asked, only half kidding.

My fiancé hugged me closer to him, and I groaned in pain. The longer time passed after our car accident, the more my muscles complained about being whipped around.

Luke frowned. "You're hurt?"

Collapsing against him despite my body aches, I told him everything about going to Fia's house, reading through Isabella's letters, and then being run off the road. A guttural roll of a growl rumbled in Luke's chest like the thunder from before, but he kept his arm wrapped around me.

After listening to me, his chest rose and sank with a long sigh. "Do you think we could start our day over again? Today has not been exactly great."

"Neither was last night," I reminded him. "But sure, as long as you can forgive me my stupid act of magic."

"No, *cara*. Forgive me for forgetting my duty first to you." He let out another loud exhale. "Before we came here, it was just you and me. Now that I've returned, I fear that I have fallen back into the life of

Luca de Rossi. And I'm not so sure I like him very much. I much prefer being Luke Manson."

"But you are both of those people," I defended, looking up at him. "You will have to figure out how much of each you can reconcile with and move on from there."

"Wise words from someone I yelled at." He kissed the tip of my nose.

Even that brief gesture of care hurt, and I couldn't stop the groan from escaping me. Luke released me from his hold and stood.

"For now, I just want to be Ruby Mae's man who takes care of her. Let me draw you a hot bath to soothe your muscles. Perhaps I should have a doctor called in," he wondered out loud.

I waved him off. "I don't think anything's broken or truly hurt. Just a little whiplash maybe. Fiametta said she'd send some soothing cream."

He nodded. "I can make sure that gets brought to you after I get you in the tub."

I let my fiancé fuss over me. Maybe I took a little too much pleasure in his fawning out of guilt, but the bath did do wonders to help relax my muscles. Taking a couple of pills for the pain, I collapsed into the bed after applying some of Fia's cream. Luke promised to wake me up for dinner and left me to get some rest.

At first, I fell into a deep sleep. But odd visions disturbed my rest, and I found myself running around the castle grounds. Except, I wasn't lost.

I knew every inch of the place, where each corridor led, how to open the secret passageways, and more. The whole place had been my playground since birth, and I loved every inch of stone. I ran around with careless abandon, giggling and crying out for my brother and his friend to find me.

A voice that sounded like Luke's but different called my name. "Isabella!"

No, that wasn't my name. And these weren't my memories. I tossed and turned under the sheets, trying to claw my way out of the dream, but the power of it pulled me back under.

The scene changed, and I was no longer a child at play. I watched a handsome man speak with my father about fixing some of the spells that protected the castle. He negotiated well, unafraid to ask for what his services were worth. My father respected him and agreed. While the stranger was allowed on the castle grounds, I found ways to watch and spy on his every movement until the day he discovered me and turned into a fox right before my eyes.

The animal trotted over and let me pet its thick fur. Its

tongue lolled out, and I laughed at the absurdity of it all. After a few brief moments, the fox disappeared and changed into the man again. He told me his name.

"Paolo Gasparotto," he said in a deep voice I wanted to listen to again and again.

Strong love grew over a short amount of time, and I shared with him all who I was. Paolo did not care that he and I were not meant to be together. We could choose each other and not have to listen to others' expectations of us.

I heard my brother yelling at me after I revealed my secret to him. His best friend glared at me like I had done something terrible. Neither of them supported me, and I realized that all I had in this world was my freedom to choose Paolo. I made plans.

My parents somehow learned about my love and have threatened me. My father did not like me ruining his plans to marry me off to some other noble. My mother refused to approve of me choosing a witch instead of a vampire. Their anger led them to sequester me in a tall tower in the middle of Perdaggia, isolating me from anyone until I gave up Paolo. They did not know the strength of my will or my feelings.

Despite my resolve, I cried every day that passed me by. And every time they checked, I refused to give in to their demands. A fight occurred. Words of anger. Fire blazed. Death came for me instead of love.

I bolted upright, panting and sweating from all the heat. Confused and disoriented, I patted the sheets to make sure none of them were actually ablaze. When I was little, if I dreamt of fire, it could set off my magic by accident. With relief, I found no smoldering holes in the expensive linens.

Everything I remembered felt like my own memory and yet not. Tugging on my own hair, I checked to make sure it was still red and not the dark brown from the dream. Popping out of the bed, I rushed over to the full-length mirror to make sure I was just plain old Ruby Mae, not a shadow of Luke's sister.

My muscles no longer ached, but the ring on my finger tingled against my skin. I twisted it off and held it in my palm. It pulsed with the same type of heat that the token did against my chest.

Isabella still remained here in some form, reaching across time to give me a message. I just had to figure out what she wanted me to learn before anything…or anyone…got hurt. Especially me.

CHAPTER FIFTEEN

I debated whether or not to continue wearing Isabella's ring. It clearly held some sort of connection to her. If I wanted to discover her secrets and the truth behind her death, the piece of jewelry was my best link to it all.

After splashing some cold water on my face to ensure I was truly no longer dreaming, I pulled on the chain of my necklace and pulled out the token.

"Granny, if you can hear me, I could really use your help right now," I said, rubbing my thumb over the relief of the elephant.

The coin warmed a bit in response, but my ghostly great-grandmother did not appear. I almost gave up in despair, but another thought stopped me.

Switching the token into my left hand, I let the ring touch the metal of the medallion.

"Come on, Granny Jo. I need someone on my side to help me out," I begged.

The token vibrated a little in my hand, but even with the touch of the ring, I could not summon my great-grandmother. But I knew a place where I could. I wanted to go back to Isabella's room to search anyway. See if I could find Paolo's letters so that Fia could help me figure out the other side of the doomed couple's written conversations.

I answered a light knock on the door and yanked on Fiametta's arm to pull her inside.

"I came by to check on you." She looked me up and down, holding onto a tray. "You do not seem to be in any pain."

Huh. I'd been so focused on the visions of the dream that I hadn't recognized that my body no longer hurt.

"I guess your cream worked," I said with my compliments. "Listen, do you think you could get me back to Isabella's room?"

Her eyes widened, and she shook her head while setting the tray of espresso and snacks down. "I do not think returning there is so good. That room usually stays locked and untouched, but someone let the mistress of the castle know that her daughter's chambers had been disturbed."

"And now, they're suspicious as to who did it. Well, grits and ghosts, that makes things a bit more difficult," I mused. "But you got me out of there using a secret passageway, right? Why couldn't we use it again?"

"Why is it necessary for you to go there right now?" Fiametta asked.

I told her about my nap and dream, explaining what I had seen. It might have been a little evil of me to include so many enticing details about her ancestor, Paolo. But I needed her help to get into the room without being detected. Something in me knew that some of the answers waited in Isabella's former quarters.

"My *nonna* told me about the witches' community helping to keep the spells cast on the castle renewed over all the centuries. But I had no idea I had a direct descendent who helped." Fia chewed on her thumbnail. "Maybe that is why I can move about with such ease."

I grasped her hand in mine. "Will you help me?"

Fiametta sighed with resignation. "Yes, but we need to wait until there are fewer people roaming about. Maybe some time tonight. After your dinner."

She handed me a thick card with fancy calligraphy on it.

I read the invitation from Luke, pleased at his fancy attempt to woo me. "The time says not until eight tonight. You Italians start your suppers late."

Fia chuckled. "We like to take our time. Enjoy every minute of the day, stretching out the pleasure."

I thought out loud. "If I get ready for the dinner first, then you could take me to the room prior to meeting Luke. We'll search the space together and see what other clues we can find. Does that sound acceptable?" Remembering my talk with Claudio, I added, "But if you don't want to, feel free to say no."

The kind young woman gave in. "I can get you there, but since I work in the kitchens, I will be needed to help prepare the meal."

"If you'll teach me the spell to use the passage-way, then I will find my own way out," I promised, a little less than fifty percent sure I could actually uphold my side of the bargain.

Fia agreed and told me to be ready by seven. That gave me a little over an hour to get cleaned up and ready. "I will meet you later," I told her at the door.

"*Ci vediamo,*" she called out as she left, her nerves making her forget her English.

Wanting to impress Luke, I spent extra effort

choosing from some of the fashionable clothes in my closet. Although a dress would be more appropriate for an evening date, I picked out a silky dark green blouse with ruffled sleeves and cream pants that fit like a glove. With my best efforts, I worked on my hair, unable to manage a fancy twist. I settled on an intentionally messy bun at the nape of my neck with tendrils hanging down by the sides of my face.

Lady Eveline's diamond chandelier earrings would have been perfect if she hadn't taken them back, but I chose my simpler studs for my ears, pleased to choose something that I'd purchased with my own money. The bracelet I'd bought at the Midnight Market would look stunning, so I slipped it on my wrist as a nice sparkly touch.

The shoes were the last item to select, and I held up a pair of high heels in one hand and my worn-out sneakers in my other. One of these things just didn't belong, which had become my story since arriving in Italy.

"If I'm going to be navigating the magical secret passages, I think rubber soles and closed toes are the way to go," I stated out loud, telling myself I'd have plenty of time to come back to the room and change before meeting Luke.

I met Fia in the hallway, wanting to keep an eye

on any staff walking around. She hustled both of us to a part of the wall with no tapestries or art. Raising her hand, she found the spot that activated the spell and opened a small entrance for both of us.

"Quickly. Follow me." She ducked inside and disappeared.

When I cleared the threshold, the door shut behind us with a thud, and I cast a light orb to join Fiametta's.

"We must hurry so I can make it back without being missed," she whispered.

Only the squeak of some rodent answered her, and I kept the rising squeal in my throat from bursting out so as not to insult my friend who could change into a mouse herself. I thought it would be smart to play a little Hansel and Gretel, so I retrieved a napkin I'd stuffed in my pocket with half of the pastry that had accompanied my macchiato.

Tearing off little pieces, I dropped them as we progressed and hoped that none of the actual mice would eat them before I found my way back.

Fia stopped at a crossroads of passages and pointed to the left. "We will head down here. When you come back, you will need to turn right."

I held up the last of the cornetto. "I've come prepared."

She smiled at my ingenuity and continued down the passage.

The ring on my finger tingled, and I wasn't surprised when Fia stopped. "Here, give me your hand."

I did as she asked, and she waved it slowly over the stone. "Do you feel anything?"

Stepping closer, I scanned my palm over the stones myself. "Here. This area feels different."

"Yes, exactly. That is the spell," she said.

"When Luke used one of the passages when we first got here, he pressed his hand against the stone and had to bleed a little to get it to open," I said, unsure if I wanted to be punctured in such a dirty place.

"Yes, that is how the vampires must access the passages," Fia said. "Whatever magic they contain for their long lives, it exists in their blood. You and I, however, can conjure at will."

She explained the spell to me and gave me the space to try and open the secret door. It took me a few minutes, but eventually, the stone gave way, and we stepped through the opening into a darkened room.

Fiametta put her finger to her lips. "There is probably a security guard who patrols the hallway outside," she whispered. "Be sure you don't make any noise."

"Ok," I mouthed back. "Thank you."

She winked and responded with a quiet, "Good luck."

As she left through the same passageway, the wall closed behind Fia with a little *kerchunk*, and I held my breath, waiting to see if somebody on the outside had heard it.

If Fiametta hadn't told me about the discovery of the room after I'd been there, I would have expected to find papers strewn about and anything not tied down to be scattered all over the place. But someone had tidied the place again and put everything back where it belonged. Risking a little of my magic, I lit several of the candles still standing to give me a little light to see by.

The token around my neck pulsed, and Granny Jo appeared next to me. "Ruby Mae Jewell," she said at full voice.

I shushed her, and she flinched a little before wagging her finger at me. "Ruby Mae Jewell," she started again much quieter. "Just because you can't see me doesn't mean I don't know what you've been up to. If I had been in your fiancé's position, findin' out you were showing off just to spite that hateful woman, I would have tanned your hide."

Not wanting to spend even a second thinking about if Granny Jo and Luke switched places, I attempted to get her to focus. "We don't have much time here, and after our last visit, I don't even know where to start."

"Why are you so obsessed with solving something that happened ages ago? Why can't you let the past lie like sleeping dogs?" she asked in exasperation.

I cocked my head to the side and stared back. "Really? Is that what you would do? Or is your last name not spelled J-E-W-E-L—"

"Oh, hush," Granny Jo cut me off. "I can sense the sister's restless spirit is still hangin' about, and yes, I agree we should help. I just don't want you to get into any more trouble. But that might be like wishing for the sun not to rise every mornin'."

I ignored her cranky retort and filled her in on everything I'd found out so far, especially from the letters that Fiametta shared with me.

"If we can find the other half of that correspondence, I think it might have the name written down of a person who directly objected to her marriage to Paolo," I said, walking over to the desk.

"You clearly don't have any kids of your own. The last place a girl like that would put some secret letters is somewhere in the desk." Granny Jo hovered as she turned about the room. "She has a special place she kept things that she didn't want found."

"How do you know that?" I asked, still wanting to dig through everything in or on the desk.

Granny snorted. "What, did you think I was born this old? I had my own stuff I wanted to keep to myself. Plus, I raised my own kids."

"And me," I admitted, hoping she never found the loose baseboard in my room at the big house. "Okay, so if she did have a hidey hole, how would we find it?"

As if my left hand didn't belong to me, it shot straight up in the air with such strength that it pulled me onto my tippy toes.

"Why are you raising your arm up like that?" Granny Jo asked.

"Uh, I'm not." With all my strength, I tried to lower my hand.

Instead, it changed positions and pointed forward, twisting to the right. I had to move with it to keep my shoulder from popping out of socket.

"I feel like one of those spinners on the board games we used to play. Like someone's flicked my arm and I'm moving around in circles," I said, a little perturbed to not be able to control my own body.

A strange force stopped spinning me and tugged me forward. I stumbled to keep upright and allowed whatever compelled me to guide me forward. My left wrist twisted up, and my palm rested in the middle of a painting.

"I think this is the spot," I said, the ring on my finger still tingling but control of my hand returning to me.

Grabbing ahold of both sides of the painting, I lifted it off of the wall. With care, I set it down on the floor and leaned it against the wall. I took a nearby candle and ignored the drip of hot wax on my skin as I inspected the stone surface.

One of the stones appeared different than the others, and I stepped a little closer to look at it. There was nothing special about the rock, but the cement sealant had been chipped away.

"I wonder," I mused, gripping the stone by its side and pulling on it.

It gave way with minimal effort, but I lost my hold on it, and it clattered to the floor and skittered somewhere behind me.

"What's inside?" Granny Jo asked, hovering closer to me.

If I tipped the candle to be able to see, I'd drip wax everywhere and leave evidence of my trespassing. With a little of my fire magic, I scooped the flame into the palm of my hand and willed it to grow bigger to provide enough light.

"There are some papers in here." I said, pulling the controlled flame away and reaching in with my free hand. Withdrawing the treasure I'd found, my heart raced at my discovery.

The paper was folded much like the letters that Fiametta had at her place. I extinguished the flame in my hand and moved over to the desk. Sitting down, I did my best to read through each one, but since I couldn't even read any Italian, I had no hope of reading these.

I scanned each line to see if I could decipher any specific names and found Luke's a few times. By the sixth letter I unfolded, I realized the folly of my mission.

"I should take these, put the stone and painting back in place, and have Fiametta or even Luke help me read them," I said. Just as I was giving up, I spotted an anomaly in the handwriting. "Wait a minute. I think this part right here is a name. But I can't figure it out."

Granny Jo broke my concentration. "Ruby Mae, I think someone is coming."

"Shh, it's probably Fia. I'll bet her curiosity got the better of her." My fingers traced over the loops of the hastily written script. "This might be an *S*. Or maybe an *O*. The next letter is definitely a lower-cased *A*. Or maybe that's an *O*?"

The secret door in the wall slid open, and I waved my hand at it. "Hey, Fia. Come see this. I think I've found the name of the person who was threatening Isabella."

"Ruby Mae!" my ghostly great-grandmother shouted.

I turned too late, and whoever entered through the secret passage got the better of me. Something hit my head, and everything went dark.

MY LUNGS FOUGHT to take in air, and I coughed myself awake. Granny Jo had disappeared, and my head pounded like someone had tried to split it open. I reached up to touch it, and when I pulled my hand away, blood covered my skin.

"That's not good," I uttered, sitting up.

Flames licked over every piece of furniture and cloth. Whoever had attacked me had also set the entire room on fire. Although a little woozy, I managed to get to my feet. The air at that level was too thick to breathe.

Falling back down to my knees, I crawled into the space in the middle to figure out my best escape. I looked at the wall with the secret passage, but a large dresser engulfed by flames sat in front of it.

To the left of the desk, velvet curtains that hung from the ceiling down to the floor smoldered and burned. But the leftover tatters revealed a windowed door to the outside terrace much like in my room.

My head ached and the room spun a little, but I knew what I had to do. I drew in a quick breath from the floor level and pushed myself to stand. Summoning my magic, I called to the fire. The tip of all the flames in the room changed direction and pointed in my direction as if I was the north to their compass. The bracelet on my wrist glowed, and I prayed it would give me a little extra boost when I needed it.

Holding out my arms wide, I concentrated and invited the fire to leave where it burned and come to me. Like a vacuum, I absorbed all of the flames in the room, letting them fill me up until I could take no more. The inferno raged inside of me, and I marched towards the windows behind the ruined curtains.

With a little energy push, the glass shattered, but the doors did not open onto the terrace. Every second I allowed the fire to burn in me depleted my magic reserves. If I used up any more power to open the door, I'd risk losing control. My skin glowed as if I was a walking ember, and if I couldn't get outside, everything I'd absorbed would consume me, and my efforts would be for nothing.

Backing up as far as I could, I ran at the door, risking a little magic to protect my body as I rammed into the wood and leftover glass shards. I felt nothing as I broke through to the other side, and as soon as I saw stars in the sky, I sank to my knees. With one big wail, I aimed a stream of flames into the air until I had nothing left in me.

With the fire gone, I didn't have to fight anymore. I collapsed onto the terrace, giving into the darkness that dragged me under.

CHAPTER SIXTEEN

I drew in a hard breath and winced at the burn in my throat. My eyes fluttered open, and my fiancé's face filled my vision.

"Welcome back," he uttered, flashing me a brilliant smile almost as bright as the sun lighting up the rest of the room. He brushed hair out of my face. "Oh, *cara*, you may be the death of me yet."

I tried to chuckle. "That's saying something, coming from a vampire."

Luke helped me sit up in bed, propping pillows behind my back. He handed me a glass of water, and I downed its contents, holding it out to ask for more. I finished the whole pitcher before my thirst came close to being quenched.

"Is your sister's room completely destroyed?" I

asked, recalling the last thing I remembered. Lifting my hand to my head, I felt for the bump from where I'd been hit and flinched when I found it.

My fiancé shook his head, frowning at my pain. "We can discuss the details later. I want to make sure you're fully recovered. May I call in the doctor to check on you?"

I agreed, too weak to protest. "I'll need some food, too," I uttered.

"First, the doctor." Luke kissed the tip of my nose. "Then I will be sure you get fed. Although I'm not sure I can find you any fried chicken like your Granny makes you."

At the mention of her name, I reached for the chain around my neck and pulled out the token. At first, it didn't respond to me, and I feared the worst. Before my worry great into full-blown panic, a slight pulse of energy responded to my touch, and I breathed a sigh of relief.

An older female entered the room after Luke answered the knock, and she examined me while my fiancé translated for the both of us. When she inspected the injury on the back of my head, I clenched my teeth to keep from groaning in pain.

She checked on my breathing and seemed pleased at the condition of my lungs. But after she examined all my limbs, her slight frown concerned me. Her voice raised as she gestured at me while talking to Luke. I did my best to keep up, but my fiancé responded for me, keeping me in the dark about his answers to her questions. She nodded and accepted whatever he said, but her eyes continued to scrutinize me with intensity.

After she left, Luke chuckled. "She's confused as to why you aren't more damaged from your injuries."

I glanced down at my skin unmarred by any burns. "I guess it wouldn't make sense to someone who didn't know about my magic."

"I told her you had managed to fight your way outside, saving you too much injury," he said. "I think she suspects the lie, but she won't question my word."

Snorting, I repositioned myself on the bed. "The benefits of being the richest family in the area."

He sat down next to me on the bed, fussing over the sheets instead of looking at me. "Yet all the money in the world will not bring you back to me if you do something that will harm you too much."

I stopped him from straightening the covers. "Are you mad at me?"

He clenched his eyes shut and sighed. "I'm doing

my best not to be. But you take such risks, and this time, you were lucky." Luke opened his eyes to let me see the hurt and anguish in them. "But what about the next time?"

A lump formed in my throat, and I swallowed hard. "I didn't mean to cause any problems. Tell your parents I will be glad to pay for any damages."

"You think I'm talking about my sister's room?" Luke scrambled off the bed, too angry to stay still. "It's *you* I'm worried about, Ruby. Things can be replaced. You cannot."

I opened my mouth to utter an apology, but a firm knock on the door interrupted us. My fiancé ran his fingers through his hair in frustration.

"That will be some food for you," he said, answering the second knock.

I heard him argue with someone at the door, and my stomach clenched when I recognized the voice. His mother strode into view and stood next to my side of the bed with her arms crossed.

"The doctor has informed me that you are recovering well from when we first found you," she said, her voice even and cold.

"Yes, I guess I just needed a good night's sleep to heal a little." I offered her a weak smile.

She glanced at her son. "She does not know?"

"Know what?" I asked.

Damiana huffed out a quick breath. She played with the ruby amulet dangling from the gold choker around her throat. "Two nights have passed since we found both you and my daughter's chambers damaged."

I pulled the sheets up around my body as if I could shield myself. "That was two nights ago?"

"Mother, I don't want you to upset Ruby Mae," Luke pleaded.

She silenced him with a single look. "If she wanted a visit with nothing but pleasantries, then she should have refrained from flaunting her powers in our home," she said to her son. "As I see it, she has done nothing but disrespect our family."

Luke frowned and replied in Italian. The two of them devolved into loud squabbling with raised voices and wild hand gestures. I heard my name enough to know I was at the center of the argument.

"Hey," I called, my voice scratchy and a little too weak to be heard. Scrambling out of bed, I stumbled a bit from an immediate wave of dizziness but refused either of their help. "I'd appreciate if you both talked *to* me rather than *about* me."

Luke's mother looked down her nose at my less-than-stellar ensemble. My fiancé had dressed me in my comfy worn-out T-shirt and a pair of old shorts with a faded logo from the tiki bar that were too holey for any other purpose than to sleep in.

"Mother believes you set the fires in Isabella's room," Luke said, crossing his arms over his chest.

I turned around, offering to let her inspect the injury on the back of my head. My fiancé insisted she feel the wound, and I hissed through my teeth when she found it.

"Perhaps someone attacked her," she said with care. "Or perhaps she inflicted this injury upon herself to cover up her true purpose. To ruin my only daughter's possessions."

"Lady, if it weren't for my efforts, half of your castle would be burnt to a crisp," I defended, too tired to mind my manners.

I wanted to appear tough and strong, but my head swam while the room spun. I wobbled on my feet, and Luke rushed over to get me back in bed. Damiana's expression softened at my weakness, and she asked her son to bring a chair over for her to sit in while we talked.

Once she got settled, she addressed me in a quieter tone. "Why were you in my daughter's chambers? I have had that whole wing declared off-limits to anyone for a long time. And yet, you found it appropriate to break in."

"I didn't exactly break in. Not the first time," I admitted, a little nervous sweat breaking under my armpits.

His mother crossed her legs, feigning indifference on the outside but failing to hide her concern with her question. "What do you mean it was not your first time? You have been in there more than once?"

I hesitated, unsure if telling her the truth would be helpful or not. But secrets and lies would only build a flimsy bridge destined to fail.

Drawing in as deep a breath as I could take without wincing from the pain in my throat, I explained about the first night after the reception. I gave her all the details about the room opening for me and my suspicions about her daughter's spirit but decided to keep Granny Jo and Fiametta's involvement out of the story for the moment.

Damiana stared back at me with a blank expression, and I thought I'd blown everything with the truth. I looked to Luke for guidance, but he watched for his mother's reaction as well.

"I would claim you were crazy if not for the stories I have heard from the staff over these several centuries," she said, busying her fingers with her amulet. "We vampires know that ghosts do exist, but I did not want to believe my Isabella had not found peace beyond this life."

Taking a bigger risk, I let her in on my growing theories. "I think she wants someone to discover the truth about her death."

Damiana's perfect mouth opened a little with a gasp. "Is she still here because of this? Have I failed her all this time?" She wrung her perfectly manicured hands together.

I glanced at Luke, prompting him to comfort his mother with some meaningful looks and a few head bobs of insistence. He placed a hand on her shoulder, and she covered it with hers.

Taking advantage of the situation, I pressed Luke's mother for more information. "What do you think happened before Isabella died?" I asked in a soft voice.

Damiana bent her head down as she spoke. "We had placed her in the tower because her father and I thought she was being too willful. Lorenzo wanted her to marry for position, and while I did not entirely agree with him, I also did not want Isabella to throw her life away."

"By marrying a witch," I added, careful not to flavor my words with too much sass.

Her eyes flashed to mine in irritation, but she sighed. "Yes. I did not think she could truly love someone who was not like us. Her relationship was tolerated as a temporary dalliance until we found out she intended to run away and marry the male witch on her own."

"Who reported that information to you?" I asked, my heart quickening.

"It was so long ago, I am not sure. Most news does not come to me directly but through a series of reports." Damiana studied me. "Why?"

I couldn't tell her the information I knew from Isabella's letters without betraying Fiametta and bringing her into things. "As a passionate woman in love, I doubt she would have told anybody her plans. Someone made sure you found out in order to keep her from succeeding. That means someone also had a reason to want her relationship stopped. A jealous lover perhaps?"

Damiana frowned. "Isabella would have told me if there was somebody else. She swore that she only loved the witch."

"Paolo," I said in exasperation. "His name was Paolo. And I don't understand your hatred of witches. Haven't you used them since this castle was built to place spells and create secret passageways?"

"Hate is such a strong word," she countered.

"What term would you use to describe your reaction to Ruby the other night, Mother?" Luke asked.

I sighed, pinching the bridge of my nose. "This is my fault we're not getting anywhere. Let's get back to my main point. Who was the one who found out about Isabella's plan to elope and made sure you knew?"

Damiana looked to her son, but Luke shook his head. "I only found out after you and father locked her away in the tower as punishment."

His mother shaded her eyes with her hand. "We only wanted her to see sense and give up her lover. It was never our intentions for her to have her life taken."

Sympathy rose inside of me for a mother who lost her daughter, and yet, I couldn't help but feel that it was the parents' choices that pushed Isabella to her end.

"When Luke told me a little about his sister, he said she was in the tower for a long time." I leaned forward and pressed the issue. "How long?"

Damiana flinched. "We meant it to be temporary.

Wanted her to suffer just enough so she would give in."

"Tell her how long, Mother," Luke insisted.

She turned in the chair to face him. "You know how stubborn Isabella was."

"I do. She was related to you and Father after all," my fiancé goaded.

Damiana blurred out of her seat and stood in front of her son, crowding into him. "Do not pretend that you were the only one wounded by what happened or that we have not been tortured by our own decisions year after year, century after insufferable century. You think you carried guilt because you were the last to speak to her? Try being the one who put her there."

The tension in the air crackled around us, and I feared if the mother and son got into a physical altercation, I would end up an unwilling casualty. Even though I still didn't have an answer to my question, I needed to deescalate the situation.

"I get it. She was in the tower long enough for everyone to have suffered," I said. "But Luke told me nobody then nor now knows the truth about her death. Only what the residents who lived at the time reported."

"Sì, the burning angel who flew from *la Torre del*

Pianto." Luke's mother collapsed into the chair. "None of us were with her in her final moments." A single pink tear ran down her cheek.

Nothing in Isabella's letters suggested she would commit suicide if she couldn't find a way to run away with Paolo. And the few times I'd encountered her here, her spirit seemed agitated, not guilty. And with her vampiric abilities to heal, she could have just jumped out the window at any time and survived.

"I don't believe she set herself on fire. Even though I never knew her, I don't think that would have been her solution to her problem." I rubbed the ring on my finger, the slight tingle against my skin giving me more confidence. "I think someone she knew did this to her. And whoever it was, I think he or she visited her in the tower after you did, Luke."

My fiancé blinked his eyes, putting together the pieces I laid out for him. He crumpled onto the bed next to me. "You mean, you don't think I had anything to do with her death?"

"No, I truly don't," I said, rubbing his back.

"Neither do I," Damiana agreed. "There may have been a time where I treated you too roughly and placed blame on you. But that was only because I found it hard to accept fault where it belonged. On me and your father."

I took Luke's hand in mine. "I'm sorry to disagree with you, Mrs. de Rossi, but if I'm right, then none of you should feel guilty. But how can I know for sure without…" I thought about the letters I'd found in Isabella's room. "Did anybody find some letters on the desk in your daughter's room after the fire?"

"No," Luke confirmed, rubbing his thumb on the back of my hand. "While you did manage to control the fire to keep it from doing any major structural damage, there still was a lot of interior destruction to my sister's possessions."

The hope I'd forged when I found the letters disappeared. I'd lost the only sure way to find the name of the person threatening Isabella. But in order to keep Fiametta safe, I couldn't reveal why losing Isabella's letters to the fire might have blown my chance to find a possible suspect.

I leaned my head back on the pillows, and Luke cautioned his mother from talking any further. "She needs to eat and then to rest," he declared.

Damiana cleared her throat and rose. "I came here with the intent to send you home. But you have convinced me that all of my beliefs that you used your magic in order to humiliate my family were wrong." She strode closer to the bed and reached her hand out, touching my shoulder. "You have proven yourself to be a woman of strength. An equal for my son."

She walked away, and I struggled to sit up straighter. "Does that mean Luke and I would have your blessing to marry?"

His mother stopped walking but did not turn around. "We shall see," she said before leaving.

Luke stared at the door. "If I hadn't heard it with my own ears, I would not believe it."

"She didn't totally say yes," I grunted, throwing my arm over my eyes to ward off more dizziness.

My fiancé stroked one finger across my skin, causing my arm hairs to stand on end. "Ah, but she didn't say no either. If you think about it, that is more than my sister received."

He had a point, but I was too tired to celebrate. Before long, one of the staff brought in food, and Luke hovered over me, making sure I replenished myself. But I figured he really wanted me to stay out of trouble if only for one day.

CHAPTER SEVENTEEN

The next day, Luke took me into Perdaggia to explore. The walled city bustled with preparations for the *Festa del Cioccolato* coming up the next weekend. Having been consumed by events at the castle, I had missed that Luke's home city was known for its chocolate!

Several vendors featured their own use of chocolate in their wares, and I stuffed my face with free samples. Luke never said a word, but he snorted when I ate another piece from a different store.

"What?" I groused at him. "I'm still recovering. Consider it my fuel."

"So, what? Now you run on chocolate?" he teased.

I stood in the middle of the road, making a scene

with my hand on my hip. "As old as you are, you'd think you'd have learned a thing or two about women," I sassed.

A few tourists who understood English razzed Luke, and he escorted me away, digging his fingers into my side to punish me with tickles.

We stopped in a few shops, and I browsed for gifts to bring back for my family. Luke assured me he would ship back a bunch of olive oil and wine, so I stuck to things that would fit in my luggage.

Even though some of it was a little cheesy, Luke helped me pick out some T-shirts and hats, even modeling a few to help me choose the best options. Boxes of assorted chocolates were a must for all my female friends, and I loaded up and purchased as many as I could hold. Luke carried my bags from one place to the next without one word of complaint.

My fiancé's willingness to indulge me so much didn't escape my notice. I appreciated his efforts to distract me a little from my ordeals, but he was trying a bit too hard. He had done his best to discover who the driver of the car that ran Fiametta and me off the road was, but without either of us girls able to give better details of the vehicle, he'd come up with a whole lot of nothing.

Maybe Luke and I deserved a break from the drama.

We hit up another store, and the hairs on the back of my neck stood up. I searched around us, seeing if I could locate the source of my discomfort. A man with dark hair stared at me for a good second or so. He stopped and went about his business, but I kept watching him as I perused the aisles of goods, wondering if he was following me. When a young woman ran over to him and threw her arms around his neck, I shook my head at my paranoia.

Luke's hands were filled with bags. "You look absolutely adorable," I declared.

"I look like a work mule," he said. "If you can pull out my cell phone from my pocket, I'll call Enzo to have someone come and take all this back to the castle."

"Front or back pocket? Because if it's the front, we might get arrested for indecent and lewd acts in public," I joked, wiggling my eyebrows at him.

He turned and stuck out his behind at me. "Back."

I slid his phone out, and he instructed me on which contact to select. I dialed the number and held the phone up to his ear so he didn't have to put down any of the many sacks full of my souvenirs.

"Enzo will send Claudio to come fetch the bags,"

he said, thanking me for helping him call. "In the meantime, there's something I'd like you to see just a little stroll up this way."

We walked away from the crowds of tourists and up a narrow street. Stores gave way to houses built on top of each other, taking advantage of every square inch the city offered. Laundry hung from lines stretched in between houses across the road from each other. A couple on a scooter whizzed past us, and I avoided a black cat who skittered across the street and ended up mewing on the front steps to another house.

"Just a little further," Luke urged, pushing us both around another hilly curve.

The street grew narrower until we reached the pinnacle of the incline. A modest chapel sat surrounded by well-kept flowers and plants. Luke entered and placed the bags near the front, holding his hand out for me to take. He led me further into the interior, and it took a moment for my eyes to adjust from the sunlight outside to the dim lighting of the structure.

My fiancé crossed the small room and stood in front of a partition that protected the far wall. He placed some money into a nearby collection box, and some overhead lights flashed on, spotlighting the paintings on every single wall.

"Holy hexes," I exhaled, marveling at the sight in front of me. "They're all beautiful."

Each surface contained paintings that captured life at the time in Perdaggia. Luke walked me around, allowing me to take it all in.

"How old is this place?" I asked in a reverent whisper.

He chuckled. "Not as ancient as me. It was built sometime after the castle, but the painting was done towards the end of the fifteenth century. It's Pinturicchio again."

"You like his style," I commented, moving to the next vignette of captured life.

"I like his bold use of colors, which he learned in an art school here. Because of his bright hues, these paintings still stand today with less fading than some of his contemporaries who trained in Tuscany," Luke explained.

I moved to the next scene and my breath caught in my throat. A tall tower climbed towards the ceiling. On the left side of the painting, the sky stood blue against the stone structure. On the right side, the darker night sky with stars covered the city. But in the middle of the dark was an angel wearing period clothing with outstretched wings that looked like flames of yellow, orange, and red.

I gasped. "Your sister?"

Luke stretched out his hand to touch the brilliant depiction of Isabella. "The townspeople thought she was a good omen. They talked of their angel and passed on stories about her to their children. If something good happened, they'd say the angel blessed them. If a child did something bad, his or her parent might tell them to behave or else the angel would come for them."

"Nobody knew she was real?" I pressed.

He shook his head. "But my parents and I mourned her from when the stories started until they morphed into town lore. I used to visit here quite often, experiencing my guilt over the loss of Isa as a form of punishment."

I stopped scrutinizing the details of every flaming feather of the angel and wrapped my arm around Luke's waist, leaning into him. "You need to stop blaming yourself."

"But something kept Isabella from trusting me. Why wouldn't she talk to me about her plans? Maybe I could have helped her instead of disappointing her," he complained.

"Or maybe those are the words coming from a

man who's matured and finally understands why his sister made the choices she did at the time," I countered. "You told me yourself, one of the reasons you could love me was because of Isabella. Because she had been brave enough to stand up for her love."

He kissed the top of my head. "You're right."

I giggled, and he asked me why. "I just like hearing those words."

Luke leaned down and whispered into my ear. "You are right, *cara*."

A shiver spread from my head to my toes, but I still giggled. "Well, if you're man enough to admit that, then I guess you're worthy of marrying me."

My fiancé swept me into a full embrace, looking like he wanted to kiss me.

I placed a finger over his lips to stop his progress. "Not in here. It doesn't seem…right."

His eyes flashed over at the painter's rendition of his sister with her arms and wings spread wide. The money from his donation ran out, and the spotlights turned off with a faint click, leaving us no view of the frescoes.

"I think Isabella would have liked you," Luke said after a weighted silence.

Her ring tingled against my finger, and I smiled. "I hope so."

We walked back to the main part of town together, both of us carting an equal share of the bags. Claudio met us with a car, and he rushed to put all of my new goodies into the trunk.

The smell of chocolate still lingered in the air, tempting me to stay. But my overall energy levels still hadn't fully recovered yet. With reluctance, I agreed to ride back with Luke, especially after he promised we could return whenever I wanted to.

Due to the location where Claudio picked us up, we drove back on the scenic route like the first time I'd arrived. The edifice of the ancestral building blazed red, and I couldn't decide if I saw it more as the home of the de Rossi family or Castle of Blood after knowing a bit more about the secrets and dark past its walls contained.

Luke gathered up a handful of the bags and headed off for my room. Claudio waited for him to leave before speaking with me.

"You must stop asking Fia for help," he said in a hushed tone while picking up my parcels from the trunk.

"Why?" I asked, a little frustrated. I'd been trying to find her for the past day or so hoping we could talk, but had been unsuccessful.

The young man kept a watchful eye on our

surroundings before speaking again. "While you were in recovery, Fia went home after work and found her house had been...upset."

"Upset?" I didn't understand his meaning.

Claudio slammed the trunk shut with frustration. "I don't know how you say it...someone not invited had been in her place."

"Oh, you mean, someone broke in and wrecked her house?" My high from spending a lovely drama-free day with Luke evaporated.

"*Sì*. I am worried for her safety," he uttered in a low voice. "You must leave her be."

Claudio left me standing by the car, gawking at him as he walked away. I caught up to him and held his arm. "Was anything missing? Did the intruder take anything?"

He frowned at me. "I am sorry, miss, but I do not want to involve you with any more details. Please, do as I ask. You cause trouble. Leave Fiametta alone."

I followed Claudio to my room but slowed my pace to stay behind him a little. It saddened me to know I'd upset him or that Fia had suffered a crime for helping me. Every ounce of me wanted to find her and grill her about what had happened, but with the young man as her protector, I would have a hard time reaching her. And I refused to use Luke's position in the household to gain any favors or force anyone to do anything. Perhaps that was what Claudio was counting on.

It bothered me that since the fire, Granny Jo didn't seem as active as before. With everything else I had to worry about, I didn't want to add the possibility that the trip and everything that had happened had taken too big of a toll on my ghostly great-grandmother. It eased my mind when the token emitted a small pulse in my hand when I held it, but I wished I could find a way to talk to her directly.

After a bit of a rest to recover from our excursion, Luke and I prepared for a casual dinner he'd arranged in the garden. I didn't remember seeing a table out there, but when we arrived, I found out just how much pull my fiancé had with the staff.

A long carpet lay over the gravel pathway and someone had scattered white, pink, and red rose petals down its length.

"This is a teensy bit more than casual, don't you think?" I second-guessed my choice of clothes for a fleeting moment before I remembered I'd worn my favorite sundress again because I wanted to feel more like myself rather than a version of me wearing an expensive outfit.

Luke's hand guided me at the small of my back. "I

thought I would surprise you a little since your time here has not gone as smooth as I'd hoped."

We approached an intimate table for two in the interior of the garden surrounded by the scent of flowers and accompanied by the sound of running water from the nearby fountain. If my man was trying to woo me, he was doing a darn fine job of it tonight.

"This looks fantastic," I exclaimed, sitting down in the chair Luke pulled out for me. "On a scale of romantic gestures, I'd say you're on your way to a solid seven and a half."

My fiancé chuckled. "So low?" He handed me a glass of sparkling Prosecco and raised his own in the air. "And what do I have to do to earn a higher score?"

I almost clinked my glass against his and then pulled it away at the last second, pretending to take time to think. "Hmm, I suppose you could earn some points based on how good the food is. Although technically, you won't have cooked it."

"But I will have given your preferences to the kitchen staff so they could prepare dishes that would please you," he countered.

"Fair enough." I tapped my glass with his and

took a small sip. "Then maybe if the food is good, it could earn you half a point."

Luke's mouth gaped open in mock horror. "Only half? That gets me to a possible eight."

I wiggled my eyebrows at him. "That's right. The other two points depend on what comes *after* dinner."

"If I find you some limoncello, will that help?" he teased, and we both laughed and reminisced about the dinner in Rome.

One of the kitchen staff brought out two small plates with various meats, cheeses, and a dish of olives. He poured us both some wine and left the bottle on the table.

"What about dinner conversation?" Luke asked. "If I stimulate you, will that be worth any points?"

I chose to ignore his poorly executed double meaning. "Depends if you can guess the topic I would most like to talk about."

His brows furrowed. "I wish to avoid anything involving my sister. At least for tonight."

The server returned with a plate filled with toasted bread covered in a mix of roasted peppers, eggplant, and tomatoes. Luke and I argued how to pronounce *bruschetta* until I took a bite. I'd happily call it whatever he wanted as long as I could eat more.

I noticed he only picked at the food and watched me consume more than my share. "Why aren't you eating?" I asked in between bites.

He sat back in his chair, and the soft glow of torchlights danced off the red amulet hanging on the black leather cord around his neck. It pleased me to see him show it off with his shirt unbuttoned rather than hiding it.

"I take great joy in seeing you indulge yourself," Luke said. "Much more pleasure than if I were to join you."

I put my piece of *bruschetta* on my plate. "It's weirding me out a little. You've eaten when you've been in my family home."

"Because that's the polite thing to do. You know I don't have to eat. I usually do it to keep everyone around me from noticing my differences," he explained. "But here, I appreciate being able to just be myself. Especially with you."

"Oh." My cheeks heated with the compliment. Much like my choice to wear my sundress, my fiancé was choosing to do something that made him more comfortable, too. "Then I guess there will be more for me."

"Don't worry," he said, his eyes sparkling with mischief. "My desire to take a bite doesn't go away."

"Who are we biting?" Amara asked. The carpet over the gravel kept us from hearing her approach.

I forced the groan in my throat down with a large swallow of wine. "Good evening," I managed without sounding too annoyed.

"Why, Luca," she said, ignoring me. "What a pleasant surprise to find you here on this fine evening. It is too bad that you are in want of good company."

"Amara, must you insist on playing childish games?" Luke replied with a sigh. "Do not disparage Ruby Mae in my presence."

The spiteful woman turned to face me and jumped back with dramatic flair as if I were a danger to her. "Oh, I did not see you sitting there."

"Then, bless your unbeating heart, you must be deaf as well as blind, sweetie," I uttered with a smile as sweet as iced tea and a voice as honeyed as butter on cornbread.

She narrowed her eyes at me. "I do not understand your American accent well. Perhaps you meant to address me by my title, Baronessa. Not...sweetie."

Cassio joined our awkward threesome, and

tonight's score for my date dropped down to a five at best. "Amara, if the de Rossis do not demand the use of honorifics, then no one should. Plus, your mother is not dead, so you have not inherited the title."

"Yet," Amara clarified.

I had no problem imagining her arranging her mother's demise to rise up in vampire nobility. She already acted like a cat in heat when around my fiancé, and I wondered if she had true unrequited feelings for him or if she wanted to use him to rise up in the ranks.

"You can clearly see this dinner is meant to be a romantic gesture. Leave Luke and Ruby alone, Amara," Cassio insisted, trying to lead her away by the arm.

She yanked out of his grip. "Do not presume to touch me."

The server stood behind the two interlopers, waiting to serve me the next course. Amara whipped the plate from his hands. She held it out to me with a widening smile. "Allow me to apologize for my behavior. Here. This is for you."

I took it from her, suspicious of her complete change in behavior. "Thank you. I'm surprised you didn't try to give it to Luke since you've been either ignoring me or insulting me since you crashed our date."

The hateful wench sputtered in protest. "Well… but…of course, the food would be for you. We vampires do not require that kind of sustenance."

I kept my eyes trained on hers, willing to match her in a staring contest if she dared. She held my gaze for an extra minute before clicking her tongue and looking at her nails.

"I find their company tedious. Come, Cassio. Let us go out and find some fun of our own." She stomped away like a bratty toddler who'd had her toy taken away.

Cassio shook his head. "She really is insufferable."

"Thank you for saving us, old friend," Luke said.

His childhood companion bowed with his hand over his heart. "My pleasure. Enjoy your evening."

The pasta dish smelled incredible, and I noticed how similar it appeared to the one Fiametta had made for me at her house. Perhaps she'd been a part of cooking tonight's meal and thought I'd enjoy eating it again.

"I love mushrooms," I declared. "I wonder if these are that one kind that can be found in the wild. Caesar's mushrooms, although I think there's a fancier name for them."

Luke gazed at me in wonder. "I didn't know you were acquainted with the favorite pastime of hunting fungi."

I shot him a playful wink. "I'm a smart cookie who likes to learn."

My fiancé laughed. "I'd be happy to take you out while we're here so we could look for other varieties that are good in pasta. Like porcini."

Isabella's ring flared to life, and I squeezed my fingers shut to shake off the sensation. The tingles crawled over my hand and down my wrist. Without warning, my fist slammed down on the table next to the plate, jostling the silverware and dishes.

"What are you doing?" Luke asked.

"I wish I knew," I said, trying to gain control of my own body. "It happened before." But I wished with everything I had that Luke's sister could wait for a better time to connect with me.

The scene I caused must have made me look like I was a lunatic. One hand acted on its own while my I contorted my body, struggling to regain control. My glass of Prosecco was lost in the battle and spilled all over my lap.

"Grits and ghosts, why are you doing this now?" I yelled, frustrated at my lack of control.

My left hand knocked the bottle of wine over as

it shot out to my left side, turning the palm to face inward. In one swift movement, it blasted to the right, knocking the plate of pasta off the table with great force. The contents splattered all over my dress and onto the ground.

The prickling sensation faded away, and I regained dominance over my left hand. But the damage to our evening had been done, and I surveyed the disaster oozing down my sundress.

"Well, I think the score for our date has just dropped to zero," I said, taking the napkin from my lap and wiping off what I could.

"Let me help you clean it up," Luke offered, sliding out of his chair and using the emptied plate and my fork to pick up as much of the ruined pasta as possible. "Wait. This is not right."

"I know, I know." I gave up cleaning myself off and waved him off. "Don't trouble yourself. It's my fault, so let me fix my own mess."

"No, that is not what I implied." My fiancé lifted the retrieved contents to his nose and picked up some of the mushroom pieces. He held them up closer to his eyes. "I was afraid of that."

"What?" I stood up to join him even though I couldn't see much of anything without more light.

He placed the plate down on the table and

wrapped me up in his arms. I protested and pushed against him, trying to keep him from ruining his expensive clothes. But he held me tight to him regardless.

"Are you going to tell me what's wrong?" I mumbled into his chest.

"The mushroom. It is not what you think," he said, rocking me back and forth.

Fear snuck into my stomach and churned the contents I'd managed to consume. "Okay, now you're scaring me," I admitted.

He let me go and drew away so I could see him. "Good. Because you need to know the truth."

"Which is?" I pressed.

Luke held up one of the slices of mushroom. "This is indeed a type of amanita mushroom."

"Yes, it's the Caesar one. Isn't it?"

He shook his head. "No, *cara*. This is *amanita phalloides*. Otherwise called a death cap. An extremely poisonous and deadly fungus."

I knocked the mushroom out of his fingers. "What would have happened if I had eaten the dish?" I asked, already guessing the answer.

"In six or more hours, you would suffer severe abdominal pain and distress, vomiting, and other unpleasant effects." Luke held me in his gaze. "But the poison attacks the liver. You could experience rapid organ failure. Go into a coma. Die."

The last word echoed in my ears. Panicked, I picked up my napkin again and wiped my dress over and over, wanting any remnant of the mushroom off of me. Luke waited with patience until the tears formed in my eyes and fell. I dropped the napkin and returned to his hold.

"Do you understand what this means?" Luke asked.

I nodded into his shoulder. "Somebody was trying to kill us."

"No, *cara*. Not us. You." He cradled my face in his hand. "Someone wants you dead."

CHAPTER EIGHTEEN

L uke escorted me back inside, but I hesitated before crossing the threshold. Ever since coming to the castle, nothing had gone right. And while I wanted to finish my mission and figure out how Isabella really died, I was less sure I wanted to sacrifice my own life for the truth. At the same time, whoever was trying to hurt me in the present must think I was getting close enough to worry whoever it was.

The link between Isabella and me grew more evident. Two women threatened. One already killed. And I had escaped three attempts to hurt me. And if Luke was right, the culprit was stooping to more sinister means to get rid of me.

Cassio caught sight of us as we hurried through

the halls. His eyes widened in surprise. "Do not tell me Amara ruined your evening?"

Luke ushered him to the side, glancing around to check for onlookers. "I need you to do me a favor, old friend."

"Of course, whatever you need," Cassio agreed.

My fiancé touched his shoulder to pull him closer. "Someone has tried to poison the pasta that was served to Ruby Mae."

"No!" he shouted, and then spoke in a quieter tone. "Are you sure?"

Luke snorted. "You and I both know our mushrooms well. Whoever made the dish used death caps."

Cassio hissed. "That is a sinister mistake."

"I don't believe it is a mistake, my friend. That's why I need some assistance to find out who made the dish," my fiancé insisted. "Will you help us?"

"Always," his old friend promised. "I shall go to the kitchens now and see what I can find out."

Luke offered him our thanks and whisked us through the halls with purpose, ignoring the odd looks from staff who stopped in respect to him. Instead of heading down the corridor that led to my room, my fiancé paused, looking down the darkened hallway that led to his sister's destroyed quarters.

"Do you trust me?" he asked.

I nodded. "Of course."

Scooping me into his arms, he kissed my nose. "Good." He used his vampiric speed to zip us down the hall to his sister's room.

He kept ahold of me while he tried to open the door. In the pitch black, I listened to his failed attempts, the door rattling as he shook it. Yelling a couple of curses under his breath, he stopped.

"They've locked it again. The only way in would be to break it down." Frustration laced his heavy words.

I patted his arm and swung my legs to encourage him to put me down. "This is why it's good to be friends with a witch," I said, casting a small orb of light to be able to see.

Luke's frown faded as he realized what I meant. "I guess we might work better as a team."

I tapped his forehead with my finger. "Now you're getting it. Let me have a crack at the lock. I do this all the time with the stuff we buy from estate sales."

Holding my hand over the lock, I focused my magic and willed it out of my fingers in search of the mechanics of the latch. I stuck my tongue out in concentration, and after a couple of minutes, I heard a couple of clicks. With hope, I tried the handle again, and the door gave way.

The smell of soot and ash hit my nose, reminding me of the other night. Risking a little more energy, I increased the size of the light orb and cast it into the center of the room. Its glow lit up what was left from the fire. I reached out for Luke to take my hand, needing to ground myself as I absorbed just how much I'd risked that night.

"It is a wonder you survived," he exhaled, squeezing my fingers in his.

I touched the fire opal of the bracelet I would be wearing from here on out. "Your sister's things are all gone. Destroyed."

Luke stayed very still, and I stopped taking stock of the damage. "Hey, what's wrong?"

He picked up my left hand and held it up. "You said this room contained some ghostly energy. Is my sister's spirit still here?"

My abilities to deal with ghosts were usually contained to the family homestead. Any encounters I'd had here were not controlled by me. I drew the token from underneath my dress and held it, but Granny Jo didn't appear as she had before.

"I don't think so. The fire must have changed things," I said with regret.

Luke pleaded with me, his eyes full of sadness and regret. He touched the ring he'd given me as a promise for our future. "Will you at least try to contact her?"

With a reluctant nod, I grasped both of his hands in mine and closed my eyes. "Isabella de Rossi, if you are present, please show yourself."

We waited in the silence, but no sound except my own excited breaths filled the room. The ring itself did nothing, and I feared the worst.

"Isa, please. This is your brother, Luca." My fiancé glanced about the room, begging. He finished his plea in Italian.

My heart sank with disappointment. "I'm so sorry. I don't know how it all works. Maybe the effort she made to take control of my hand and stop me from eating the deadly pasta took too much energy."

Luke's eyebrows furrowed. "That's a good probability. Perhaps I'm asking too much of her."

Taking care as I moved around the room, I walked over to the remains of the desk. Only ash scattered over the marred wooden surface remained. My finger traced patterns through the black dust as I tried to remember the pattern of the handwriting where I thought I'd spotted the written name. If only I had stashed the letters on me before everything burned, we might have had a solid clue to go by. Right now, all we had was my suspicions and no idea what to do next.

Luke approached me from behind and wrapped his arms around me. He placed his chin on my shoulder. "What are you thinking?"

"That I've got very little left to investigate. The one solid lead I had burned away," I pouted. "And I don't want to get Fiametta in trouble after Claudio told me her house was broken into and asked me not to involve her anymore."

My fiancé released me from his embrace. "I didn't know anything about this. The young man has no right to ask you to do anything."

"Don't get all high and mighty," I said, waving off Luke's sudden offense. "He's in love with her and is only trying to protect her. You should understand his motives."

"Still. I could force a situation where she has to speak with you if you think that's what you need," he offered.

I thought about what Fia might be able to add. Her biological connection to Paolo could be helpful in trying to summon Isabella again. But if the letters

Luke's sister wrote were lost in the break-in, then there wasn't much else she could do.

"I may need her assistance at some point, but for the moment, can we think of anyone else who might have information we're missing?" I asked. "Who is still here that lived back then?"

"This may sound awful, but I don't know the history of all of the staff," Luke admitted.

I thought about Fia's information she shared about how the castle was run. "Many were probably not vampires, so they wouldn't have been here all those years ago. I'm talking about those you know for sure existed then and are still around now."

He tapped his foot on the floor while he thought. "Other than me, there would be my parents. And Cassio."

"And Amara?" I asked.

Luke sneered at the mention of her name. "Yes, her as well." He paced the floor until he stopped and snapped his fingers. "I know who we need to talk to! Enzo. He's been around all of my life, and no one would know more about what went on here than him."

I thought of the kindly gentleman and realized what role he truly played in the household. "In essence, he's the one who nobody notices but who knows everything."

"Precisely," Luke said. "I'm actually disappointed in myself for not considering talking to him before."

"Is there a way for us to speak to him tonight?" I insisted. "He may provide us another avenue to approach the investigation."

Luke stood straighter, agitated with purpose. "I can take us to him right now." He beckoned for me to hop into his arms.

I took one step forward but stopped. "No, wait. We're so focused on finding out more information that we're not looking at the whole picture." An alarming theory formed in my mind and took root.

"What do you mean?" Luke asked with impatience.

Gazing at him, I spoke words I'd only heard in old black-and-white films. "What if the butler did it?"

At first, my fiancé dismissed my idea with a scoff. But his head tilted once he considered the possibility. "I have known the man all my life, and everything in me says he would rather die himself than do any harm to a member of our family. But you may be right. Out of all people, he would have the best access to everyone involved."

I groaned. Even though I'd started my mission with good intentions, if I continued pulling on threads, it was possible I'd unravel the whole foundation of Luke's family rather than helping them find some peace.

"If he is involved in any way," Luke continued, "then I wish to hear it from his own mouth. Wait here. I'll be back in a moment."

I spent the time alone assessing the damage of the room and trying to piece together the fragments of what happened. I had been too busy trying to decipher the name in the letter that I hadn't paid attention to the person who'd entered the room. But they hadn't used the door. At least, not the usual one.

The dresser that had been moved to block my use of the passage as an escape still sat in front of the secret entrance, although the wooden remains were badly singed. Whoever came in had intimate knowledge of the castle and its hidden mysteries well enough to get around without being seen.

Except, the person who'd hit me over the head had been seen. But not by a living being. I retrieved the token and wrapped my hand around it, trying to coax my ghostly great-grandmother to appear. A light pulse of energy let me know she still existed, but whatever power she had to manifest in this room was long gone.

I paced the floor, trying to put the few pieces of the puzzle we had together. Whoever was behind all the attempts to hurt me had to be someone who belonged in the household. Someone that others would not question if seen. My concerns about Enzo grew, and I questioned whether or not talking to him alone would be beneficial or dangerous.

Luke blurred into view with Enzo right behind him. The latter shut the door, and my heart rate increased with my new suspicions.

"Master Luca tells me you have some questions," the family's right-hand man said.

An idea popped in my head. "Before we speak, I'd like to make sure nobody can listen in."

With a flourish of my hand, I cast a simple bubble of privacy around us. It would not hold for very long, but it would keep anyone who had the ability to eavesdrop from hearing anything as long as it held.

"I don't understand," Enzo said. "But if there is something I know that can help either of you, I'd be happy to share if possible."

Luke nodded at me to take the lead, and I jumped in the deep end right away. "Were you the one that found out about Isabella's plan to run away and marry Paolo? And did you tell her parents?"

Enzo's eyes widened and he stammered. "You think that I...I would never..." He cleared his throat. "I have served the de Rossi family faithfully as have all of the Morandi line I descend from. My nephew Claudio will take over my place when I deem him ready. For you to imply that I would betray a family member's trust is...an insidious accusation."

Luke touched the older man on his arm. "There are reasons to her questions. She doesn't mean to cause offense. But please, answer the question."

"No. I was not the one who informed your parents of Isabella's intent," Enzo replied. "I wish she had confided in me as she used to, for I might have assisted her in coming up with a way to soften the blow and make things easier."

"Do you know who ratted her out?" I asked.

Luke had to explain what the term meant, but as soon as he understood, Enzo continued. "I did not become aware of the situation until Isabella was being sent to the tower."

When he uttered the last word, the ring tickled my finger. Our conversation connected with Isabella, and I did my best to keep it going.

"In all of her time in isolation, did you ever go see her?" I asked.

Enzo sighed. "*Sì*. Many times."

"I didn't know that," Luke said in surprise. "I thought I was the only one who snuck up there."

The older man chuckled. "Who was it that taught you about the secret passage to get there from here? You think I would show you the way and not use it myself?"

"Why did you visit her?" I asked.

"Isabella was strong in will, and her refusal to give in only provoked her parents. I allowed her to tell me everything. Listened to her every word." He shook his head. "If only her parents had seen past their anger, they might have come to the same conclusion that I did."

"And what was that?" Luke asked.

"That if she was ever to find happiness, she needed to be allowed to live the life she wanted," Enzo finished. He dropped his head in shame. "The day before the night she perished, I made her a promise. That I would help her talk to your parents and convince them to let her go."

The ring reacted again to his words, and I twisted it on my finger. "Why didn't you just help her escape?" I pressed.

Enzo snorted. "She could have left at any time she wanted to, and she knew it. No, I understood she did not want to break her parents' hearts. If I could help her fix things, then I would do so."

"Did you talk to her before or after I went to see her?" Luke inquired in a low voice.

"Before."

"Why did you not tell me of your plan?" my fiancé pushed. "If I had known—"

"Would it have really made a difference?" I interrupted.

Luke blew out a long breath. "No, probably not. I yelled at her for being stubborn. Maybe even took our parents' side because she wouldn't budge. She could be so annoying."

"And she planned to wait for Enzo's assistance. So, if Isabella had no intentions of leaving, then someone else came to her the night she died." I needed to pace to think, but the spell I used to keep anyone from hearing us prevented too much movement. "I think there's a way for us to get answers and catch her killer at the same time."

"Whatever plan you can come up with, you can count on me for help," Enzo said. "I have carried the burden of Isabella's death inside me as much as her family has. I would do anything for the pain to be lifted from all of us."

I grimaced when I looked to Luke. "You're probably not going to like my idea."

"Probably not," he agreed with a slight grin.

"It could be very dangerous," I warned.

My fiancé sighed. "Like that has ever stopped you. What do you have in mind?"

With a flick of my fingers, the bubble of privacy popped. If anyone was listening in, they would hear everything I said.

"I think there's one place that holds the key to everything we want to know." I moved toward the door, ready to take action. "We need to go to the tower."

CHAPTER NINETEEN

L uke, Fiametta, and I walked through the busy streets of Perdaggia, navigating through the crowds of tourists still out walking the streets. I'd risked involving the other witch for my backup plan, and as soon as I'd talked to her, she'd insisted on helping despite Claudio's objections.

We found ourselves getting closer to the bottom of the tower and fell behind a tour group. Too many of them stood in our way, so we had to wait until they moved on in order to keep any unnecessary attention off of us.

The leader held a glowing sunflower in her hand so they could follow her. She spoke in a loud voice so the people in the back could hear.

"Now, this is the Weeping Tower, or *Torre del Pianto*," she explained in a clear tone. "The legend tells of a princess who lived in the castle. And she fell in love with someone her family didn't approve of. Because of this, they locked her away for a long time. The villagers down below could hear her crying, which is where the tower gets its name."

A little girl from the middle of the crowd raised her hand. "Was her name Rapunzel?"

The guide smiled. "No, little one, that is only a fairytale. This princess was real. Nobody was ever seen going in or out of the tower. And then one night, those who lived here looked up and saw the princess. Except now, she was a shining angel who rose to heaven in a brilliant flame."

The father of the little girl crouched down beside her. "You know this isn't true, right? They just make up the story so the building seems more interesting."

The guide stepped forward and spoke in a spooky voice. "Some say that on a still night, when you walk by the tower, you can still hear the princess weeping."

"You won't lock me up like that, will you, Daddy?" the little girl asked her father.

Her mother reassured her that would never

happen, but I caught the father's mumbled words before the tour moved on.

"Depends on how many dates show up at our house," he muttered, keeping up with his family as they left the area.

Luke stared after them for an extra beat before ushering Fiametta and me around the back of the building. "This way."

We followed him to the entrance to a closed store. He pulled open a panel, revealing a keypad, and punched in some code. The door unlocked, and he held it open for us.

Fia and I stepped into what looked like a bookstore. Luke didn't bother with any of the products but rushed past all the displays and stacks of books until he reached the back of the business. We entered the stockroom but found no books or other goods. Instead, the large space was empty.

"This is the original structure that we used to access the tower from outside the castle," my fiancé explained. "The storefront was built in more modern times. It's gone through several different businesses, but we've maintained control of all of them."

For someone who claimed he didn't want to take over control of the family business, Luke sounded like he had good knowledge of how things worked. So many other things had distracted us since we'd arrived that neither of us had addressed his parents' desire for him to stay.

I shook off those concerns and forced myself to worry about them later. Right now, I had to stay focused on my plans to see if we could set the trap to catch the killer.

Luke used a very heavy key to unlock a door at the back corner of the empty space. He walked us through into yet another dark corridor.

"This is where I stay," Fiametta said. "Good luck." With a small wave of her fingers, she cast her spell, and her body shrank down until a small mouse squeaked at the two of us.

"She should teach that trick to your cousin," Luke stated, waiting for me to create a light orb to guide our way.

"I'll get around to asking her about it if we get out of this unscathed," I said, pushing forward until we crossed a final threshold. "Whoa."

My floating magical sphere provided only enough light to see halfway up the inner structure of the tower. I looked for a way to climb but couldn't see any stairs or ladders.

"How in the world is anyone supposed to get up

to the top?" I asked, sending the light orb as high as I could without losing it.

"The tower wasn't built for just anyone," Luke said. "Take a closer look at the sides."

Pulling my source of light closer, I found the tiniest ledge carved into the stone. The path it took spiraled higher and higher, and I realized why Isabella's lover could never have reached her at the top.

"Well, if that's how I have to make it, then we won't have to wait for the killer to find me. I'll die if I have to shimmy up that way," I claimed.

Luke chuckled. "If my lady will permit me, I would be happy to carry you."

He didn't have to ask me twice. I hopped into his arms. "Okay, Prince Not-So-Charming. Make it worth my while. And don't drop me."

Luke flashed me his best smile, showing off his fangs to me. "My pleasure."

Using his vampiric speed, he rushed up higher and higher. The rapid twists and turns made me dizzy, and I squeezed my eyes tight to keep from getting motion sick. By the time we reached the top, I clung to my fiancé's neck like a barnacle on the pier at Atlantic Beach back home.

Luke patted my back. "You can get down now. We are on solid footing."

With great caution, I raised my head from his neck and risked a glance. Pitch black darkness met my eyes, and I couldn't tell the difference between having them open or shut. Peeling myself off of my fiancé's body, I trusted him and planted my foot on something wooden.

Another light orb allowed me to observe the modest room where we stood. Luke closed the heavy wooden door behind us.

"Now what?" he asked.

"I guess we wait to see if we were being followed." I pulled my family's token out from underneath my stained sundress and held it.

Hot energy pulsed against my touch, and I appreciated Granny letting me know she was still with me. A part of me wanted her to manifest in her spectral form, but we needed to keep things less complicated in order to be ready if our trap worked.

My engagement ring sprang to life as well, and it vibrated on my hand. "I think Isabella is here with us."

Luke swiveled around, watching me. "Do you think she can hear me?"

"I don't know." Although I tried my best to interpret the slight connection I held with the ghost, I really had no clue. "Why don't you try and reach out to her. See what happens."

"How do I do that?" he asked in a quiet voice.

"Talk to her," I suggested. "Tell her everything you wish you'd said to her the last time you saw her."

Luke strode into the center of the space. His mouth opened and closed several times as he tried to find the words. Finally, he began to speak in Italian. The more he said, the faster his pace sped up. He paced back and forth, his hands gesticulating into the air. At some point he stopped moving and turned in circles, looking for any type of reaction. When nothing happened, his shoulders drooped.

"What did you say?" I prompted, closing the distance between us and touching his arm.

A pink tear fell from the corner of his eye. "I apologized and told her I should have helped her fight for her love. And that I wish she understood that all I wanted when I spoke to her that night was for her to come out of the tower and come back to us. I never meant for her to think I was mad at her or that I agreed with our mother and father."

I rubbed his back to comfort him. "I'm sure she knows all this."

"I also told her about you," he continued,

giving me a weak smile through his sadness. "How you have brought love into my life. How it's so strong, and that I understood why she fought so hard for what she wanted. And then I told her if she needed to, she should move on and be at peace."

"Maybe that's all she needed to hear. Because I don't feel any—"

The ring on my finger buzzed with a strange cold energy. I stumbled away from Luke and held my hand. The tingles spread down my arm and flowed over my body, covering me in the foreign substance and filling my insides until I thought I might get sick.

"Ruby Mae, what is happening?" Luke moved to come to me, but I stopped him.

"Don't," I panted. "Just…wait." My left hand lifted in the air, no longer in my control.

A strange sensation overwhelmed me, and instead of fighting it, I invited it in. It fed off my own magical resources and the power being in this location gave it. A form billowed out of the ring like smoke until it took the shape of a person.

"Isabella?" Luke exhaled.

"Luca," the spectral figure sighed.

My fiancé fell to his knees. "Isa," he cried.

The ghost of his sister opened her mouth and said something to him.

"She wants us to watch," Luke translated.

The space around us changed. A simple bed lay behind me. I found myself standing next to a young woman with hair the same color as Luke's but eyes like his mother's. She sat in a chair, gazing out a window opening. Something caught her attention, and she spun around and stood up.

A man about the same height as Luke, but with much longer hair and a beard, entered. He spoke to Isabella, his body rigid with purpose.

"No, I don't want to see this," Luke complained, waving his hands in front of him as if he could banish the vision. "Please don't make me relive my mistake."

Isabella grabbed the younger version of my fiancé by his sleeves and fell to her knees. She cried, but Luke would not comfort her. He yanked himself out of her reach and left. His sister collapsed on the floor in tears.

"Are you showing me this to punish me? Have I not suffered long enough?" Luke wailed, fresh pink tears streaming down his face.

"No, wait. Look," I instructed.

The spirit of Isabella had sped up the time. She

no longer wept on the floor, but she stood in the window frame, staring down at the ground. Her right foot hovered out into the air as if she contemplated jumping, but at the last second, something startled her.

Another figure entered the room, and Isabella stepped down from the window to face the person. The hairstyle and facial hair were different, much like my fiancé's.

"No. It can't be," Luke uttered, watching the rest of the scene unfold.

Although I couldn't hear the male speak, I recognized the face.

"Cassio," I whispered.

CHAPTER TWENTY

I turned to my fiancé. "Did you know he visited her?"

Luke pushed himself off the floor and wiped his face with the back of his hand. "No, he never told me in all these years. What was he doing here?"

The transparent form of Luke's best friend knelt on one knee in front of Isabella, holding her hand.

"That looks like a proposal to me," I stated, watching the young woman's face for her reaction.

Isabella yanked her hand out of his hold. She pointed at the door, and as best as I could tell, she refused Cassio. He stood but approached her again, tugging on her arm to get her to face him. When she turned, she slapped him across the face, drawing blood. He wiped his cheek and licked the contents off his finger. His eyes narrowed as he confronted her with anger in his gaze.

She pointed at the door again and waited for him to trudge in that direction before turning back towards the window. At the last second, Cassio turned. He picked up the nearby oil lamp that provided light for the whole room. In a fit of passion, he threw it at her.

Isabella shielded herself with her arms, but the glass shattered against her, covering her in oil. The flame from the lamp caught the oil on fire, and her whole body burst into flames. Cassio stared at what he'd done but did not move to help her.

"No!" shouted Luke. "Help her!"

Flames consumed the vision of his sister, and her mouth opened in silent screams. The figure of Cassio stood and watched. Isabella stumbled backward and steadied herself by clutching the stone edge of the window. She pointed at the cruel man, and I found my same hand pointing as well. Whatever she said displeased him, and he rushed towards her. His hands hit her shoulders, and she tumbled out of the window behind her.

Luke roared out curses in Italian as he observed the demise of his sister and accepted the identity of the true killer. The vision disappeared, and I bent forward, drained and panting to catch my breath.

"That is a neat trick," Cassio said, clapping his hands as he entered the room. His hair was cut to modern standards and he wore a well-cut suit. "It is too bad that nobody will believe you if you try to tell them what really happened."

Luke's body tightened, and he stood like a predator about to spring on his prey. "Do you honestly believe you will live another second outside of this place?"

His former friend sneered. "I have survived over all these centuries and garnered much favor within the ranks. There was a time when the golden son of the de Rossi family would inherit everything, but now, things will be changing."

"As if I would allow you to assume any power. I have seen the truth, and you will pay for what you did to my sister," Luke promised, curling his upper lip back to show off his fangs with a hiss.

"Ah, but you forget. I know every move, every trick you use when you fight. We trained together. Fought side by side. There is nothing you can do that will catch me by surprise," Cassio taunted. "Do you honestly believe that you won every match we ever played against each other? Every fight?"

"He's lying," I accused.

"Be quiet, witch." Cassio spit on the floor in disgust. "You and your kind should have been wiped out ages ago."

"You just have a thing against us because you couldn't compare to Isabella's man. Paolo outmatched you in every single way. Especially as a potential lover." Provoking the remorseless killer might not be the best plan, but I needed to buy us a few more minutes.

"Do not speak his name!" Cassio cried out. "He could never love her as much as I did. I would have provided her stability, and the two of us could have ruled when it was our turn."

"Why did you never tell me?" Luke asked. "You were my closest companion outside of Isa."

Cassio scoffed. "You have believed that to be true because that is what I wished for. I came from nothing, but I aspired to much more than my lack of position the vampire ranks would allow me. The only way I could rise was by befriending you."

My heart broke for Luke as the truth cut him to his core. A keening noise escaped from my fiancé's lips, and he rushed toward the traitor in front of him. He slammed Cassio against the wall with brute force, and a crack spread from the point of their impact up to the ceiling.

Instead of grimacing in pain, his former friend sneered, holding up a knife in his hand with my fiancé's blood dripping down it. "That will hurt, my friend."

Luke stumbled back, clutching his stomach. "What good will it do? You know I cannot die."

"Ah, but I have laced the blade with a poisonous mixture boiled down from the death cap mushroom." The villain shrugged. "It may not kill you, but as your metabolism tries to burn through it, you will suffer its effects until it is all gone."

I rushed to Luke's side and tried to catch him as he stumbled again. "You are a fool if you think you can escape the consequences of your actions, Cas."

The man reached inside his suit and pulled out a vial full of liquid. "I may not have an oil lamp to use this time, but I did find a very effective accelerant. When your parents hear how your witch got upset when you told her you were leaving her and set the two of you on fire, they will mourn your loss. But they will have no one else to turn to except me and my entourage of supporters."

A low chuckle burst from my lips. A tittering

giggle followed until I devolved into full cackles. My sides ached from the uncontrolled laughter.

"I see nothing funny about your situation unless you are simply losing your mind," Cassio said with contempt.

I sighed out loud just to annoy him. "You've been scheming for so long, you haven't paid attention, have you?"

"To what? The fact that your display of power to Amara gave me this brilliant idea?" he asked.

"No," I countered. "To the fact that I can control fire. It can't hurt me."

Cassio fake pouted for a second before crowing in glee. "Maybe not, but the same cannot be said of your beloved." He shook the contents of the vial. "I throw this on him and light a match, and you will have a hard time saving him from the damage."

I stood in place, unsure of my best options for attack. At this point, I hoped our other players in this game had done their jobs.

Cassio, emboldened by my hesitation, shook the dagger at me. "And if I stab *you* with the poison, then there's nothing that will save you. The two of you will burn and become another legend to be spread amongst the tourists of Perdaggia."

Movement across the floor caught my eye, and I

relaxed a little. A tiny mouse scampered into the space behind Cassio.

I held up my hand, conveying a silent message to the animal, but Luke's former friend misinterpreted my meaning. "It is too late to beg, witch."

Shaking my head, I tightened my hold on Luke as my fiancé succumbed to the effects of death cap poison.

"It is time to accept your fate," Cassio added.

With Luke collapsing to the floor, I stood straighter and held up both of my hands. "I couldn't agree more. Now!" I shouted, releasing a spell to freeze Isabella's killer in place.

The little mouse shifted into the figure of Fiametta. She placed her hands in front of her and added her own magic to mine to bind Cassio. She called out Claudio's name, and the young man opened the door.

"What is this?" Cassio grunted, struggling against the magical hold. "Young Morandi, these witches are attacking me," he accused.

Claudio pointed to his ears. "I have heard everything. My uncle has already returned to the castle to inform the authorities and Master Luca's parents. It is over."

"No!" shouted Cassio, trying to move but finding it impossible with our spell.

Luke rolled over and grimaced. He laughed through his pain. "How tragic. You lost my sister's affections to a witch and now you will lose again. It is your disregard for them that brings about your downfall." As soon as he finished his last insult, he curled into himself and moaned in agony.

"There is no proof of what I did to your sister. If I am punished at all, I will outlast as I always have," Cassio promised. "And I will make it my life's mission to bring misery to all of you and the generations that come after."

The same sickening cold power from before rose in my body. Emotions that did not belong to me clouded my vision. Blind rage filled every crevice inside my body, and the spell I cast to hold Cassio dissipated.

"Ruby, I do not know if I can hold him by myself," Fiametta shouted through gritted teeth.

Strange words came out of my mouth, but I understood the language even though it wasn't mine. "Cassio, your ego will be your doom."

Isabella's spirit filled me, and I felt her access my fiery magic. Flames ignited in my upturned palms. I wanted to order Claudio to get Luke out of the room, but I could not control my own body. The angry ghost made me take halted steps closer to the man who killed her.

"Isa?" Cassio asked, his arrogance contorted into a little wonder.

"I lost everything because of you," my voice uttered.

Fia and Claudio both shouted something, but I could not hear them. The spirit inside of me focused solely on her killer.

"You would not return my love," Cassio responded.

I snorted. "Love? You admired me in secret. Never declared your feelings because you did not possess the heart to fight for us if anyone stood against the relationship. I owed you nothing and you took everything," Isabella repeated, using me.

"If I could not have you, I would not let you live your life with that witch," Cassio defended. "Better for you to die than to taint yourself with him."

Fiametta shrieked and doubled her efforts. Claudio was caught between watching me and wanting to protect her.

Flames licked over my skin, too hot and wild. "If I cannot go to Heaven, then you will join me in Hell,"

I promised, my body poised to embrace the man who took my life.

Strong arms wrapped around me, holding me back from my attack. I screeched in protest and kicked to break free, the stench of burning flesh filling my nostrils.

"Isabella," Luke grunted into my ear, struggling to restrain me. "Let Ruby Mae go. I will make sure Cassio is punished for what he did. Be at peace."

The fire that did no damage to my skin licked over his. Cassio used the moment of distraction to break free from Fia's spell. At the same time, guards from the castle broke into the room and detained the man, keeping him from escaping the justice he had earned so long ago.

My body stopped fighting Luke's hold. Fia walked over to me and spoke. "I am Fiametta Salvatori Gasparotto, Paolo's descendent. He is waiting for you on the other side, Isabella. Go to him."

I sighed in relief, and tears that did not belong to me streamed down my face. "At last," I uttered. "Thank you."

The spirit of Isabella de Rossi lifted out of my body, and I came back to myself, regaining control. Breaking free of Luke, I willed the fire crackling over his body to come back into me. Closing my eyes and gritting my teeth, I forced the flames to die down. The power dissipated little by little until it was extinguished.

Luke's burnt body crumpled to the floor, and I rushed to his aid.

"Why did you do that?" I asked, my own tears joining the remnants of Isabella's.

"Because…you did not need…his death…on your conscience," my fiancé wheezed.

More guards and the presence of Luke's parents caused a commotion behind us, but I ignored everybody else but my love. I cradled his head in my lap. "I would rather he burned than you."

Luke drew in hard breaths. "I will heal in time."

"He needs blood," his father stated. "We should take him back to the castle."

Damiana pushed past her husband and stood over me. "In his state, that may do more damage."

I glanced up at her. "You have a source right here."

"It may require a lot. Are you willing to risk your well-being for him?" she asked.

I stroked his hair and smiled down at him. "For him, I would risk everything."

"I do not agree that he should take from a witch," Lorenzo protested.

Luke rattled a chuckle. "It…would be best…if you don't…underestimate…a Jewell woman."

"That's right," I said, grinning. "We're made of strong stock and tend to make our own choices in this world."

Damiana took my left arm and positioned it in front of her son's mouth. "We de Rossi women are much the same." She touched the ring on my finger. "Perhaps the joining of the two families will not be such a bad thing."

As my fiancé took what he needed from me to heal, I basked in the glow of victory until the world faded away and I could rest.

"I still can't believe Cassio challenged the charges brought against him. Fia and Claudio actually witnessed his confession and actions at the tower," I stated from inside my closet, sifting through the many outfit choices.

Luke called out from my bedroom, "He tried to claim self-defense and wanted to press counter-charges against you as well. His strategy was to use the longtime prejudices against witches here as his shield."

I popped my head out. "Fiametta's not getting in trouble, right?"

"No, his attempts to blame her for the deadly pasta backfired." The corner of Luke's lips curled up. "In fact, I was going to tell you a fun detail at another time, but maybe it will help lighten your mood now."

Placing my hand on my hip, I stomped my foot on the ground. "I'm not being moody. I just want to know what these secret plans are for tonight. How am I supposed to choose what to wear if you won't tell me what we're doing?"

My fiancé chuckled. "Of course, *cara*, but if I told you, then it would take away the element of surprise. And I would not do that for anything in the world."

I narrowed my eyes at him in irritation. "Fine. What was it you wanted to tell me?"

"Oh, I think you will like this. Guess who was involved with the poisonous pasta?" he asked with a twinkle in his eyes.

"Not Cassio?" I replied, confused as to who else it could be.

Luke shook his head. "Well, he was, but not directly. Turns out, he convinced Amara that she could have me if she helped him get rid of you."

My mouth dropped open. "You mean, she was willing to *kill* me to get to you?"

"She did not know just how deadly the death cap was," Luke said. "Cassio gave her the mushrooms to put in the dish. Amara was the fool who did as he asked."

"Pretty please with cherries on top, tell me she's getting punished, too," I begged, clasping my hands together in a plea.

My fiancé laughed at my dramatic display. "Because it was only an attempt on your life and she was coerced by Cassio, my parents have banished her from this region forever."

I frowned. "That doesn't sound that bad."

"Oh, but it is." He held up a finger. "She no longer has the protection of any vampire from this region or any others. And for one hundred years, no one is allowed to assist her. She is, in essence, by herself. And Amara has never done well by herself."

I let out a long sigh. "I guess that's enough."

"Cassio's sentence…that is another thing." Luke leaned against the edge of the dresser. "He forgot the abilities my father and I share. All of his protests were worth nothing once we both tasted of his blood."

I had learned about my fiancé's ability to read blood before when we'd found a dead body on my family's property. In a few drops from a regular human, he could read the life of whoever it was in a few moments. I didn't want to think about how much blood he and his father had to drink from

Cassio in order to reach back centuries to see him murder Isabella.

"Why did your father not read his blood back then? If it were my daughter, I would have drunk from everyone," I said, still a little uncomfortable with the vampires' style of justice.

Luke looked down at the ground, a little guilt still eating him up. "Cassio was so close to me. Like a brother. We never suspected he could do anything like he did."

I crossed the room to throw my arms around my man. He buried his nose into my hair and drew in a calming breath. My arms encircled him, and I rested my head against his chest.

"Enough," I declared. "If we keep holding onto the past, it'll drag us down like an anchor. Better we let it go."

He brushed his lips against my forehead. "You are very wise for your age."

"Why thank you, kind sir," I teased. Lifting up on my tiptoes, I pressed my mouth against his, taking my time and lingering until he got a little hot under the collar.

"I know what you are trying to do," he said, resisting my charms. "And I am not going to tell you what the surprise is."

I broke away from the kiss. "Dang it. Then you'll have to put up with whatever it is I choose and live with it."

Luke swept me into his arms and dipped me like they used to in old films. "My pleasure," he purred, grazing his teeth against the skin of my neck.

"Help, help," I mock yelled, giggling and flailing in his arms. "I'm being mauled by a vampire."

He righted me, setting me back on my feet, and smacked my behind. "Hurry up and get dressed, *cara*. Trust me, you do not want to be late."

I stuck out my tongue and pouted. "Fine. But no complaints if I'm either too dressy or not fancy enough."

I RAN my hand down the front of the red A-line dress I chose. Despite not having any guidance from my fiancé, I didn't want to chance embarrassing him or myself if I showed up to another event like the first one I attended.

"Stop fidgeting. You look gorgeous," Luke said, kissing my cheek.

"And I'll fit in, right?" I checked. "Even these?" I lifted up my foot to show off my cowboy boot. The dress may have been a designer label, but the boots were all Ruby Mae Jewell.

He squeezed my hand and slipped it around his arm. "Everyone will be very pleased. Now, stop dragging your feet."

We exited the castle and entered the gardens. The last time we were there, someone had tried to poison me. I hoped this time, there would be fewer murder attempts and more fun.

Damiana and Lorenzo greeted us by the rose-bushes. Luke's mother embraced me and then kissed me once on both cheeks. "You look lovely this evening, Ruby."

"Yes, and I especially enjoy your footwear," my fiancé's father added.

Ever since he saw the aftermath in the tower, Lorenzo had changed his attitude towards me and accepted my relationship with his son. It pleased me to no end to have his parents' approval, even though we'd yet to receive their blessing for marriage.

"If you come visit us back home, I can make sure to get you a pair for yourself," I promised, figuring they would never trade the luxury of their castle for my family's simple digs.

"We may take you up on that offer sooner than you think," Lorenzo said. "But first, my wife and I would like to give you something. A token of our gratitude for everything you have done for us." He slipped something out of his jacket pocket and handed it to his wife.

Damiana stepped forward and presented me with a velvet box. "Before you came, my family had been functioning but was broken. Missing out on living life to its fullest because of our grief and guilt." She flashed her eyes to her son. "And while your arrival here may not have been welcomed, I hope that this gift will show you how grateful we are."

She flipped open the lid, and the earrings inside made of rubies and diamonds sparkled. "Holy hexes," I exhaled. "That's too much."

"What you gave us—the knowledge of how our daughter died, the capture of her killer, and the return of our son—is priceless. These trinkets are small compared to the debt we owe you," she said.

"Try them on," Luke insisted.

With shaky fingers, I placed them on my ears and felt them dangling from my lobes. "Thank you," I whispered.

Damiana cleared her throat to hold back her tears. "They once were mine, given to me by a man who loved me with all his heart." She held out her hand for Lorenzo to take it. "And I gave them to my daughter. They match the ring, and I thought it appropriate for the set to stay together."

"Maybe they can even be passed down to your own child someday," Luke's father added.

My eyebrows rose into my hairline, and I stammered at the thought of a future too far away to think about.

Luke snorted at my reaction. "Perhaps we can talk about the possibility of grandchildren another time. I would really like to give Ruby Mae my gift."

I gazed up at him. "You mean, the earrings weren't the surprise?"

Luke's parents moved out of our way and followed behind as my fiancé led me down the gravel path and around the fountain to the other side.

"Surprise!" a whole host of people shouted at the same time. They clapped and whooped, whistling with their fingers and laughing at my stupefied response.

Looking around at the faces, I almost fainted at the sight. Instead of a bunch of strangers doing their best to speak English, my immediate family and friends stared back at me.

"What...how...when..." I faltered.

"Ooh, we should do this more often. We've

finally found something that makes Ruby Mae speechless," Crystal teased, holding onto her big bear shifter of a husband, Odie.

"Yes, please fly us to Italy in a private jet more often, Luke," Cate added. She raised her flute of Prosecco in cheers to my fiancé.

Aunt Celia and Dani Jo rushed over and smushed me between the two of them. My aunt gushed over my earrings.

"Where's Uncle Jo?" I asked.

"He decided to stay home," she said with an apologetic grin. "He didn't want to leave Deacon behind on his own. Plus, that little elf of a girl was coming by to check on him."

Dani bumped her mom's hip with hers. "Misty's been visiting him a lot."

"It'll be interesting to see what happens between those two if we can ever change him from a pig back into his regular form," Aunt Delia said with a cheeky expression on her face.

"Remind me to introduce you to that woman right over there." I pointed at Fiametta standing to the side, talking with Claudio. "I think she may be able to teach Deacon a thing or two to help."

My father waited with patience to approach me,

but I launched myself at him the second I saw him. "Hey, Daddy."

"Hiya, butter bean." His strong arms embraced me. "I sure did miss you, but from the stories they're telling here, it sounds like you were in the right place at the right time."

The token hanging against my dress warmed between the two of us. "I had a lot of help," I said, picking up the medallion in my fingers and stroking the elephant. When it pulsed back, I let my father feel the energy to reassure him of Granny's presence. "I'll bet Granny's good and ready to get back to her kitchen."

"It'll be good to have you both back there. But I'll enjoy spending some time with you and Luke. Get to know his family a bit more." He nodded at my fiancé laughing with his parents. "Maybe eat some new things and see some interesting sights."

"Sounds like a good plan." I hugged him again.

Lorenzo and Damiana led everyone to a long table set for the intimate party full of friendly faces and family who loved me. Luke and his parents laughed and joked with my father, and I watched with intense pleasure. No longer burdened by the loss of Isabella, the three of them seemed lighter and more able to face the world with a smile instead of a frown.

There would still be things they'd have to work out amongst them—like whether or not Luke would take over as head of the region—but those negotiations wouldn't take place tonight. Instead, we celebrated with good food, good wine, and plenty of loud and lively conversation.

My father whispered something to Lorenzo, who nodded in agreement. Dad backed his chair up and stood, holding his glass in the air. "Most of y'all know I'm a man of few words, but when it comes to talking about my Ruby Mae, I could blabber on until the cows come home about how proud I am of the woman she's become."

I blushed at my daddy's compliments and glanced away. Luke's father listened with great intent, nodding his head in agreement to what a blessing a daughter can be to a father. I let my fingers stroke my engagement ring that no longer tingled, a little sad to have lost that connection with Isabella but happy, too, that she had found peace after so long.

"We'll have more days to spend together, but tonight, I want to toast my daughter and her choice for her future husband." Dad held my fiancé's gaze.

"Luke, you come from a fine family, and yet, you have never treated me and mine as anything less than royalty. I wish the two of you all the happiness in the world."

Several people cheered and vocally added their congratulations again. A few clinked their silver utensils against the crystal, and Luke and I obliged them with a chaste kiss.

Dad sat back down and winked at me. "Love you, butter bean," he mouthed across the table.

"Love you, too, Daddy," I mouthed back.

Damiana took the honors for speaking for herself and her husband. "Ruby Mae, thank you for everything you have done. For loving my son so much that you stayed when most would have run away. For giving me back my family and the promise of it growing once again. May you and Luca live the future of your dreams, wherever it may take you."

She reached across to clink her glass with mine. "And may my son know how special it is to be loved by a strong woman," she added with a wink.

My heart burned with joy at receiving the acceptance I so desperately wanted from Luke's parents. This trip afforded me a chance to get to know my fiancé better than I ever had. And although I knew things might be a little different when we returned to our unpretentious lives back in the South, I no longer worried about secrets hindering our future.

After much wine and Prosecco was consumed with our food, the staff brought out tiny glasses and limoncello. Luke and I made our rounds around the table, talking and gabbing with everyone. Azalea pushed me to call Ms. Robin to have her design my wedding dress while Harrison wanted to find out how he could order some of the wine from Luke's uncle's vineyard for the tiki bar. Cate, Crystal, and Dani teased me about finally setting a date, and I promised them we could go into full wedding mode as soon as we got back home.

With everyone occupied and entertained, Luke sequestered me behind a statue of some Roman god to steal a moment between the two of us.

"Are you happy, *cara?*" he asked.

"Deliriously," I replied with a little giggle. "And maybe a little tipsy. Don't let me say anything stupid in front of your parents," I begged.

My fiancé chuckled, brushing the back of his hand down my cheek. "I don't think there is anything you can do that will change their minds. Face it, they are determined to see you one day become a de Rossi."

I shook my head. "Mm-mm, you're going to be a Jewell," I insisted.

Luke pulled me into a warm embrace. "We will negotiate terms later. Tonight, we celebrate us."

Under the stars and in the arms of my vampire fiancé, I knew we didn't have to make any big decisions right now. We had all the time in the world to plan for our happy ever after.

DEAR READER -

Don't miss out on Ruby Mae's next adventure, when a little ghost problem turns into a possible big disaster in the fifth book of the series, Bargain Haunting!

THANKS so much for reading *Vintage Vampire,* the fourth book in the Southern Relics Cozy Mysteries series! If you enjoyed the book (as much as I did writing it), I hope you'll consider leaving a review!

Preorder Bargain Haunting as well as the next book in the Southern Charms series, Preserves & Premonitions: Book 7, and make sure to sign up for my newsletter if you want to hear news and updates!

NEWSLETTER ONLY - If you want to be notified when the next story is released and to get access to exclusive content, sign up for my newsletter! https://www.subscribepage.com/bellafallsrelics

NEWSLETTER & FREE PREQUEL - to gain exclusive access to the prequel to the Southern Charms Cozy Mystery series *Chess Pie & Choices*, go here! https://books.bookfunnel.com/bellasubscriberhextras

HEXTRA FREE STORIES

Want to read more about your favorite characters? Check out the free "hextra" stories available to all subscribers to my newsletter or members of my reader group Southern Charms Cozy Companions!

Click here to subscribe:

https://books.

bookfunnel.com/bellasubscriberhextras

Click here to join:

Southern Charms Cozy Companions

Southern Relics Cozy Mysteries

Southern Charms
Cozy Mysteries

Magic and mystery are only part of the Southern Charms of Honeysuckle Hollow...

Suggested reading order:

Chess Pie & Choices: Prequel

Moonshine & Magic: Book 1

Lemonade & Love Potions: A Cozy Short

Fried Chicken & Fangs: Book 2

Sweet Tea & Spells: Book 3

Barbecue & Brooms: Book 4

Collards & Cauldrons: Book 5

Red Velvet & Reindeer: A Cozy Short

Cornbread & Crossroads: Book 6

Preserves & Premonitions: Book 7

ACKNOWLEDGMENTS

I really loved writing this book for several reasons other than getting to focus on Ruby Mae and Luke's relationship. One of my favorite places the Navy ever sent my husband and I was Italy. I fell in love with the country and the friends that would become like family to me. It's a privilege to put a little of what I enjoyed into this book. While the town of Perdaggia isn't real, the area it's based on is. It was a blast getting to "live" in Italy again while writing *Vintage Vampire*. So, a hearty *Thanks* goes to the Navy for sending us there for almost four years!

I also need to thank my sprint groups who've helped push my writing to another level. Thanks to my Chatzy group and to Malorie Cooper's live sprint crew.

As always, I thank my family for their unending support. Can't believe y'all still read my books!

And to my husband—thank you for giving me the space to do what I love, for feeding me and the cats when I forget to, and for being my constant support and person who has to hear my crazy plots and help me out of the corners. Who else would force me to take breaks and go for walks to make sure I don't get "too weird?" Love that I got to put a little of our Umbria into a book!

ABOUT THE AUTHOR

Bella Falls grew up on the magic of sweet tea, barbecue, and hot and humid Southern days. She met her husband at college over an argument of how to properly pronounce the word *pecan* (for the record, it should be *pea-cawn,* and they taste amazing in a pie). Although she's had the privilege of living all over the States and the world, her heart still beats to the rhythm of the cicadas on a hot summer's evening.

Now, she's taken her love of the South and woven it into a world where magic and mystery aren't the only Charms.

bellafallsbooks.com
contact@bellafallsbooks.com

facebook.com/bellafallsbooks
twitter.com/bellafallsbooks
instagram.com/bellafallsbooks
amazon.com/author/bellafalls
bookbub.com/authors/bella-falls